BLUE CHRISTMAS

LORD & LADY HETHERIDGE MYSTERIES BOOK #6

EMMA JAMESON

For my family
For my friends
and
For my readers
With a grateful heart.

Emma Jameson
2019

CHAPTER 1

You can do this, Kate Hetheridge told herself, for perhaps the twentieth time that day. *It means a lot to him.*

Her husband, Tony, also known as Lord Anthony Hetheridge, the ninth Baron of Wellegrave, was trying, and very nearly succeeding, to project the bland neutrality of one who doesn't give a fig how his wife responds to his choice. In this case, his choice of a holiday let in the heart of London. Though it was only the sixth of December, the old city was already bedecked in the usual way: fairy lights, wreaths, shiny tinsel, and a towering Christmas tree in Trafalgar Square. And although the United Kingdom had been through its share of travails in the past few years, the holiday spirit was alive and well, perhaps even a touch more intense than in less fraught times. The very fact that Tony had discovered a rental property for them on short notice was a testament to his determination to make this work.

Kate, too, wanted it to work, at least on paper. She'd made promises, and she meant to see them through. But even though seven full days in the city felt insurmountable to her, she knew Tony wanted more. He wanted to live and work in London again.

If I can't, what does it mean for our careers? For us?

CHAPTER 2

When Tony Hetheridge embraced a new career, private investigator, the welcome had been less than rapturous. In the run-up to hanging out his shingle, as it were, he'd interviewed a handful of London PIs. Most were emotionally situated somewhere between disgruntled and despairing. One had told him flat out: "It's a dirty business, mate. Life's too short. Especially for a bloke with one foot in the grave."

Fortunately Tony, who'd recently turned sixty-one, no longer gave one-foot-in-the-grave rubbish a second thought. By his reckoning, his full plate of responsibilities required him to delay the onset of decrepitude until ninety-three, and death itself until one hundred and eight. He had a young wife. A grown-up daughter he barely knew. An adopted son, brilliant and increasingly cheeky. A challenging brother-in-law with whom he'd gradually achieved détente. And a myriad of other friends, enemies, hopes and dreams. So he'd kicked off his professional second act with gusto. The case had concerned a pair of brother-sister twins, one dead, the other vanished. Getting to the complicated truth of what had befallen the twins had been a stunning success. It also nearly got him killed.

Tony's police career had been long, distinguished, and physically uneventful, with a couple of near-misses but no life-threatening injuries. At the outset of his PI career, he'd narrowly escaped death, but was beaten so badly he almost lost an eye. A period of recuperation, quiet, and reflection had been essential.

It had been ugly. It had been tough. Nevertheless, Tony believed he'd processed the event. Was it because he'd killed his adversary? Because he'd literally cast him down? Perhaps. The evildoer who'd tried to annihilate him, Kate, Henry, and Ritchie, plus his friend and colleague, Deepal "Paul" Bhar, was dead and gone. Perhaps that triumph had permitted Tony to attain a minimal safe distance, emotionally speaking, from the worst of the memories.

The same could not be said for Kate.

It was the sixth of December. Tony and Kate's first wedding anniversary, 25 December, was coming up fast. He wanted very much to mark the occasion, as well as Christmas Day, with optimism; with a feeling of moving forward, if at all possible. Plainly put, he wanted to see the back of Briarshaw, his ancestral estate in Devon, and not come back for a span of anywhere from twelve months to the rest of his life.

That was possibly an overreaction. Tony and Kate had been married at Briarshaw, in the great house's tiny chapel, with fresh-cut evergreens and fairy lights twinkling from the hall. As old heaps surrounded by hills, hedgerows, and sheep went, Briarshaw was tolerable. (Translated from English understatement, "tolerable" in this case meant pure heaven.) The original plan had been to return to Devon in mid-December, meaning next week, and mark the happy occasion where they'd tied the knot. Then "the rooftop," as the family euphemistically called it, had happened.

"The rooftop" had changed everything. It had even landed Tony and Kate in Devonshire in May, eight months ahead of schedule, for what felt like an endless recovery—two minor surgeries for Tony, three orthopedic boondoggles for Kate. After an extended relationship with St. Thomas' Hospital, retreating to the country had been the best possible medicine. Briarshaw had swiftly become a haven, a spa, even an extended family getaway. And, so Tony believed after months of observing his wife, a sort of delicious limbo for Kate, unencumbered by challenges or traumatic memories. In Briarshaw's drowsy green grass, watching rose-gold clouds gather behind a three-hundred-year oak, Kate had rested. She had allowed her body to heal. But even the best medicine can turn toxic, if taken too long.

By July, Tony had begun entertaining doubts about Kate's progress. By September, he'd become convinced she was deliberately ignoring every overture from the outside world, including her chosen career, to bring her back into the fold. Like him, Kate had chosen the Metropolitan police service over the objections of her family, all of whom had thought she was mad to try it. Also like him—although from the opposite side of the equation—she'd had to fight for her place against naysayers, saboteurs, and those who had a vested interest in preserving mediocrity. Finally, like him, she'd loved detective work, the thrill of a tough case, of clues that initially refused to line up, of gimcrack alibis that exploded under the correct pressure. He loved it still, unreservedly. Did she?

By October, Tony had still failed to dredge the answer out of Kate, who was apparently content to feed goats and count clouds. Meanwhile, his regard for Briarshaw regressed to his teenage view: a cursed old heap, a thousand miles from any place of even fleeting interest, where bluebloods with superior deductive reasoning went to die. No one needed a policeman, much less a detective, in that bucolic corner of Devon. *Midsomer Murders* made the English countryside seem like a hotbed of sex and slaughter, but Briarshaw's nearest village, Shawbridge, had yet to get the memo.

Close to Bonfire Night, the village's weekly newspaper had

run the following headline: *KNIFE CRIME STUNNER.* Upon investigation, this referred to the theft of a pen knife that had been filched from a high street shop. The culprit, a pensioner suffering from Alzheimer's, had been identified the following day. The knife, returned without incident, was valued at £7.

Tony's hopeful overreaction to the headline, his immediate desire to sort of parachute into Shawbridge and take charge of the situation, coordinating with local authorities and hauling off the guilty to face justice, was a wake-up call. Had Wellegrave House, the London townhouse he'd lived in for most of his adult life, been in any fit state, he would've dragged Kate off to a London weekend. The pitch would've been so easy. First, a relaxing railway journey in the quiet car. Lunch at Juno's, their favorite hole-in-the-wall near Paddington Station. Then two days indoors, if Kate preferred. But alas, Wellegrave House was still weeks away from completion.

After the fire—and what a year it had been, when a major housefire became a mere afterthought—it had taken months of back-and-forth with builders, suppliers, designers, and The Powers That Be (as Tony had come to think of those rules that govern the restoration of Grade II Listed houses) to remake Wellegrave House. It would be mid-January before the house's CCTV cameras, infrared monitors, and other security measures went live. And Tony knew that until they did, Kate would refuse to spend so much as a single night there.

She's not wrong, he reminded himself. On the contrary, an abundance of caution was both sane and wise. Security failures had led to that hellish experience on a rooftop. And while Tony had killed the evildoer, he had not eradicated him.

In life, the man who'd attacked and nearly annihilated them had been a celebrity. In death, strange and hideous conspiracy theories had grown up around him, rewriting his true biography, transmuting him from the base metal of psychopathy and evil into the pure gold of—well, whatever his fringe cult needed him to be. Clinical madness was begetting voluntary madness. And it was hardly the first time, in the long annals of human history, that such a sad and destructive alchemy had occurred.

Of course, given their career backgrounds, they had all the information and reassurance a flawed world could offer. From the unit that routinely keeps tabs on potentially criminal groups and gatherings, Scotland Yard had created a special task force to monitor the evildoer's groupies and copycats. While the risk of a revenge attack on the Hetheridges from "the Fan Club," as it was called, was judged to be low, the number wasn't zero. It would never be zero.

CHAPTER 3

*I*n early November, Metropolitan Police Assistant Commissioner Michael Deaver, Tony's longtime friend and ally at the Yard, had traveled to Briarshaw to brief them in person. Although Kate pretended ignorance, she and Tony both understood that Deaver was there not only for a social call, but to assess Kate's readiness to return to service. Physically, she was already cleared. Her promotion to Detective Inspector had gone through. Moreover, her place on the "Toff Squad," the Scotland Yard unit which dealt with serious crimes that intersected with the lives of the titled, monied, and famous, was assured. Since August, Paul Bhar had been calling her regularly for help, advice, or simply to complain about his caseload. Kate always took his calls, and Tony had overheard enough of their substance to know she took Paul's requests seriously, and did the best she could to assist him from a distance of one hundred and seventy-five miles. Yet still Kate hadn't so much as hinted at being ready to return to London.

Deaver went away confused. Paul called Tony, demanding to know what was up. And when Tony finally decided to press the issue, Kate had frozen him out. It was a first.

To return to good old English understatement, a situation where *Kate* turned emotionally unavailable was something of a role-reversal. Tony had been at a complete loss. For the whole of his life, he'd been the distant one. That had been his entire M.O., pursuing women when it suited him and turning cold when it didn't. For a long time, he'd assumed his blood just ran a shade cooler than the norm; that only intellectual pursuits truly captivated him. Then came Kate. And a large part of what made her so irresistible to him, that had driven him relentlessly even when he disbelieved she could ever love him, was her fiery red core. The live ember within the ashes. When Tony was close to Kate, he felt more alive, more passionate, and more willing to risk himself than ever before. The realization that perhaps she was drifting, that the fire would fade and he would be helpless to stop it, had forced him to take drastic action.

He'd told her he wanted to see a therapist. That he was going against his upbringing, not to mention his habitual way of handling painful feelings—by ignoring them—but he believed it was imperative. Yet he couldn't muster the willingness to go it alone. He needed her to go, too.

Not as a couple, not to compare notes, not to achieve some sort of relationship breakthrough. He just needed her to support him by choosing a psychotherapist, booking a month's worth of sessions, and going to them. If she did that, he claimed, he could marshal the strength to do the same.

Had Kate seen through him? Perhaps. Had she seemed surprised? Poleaxed might be a better word for it. But she'd borne up, made some inquiries, and found a suitable practice in Plymouth.

As promised, they'd traveled there together twice a week, seeing different psychologists. Tony had concluded after eight sessions. Kate was still going—and while she revealed very little of what was discussed inside the therapist's office, she admitted the general topics were the same: flashbacks, intrusive anxiety, and the sort of helpless rage that all too quickly becomes depression. For the month of December, her therapeutic "homework" turned out to be an assignment beyond Tony's wildest hopes. Kate's therapist wanted her to return to London and spend at least a week there. Overnight—no railway trips to the suburbs, much less Briarshaw.

Tony had done his best to receive this information neutrally. He'd failed, of course, with Kate tartly informing him over breakfast that while he was allowed to be happy, he ought to have the decency to wipe the offensive smile from his face. Determined not to overplay his hand, he'd promptly shaken open the *Independent*, started reading about the current state of things—an act incompatible with smiling—and allowed the secondary track in his brain to start chugging away on the question of London. Wellegrave House was out of the question. So where would they stay?

CHAPTER 4

*I*t took him six days, seven phone calls, two emails, and two daytrips to London to sort through the flood of holiday lets and second homes offered by solicitous friends. Though Tony was embarrassed to fully acknowledge it, even to himself, the outpouring revealed something Paul and AC Deaver had hinted at: to the Met's old guard, Tony was now viewed as a bit of a hero.

To his fellow dinosaurs, some still clinging desperately to the apex of the food chain, others already retired and heckling the modern service from the sidelines, Tony was an inspiration. He'd given thirty years in service to the Met, only to be forced out as the top brass replaced seasoned, independent operators with the young and pliable. Then as a private citizen, he'd faced the nightmare of personal retaliation by a killer he'd tried to send down. It was a fear every detective who'd worked on high profile cases had dealt with, but ninety-nine out of a hundred times, the only thing they truly had to worry about was a civil suit. Barring that, a good old-fashioned hit job by the tabloid press. But Tony and his family had actually been marked for death and survived.

That meant something to his contemporaries. It even meant

something to his relatives—with the exception of his nephew Roderick Hetheridge, the man who was, through the creaky Middle Ages magic of primogeniture, his legal heir. Roddy wanted Tony to snuff it, posthaste; indeed, he'd never forgiven him for living this long. The only thing that kept Roddy happy was the knowledge that Tony had no son. Henry didn't count; the Barony of Wellegrave passed only to sons of the body. But apart from Roddy Hetheridge, the warm welcome had been quite gratifying, with invitations and offers thick on the ground.

When it came to the security arrangements of those offered properties, however, most were unsuitable for Kate. And since making Kate comfortable in the city was the entire point, Tony had politely and gently refused all offers that came with promises to visit, or a welcome party, or "dropping by for drinkies." Tony suspected that all day, every day, some part of his wife was still on that rooftop: injured, terrified, and facing down death, not only for herself, but for those she loved. A woman who saw herself as cornered wasn't likely to respond well to people she barely knew dropping by for "drinkies," even if they brought the bottles.

The railway journey to the city had gone well. Kate immersed herself in a novel and hardly said a word. The ride to Marylebone in a Black cab was unremarkable, although it fell to Tony to keep up most of the conversation with the pleasant, well-informed driver. Then they were there, at Strange Mews, a freehold brick mews house that was painted a clean, soft white. The cabbie insisted on helping them get their luggage into the mews house's foyer.

"Smart tree, that," the cabbie said, nodding at the six foot artificial Christmas tree, slim enough to fit where a coat tree might usually stand. The white fairy lights and rustic wooden ornaments—toy drums, simple dolls, bears, and alphabet blocks—fit with the tree stand, an old-fashioned sled.

"Cheers. Happy Christmas a wee bit early," Tony said,

pressing a tip into the cabbie's hand. Then he closed the door, reset the alarm, and regarded Kate with the bland expression he'd once turned on hardened criminals. He didn't have to give her a sales pitch on the security system; he'd downloaded the specs a day early, allowing her to read them over at leisure. It was quite simply the finest money could buy.

As expected, she made no complaint. But she was looking at the interior of the fully refurbished mews house as if she'd landed on the surface of the moon.

She didn't seem inclined to speak. That left him to do it.

"Let's have a peek at the living room, shall we?"

CHAPTER 5

*K*ate followed Tony out of the foyer and into the wide space that encompassed living room, dining area, and kitchen. Though the window offered what looked like a respectable view, he didn't drag her over to inspect it, or insist she look at the gleaming stainless steel cooker and fridge, both the very definition of the term "mod-cons." She appreciated that. After the long sanctuary of Briarshaw, arriving at Strange Mews —why would anyone name a house that?—was a bit overwhelming. She didn't need Tony to narrate all the features her detective's eye had already registered.

Heart-of-pine floors, polished to a warm glow. A lovely old fireplace, the small, stark kind, with a pitch-black firebox nestled inside a white marble mantlepiece. A sofa, white with jet-black throw pillows, a stylish nod to the hearth. Over the mantlepiece hung a large, rectangular mirror, unframed apart from its beveled edges. The surfaces were mostly uncluttered. Apart from a pair of silver candlesticks, the living space was an empty canvas.

"Lots of sunlight coming from the first floor," Tony said, finally driven to break the attenuated silence. He pointed up at a long plate glass window, spilling light down the iron spiral staircase and across the heart-of-pine floor. "You can't see it from here, but just under the window you'll find a door that opens onto a private roof terrace. Very snug. There's a table and chairs out there. A couple of potted evergreens for color, too. Might make a nice breakfast spot."

Say something, Kate coached herself. *Don't leave him at sea, floundering.*

"I don't want to stay here," she blurted, and cursed herself for sounding like a spoiled little girl. Taking a deliberate breath, she started over, careful to speak like a grown woman. "I mean, not through Christmas. We said a week. Seven days. Not through Christmas."

"I wouldn't dream of suggesting otherwise."

"There's a Christmas tree."

"Holiday lets," he said dismissively. "Agencies buy decorations in bulk, stage the properties, lure in the punters, and move on to the next job. The tree in the foyer must've been set up by the agency. I was as surprised to see it as you were."

His eminently reasonable tone made her feel like a right cow. She'd been mute throughout most of the trip, too caught up in her own emotions to think about his. On days like these, she wondered how he put up with her. The thought triggered the impulse to throw herself into his arms, prompting a low chuckle as well as a good hard embrace.

"I'm sorry, love," she whispered. That day she was wearing flats, meaning they were exactly the same height, and fit together perfectly. "But I made it almost four hours without complaining or running away."

"You did." He kissed her gently, then held her at arms' length. "Now tell me your honest reaction. Love it? Hate it?"

"It's nice," Kate said, striving for positivity. She'd promised Alix a good faith effort, and heaven knew Tony, of all people, deserved it. "You know I love living at Briarshaw. But this makes a change. I must say, it's bigger than I expected." She turned, taking in the ground floor. "What's down that hall?"

"The loo. And a guest bedroom."

"How many rooms upstairs?"

"Four. Five, if you count the terrace."

"Bigger than we need."

"Holiday lets. You get what you get." Tony gestured to the elegant spiral staircase. "Shall we venture up?"

"Sure."

Kate went first, noting that the staircase's modern design, with a wide initial curve and pine treads that matched the floors, was easier to climb than most of Briarshaw's steep inclines. Emerging headfirst into the upper floor was a bit like ascending into a loftier realm. Warm, bright yellow sunlight streamed through the plate glass window, flooding the landing and revealing dust motes, dancing merrily in celebration of the midafternoon.

"The terrace door is identical to the entryway," Tony said, going through the same procedure to disarm the electronic lock. "Have a look at the view."

It was brisk but pleasant on the walled terrace. The walls were a paper bag brown, not the sort of color Kate would've chosen, but she had to admit it looked well enough with the lacquered white trim and potted miniature evergreens. The metal bistro table and folding chairs looked like Asda specials. Spray-painted a jaunty parakeet green, the set was cheerful and unfussy. Kate could see herself eating breakfast at that table, scrolling through the morning news on her phone or texting Paul. Maybe even going over case notes….

That thought triggered an emotion, which gave rise to a geyser of related emotions, like an earthquake under the sea. Fearing the tsunami, Kate searched frantically for a material distraction. She hit on three.

"I don't like that big window. One man breaks it and his gang climbs through. And the inset glass pane on the door could get them off the terrace and into the residence. I know the alarm will sound, but think of all an intruder can do in the time it takes for patrol response. We're only the length of an extendible ladder from the street. Anyone determined to get up here could—"

Tony coughed.

Kate stopped. "Sorry," she said, smiling. The outburst had done its job, sweeping away difficult emotions and replacing scary thoughts with more comforting ones. During her long recovery, she'd become something of an amateur security expert. But, so had Tony.

"The window is polycarbonate. Indistinguishable from glass, wouldn't you say?" His gaze swept over it appreciatively. "Same with the panes on the door. As for an intruder entering the house via this terrace, look at the construction of the inner wall."

Kate did. The smooth curving inside lip provided no crease, nook, or porous surface. Even Henry's favorite superhero, Batman, might be stymied by the approach.

"A determined intruder could drop in from a height. From a rented cherry picker, maybe," Kate said, not really believing it, but determined to name something that *could* happen, even if it beggared belief. "Jump down on the terrace and go at the polycarbonate with a sledgehammer...."

She sounded like an idiot. Once upon a time, Tony would've laughed at her. Now he didn't even smirk. He'd become exquisitely careful of her feelings, which was wonderful and terrible at the same time.

"I don't deny that a very determined person might move heaven and earth to get on this terrace," Tony said. "Which is why there's a perimeter alarm that's automatically engaged whenever the door is locked. Anything heavier than five pounds will trigger it. It's a hundred and forty decibels. Loud enough to make any intruder feel exposed."

Kate chuckled. If Tony wouldn't laugh at her, she'd do it herself. "This place is a fortress. How did you find it?"

"Lady Margaret and Lady Vivian, of course," he said, meaning his longtime snout in London society and her amour, an equally well-connected lady of a certain age. Lady Margaret was known for her blistering tongue and her encyclopedic knowledge of pedigreed English families. Kate didn't know Lady Vivian well, except to note she was stylish, more light-hearted than her companion, and perhaps the only person who could tell Lady Margaret to shut it with impunity.

"They put me in the hands of an estate agent who spoke almost entirely in innuendo. The story he told me about this place went something like this," Tony said, putting on a sort of hard-sell manner that made Kate giggle.

"'Do you recall that American singer? The one who came from Detroit but always tried to sound like she was born in Shepherd's Bush? She lived here for a time with her husband, the one in the cinema business. They hired an international security firm to harden every mews house in the row. Based on the box office receipts, no one in London cared where they lived or what they were up to, but they still had ex-Mossad agents crawling over the property for a month. When they sold the block, most of the houses were snapped up right away. It's a miracle this last one is available to let.'"

"Oh, good grief," Kate said, pretending to be exasperated by the excesses of film stars. The Hollywood set had been "mews-o-philes" since the swinging 60s, when Michael Caine famously took one in Hyde Park. But in truth, the idea of a bespoke security firm hardening the entire row of mews houses to eliminate weak points struck Kate as brilliant. During Tony's amusing recitation of the estate agent's sales patter, those rumbles of fear in her belly—deep in her bowels, to be painfully honest—had disappeared. For the first time since alighting from the train into the bustle and noise of Paddington Station, she felt safe again.

Secure. She asked, "Dare I inquire how much you paid for the privilege of booking us these seven days?"

"No." Taking her hands, Tony pulled her close enough for a peck, then all the way into his arms for a longer, deeper kiss. "The look on your face is worth every ha'penny."

CHAPTER 6

*K*ate enjoyed the rest of the tour. Strange Mews was bright and lovely, filled with little details that had nothing to do with security. Once they penetrated Kate's attention, she began to delight in them. The living room's cream walls and navy crown molding; the kitchen's posh mod-cons, including a microwave and a wine cooler integrated almost invisibly into its central island; the master bedroom's gorgeous marble-enclosed fireplace, which turned out to be infrared.

"I trust there's no objection?" Tony asked, showing her the remote.

"Nope." One of the many things Kate loved about Briarshaw was crackling wood fires on crisp nights, but they were a lot of work. Especially since she'd made it part of her daily physical therapy to gather the wood and lay the fires herself.

In the copses surrounding Briarshaw, fallen branches were abundant, but Kate had to load them onto a wheelbarrow, then push it uphill all the way back to the woodpile. That pile was situated by the old stables, now in a state of picturesque decline and stabling nothing but tractors and hay balers. Once Kate made it there, she got her breath back by sitting on the flared stump that served as her chopping block. Then it was time for the wood-splitter, and the ax.

What she'd initially assumed to be an upper body workout turned out to be a challenge for her calves and quads, too. Steadying herself during each swing had been frustrating at first. She still limped a little, especially when it was wet or cold, despite the built-in orthopedic lift in her right shoe. She'd had all her shoes fitted with such lifts, which were costly but not too noticeable. They smoothed her gait, which was necessary, since multiple surgeries had shortened her right leg.

Another challenge to chopping wood was her inability to plant herself firmly, even after weeks of rehab. To keep from losing her balance while chopping wood, she had to push the toe of her right foot against an exposed tree root and brace herself as she brought down the ax. It worked, and that was all that mattered. Her surgeons had done brilliant work and she'd healed well. But the fact was, the architecture of her leg was different; the geometry of her knee's flexion was different. Now her job was to adapt to those differences, not pretend they didn't exist.

"This window is polycarbonate, too?" she asked, looking down into the alley between Strange Mews and its neighbors. The neat red brick exteriors and cobblestone streets almost transported her to an earlier era. Except the inevitable modern intrusions: wheelie bins, a plastic Fisher-Price push-buggy, and a *very* smart red Porsche Boxster idling a few doors down.

"Yes. And watch this." Motioning for Kate to step back, Tony brandished the same remote that controlled the infrared electric fire. With a soft hum, motorized shutters rolled down, clicking into place.

"Aluminum?" Kate teased, knowing better.

"Steel. There's no point spending a week here if you don't sleep well at night."

Kate gazed on the man she loved. It ought to be against the law for a man to celebrate another birthday and look better.

Fitter, more energetic, and possibly more confident, although in Tony's case he had hit his limit in confidence some time ago. He chalked it up to a happy marriage. She thought he'd made a deal with the devil. Either way, she won.

"When you decided to make this week work, you didn't fanny about, did you?"

"I did not. Now tell me the truth. Does it pass muster?"

"Yes," Kate said. Now that she'd seen all of Strange Mews, she wanted very much for the experiment to work. She'd been born in London, she knew it well, and she wanted her old life back. She wanted her old self back, light and sharp and fearless. And if that was impossible, she wanted a new self—one that trusted London, and belonged there.

"That bed, though." Surveying the tall, upholstered headboard, she flicked off a bit of white fluff marring the navy satin. Turning back the snowy duvet—goosedown, if she was any judge—she sat on the queen mattress and bounced gently.

"What about it?" His tone was deadpan, but a finger had already hooked into his necktie, loosening the Windsor knot.

"I think we should test it before we unpack." Kate smiled up at him. Her mind was busy formulating more slyly provocative remarks, but Tony's tie was already off, and as it turned out, no more words were needed.

CHAPTER 7

"Your mobile's vibrating," Kate murmured.

"I'm asleep," Tony said. His eyes were closed. His breath was slow and even. His face, in repose, was perfectly untroubled.

"What if it's home?" she asked, meaning Briarshaw. Or more specifically the people they'd temporarily left behind there: their adopted son, Henry; her brother, Ritchie; her sister, Maura; and Tony's personal assistant Mrs. Snell, who'd joined them in Devon during Tony and Kate's convalescence and stayed on to help run the expanded household. There was always something to manage in Briarshaw; the staff, accustomed to looking after the house, the farm, and the grounds, were not accustomed to a nine-year-old boy, a mentally-challenged man, or the whirlwind that was Maura. Kate would never have left them, even for a week, if not for the assurance that Mrs. Snell was there, steely behind her large magnifying glasses, as tightly wound as her permed curls and capable of managing everything with an iron hand.

"It's not home," Tony said.

Kate, curled against him, lifted herself enough to peek at his iPhone, which lay next to the bedside lamp. She couldn't make out the name on the screen. Tony had never bothered to personalize his contacts so that a photo appeared. He was perfectly comfortable keeping his phone silenced when not on duty. Like the *Tyrannosaurus Rex*, the *Apatosaurus*, and other stone age titans, he seemed to believe he had a right to disconnect, and to remain disconnected for as long as he pleased.

The mobile stopped vibrating. Kate had just got comfortable again—the bed had passed muster, and Lord knew the company was divine—when the rattling burr started over again, gently infuriating.

Kate sat up. "I really think it might be home."

Tony opened his eyes. Rather than looking at his phone, he looked at her. There was plenty to see, since Kate, sitting up, had pushed aside the duvet.

"It's not home. It's Paul."

"How do you know?"

"I can feel it."

"But Henry looked a bit peaked this morning. Complained about his tum…."

"He always complains about his tum when there's a maths quiz looming."

"And Ritchie's due for a setback. He's done so well with the new center," she said, meaning the Teen and Adult Clubhouse her elder brother visited three times a week. Ritchie wasn't one to make friends or warm up easily. Still, he'd adapted to the Clubhouse with surprising rapidity, possibly because one of the activity rooms had a wall covered with LEGO tape. The tape's depressed tubes and short protruding knobs allowed LEGO artists like Ritchie to build in creative new ways. He also liked the Clubhouse's snacks, as he'd informed Kate roughly two hundred times, usually when she was making him sit at the table and push veg around his plate. If he had his way, he would've subsisted on fizzy soda, fruit rollups, and prawn crisps, and would've never eaten another vegetable, except perhaps McDonald's French fries.

"I keep waiting for the other shoe to drop," Kate went on. "What if he's having a meltdown Mrs. Snell can't handle?"

"Mrs. Snell could handle the Persian Order of Assassins, should they elect to make a comeback. And don't underestimate Maura."

Tony had her there. When it came to sobriety, Maura was making a go of it. She'd had one setback—a Saturday night in Devon that was supposed to be a non-drinking dinner with an old mate that turned into an all-night gin binge—but by Sunday afternoon, she'd tearfully hauled herself into a meeting, told the group what happened, accepted another beginner chip and started again. Kate, who'd accompanied Maura to the meeting, had sat silently in the back, amazed. She'd always expected her sister to fail. She hadn't expected Maura to admit she'd slipped, hold herself to account, and try again. That impressed Kate far more than a sudden and effortless conversion, and when the time was right, she'd told Maura so. That conversation, though brief, had changed their relationship, and apparently steadied her elder sister, who seemed to feel looked up to for the first time in a dog's age.

"You're right," Kate admitted. "They're fine. Everything's fine." But as she said it, she felt just the opposite. A wellspring of unease seemed to lurk just beneath her diaphragm, never completely dormant, always ready to lock onto any mundane thought and turn it into a pitch-black omen. Hadn't she felt fine in those last seconds before the attack? Hadn't she waltzed right into the deadliest peril of her life, never guessing until the trap was sprung? Funny old life, that she had the nerve to go around distrusting Maura, when the primary person she couldn't trust was staring back at her in the mirror.

Tony's mobile, dormant for less than thirty seconds, started vibrating again. "Enough," he growled, sitting up, and snatched the iPhone from the bedside table. He punched the speaker button before answering.

"Good afternoon, Paul," Tony said, in that determinedly bright tone that everyone who'd ever worked for him feared. "It had better be murder."

"It is." Paul Bhar sounded grimly excited. In most people, anything less than sober neutrality in the face of a fellow human's extinction was distasteful. In detectives, it was just a flaw to be overlooked, like an inability to achieve career-life balance, or an addiction to sugared pastries.

"Hot scene?" Tony asked.

Kate slid out of bed and began gathering her clothes. Her husband had a sixth sense for these things.

"I can't say. It's like Covent Garden in here. We had the personal assistant, the bloke next door, the couple from across the street, and who knows how many other neighbors trooping through until the uniforms secured the scene. As I speak, we have one corpse, one murder weapon, five people awaiting interview and one who may have fled the scene."

Kate had never seen Tony wearing his current expression. But she'd glimpsed it in Henry's face on his birthday, when he'd unwrapped an official Star Wars electronic light saber.

"How's Kate?" Paul went on. "I hope she isn't dragging her feet. I warned her about being a giddy goat."

"You said no such thing!" Kate bellowed, buttoning her blouse.

"I'm on speaker?" Paul sounded betrayed.

"How many times have I told you," Tony said. "If you speak to the husband, you speak to the wife, and vice-versa. Did you say a group of neighbors discovered the body?"

"So they tell us, guv." Paul, unable to bring himself to call his longtime boss by his Christian name, despite multiple invitations to do so, had settled on addressing him as "guv." Naturally, his literal governor was DCI Vic Jackson, now in charge of the Toff

Squad, whom Paul differentiated from Tony by calling him "Chief."

"Don't you read the *Telegraph*?"

"I don't," Tony said unapologetically. "But I seem to recall hearing something about an additional twenty thousand coppers being hired to the force."

"It's the service nowadays, grandad," Paul said with his usual cheery insolence. "And I'll believe that pie-in-the-sky puffery when I see it. We're down five thousand, by my reckoning. Can't retain the sorry buggers. They're too smart to put up with the abuse the three of us did."

Tony laughed. "Get another promotion or two under your belt. That's where the true indignities begin."

"Not for you. You've passed into the great beyond. You're a consultant, untouchable." Paul, who'd increasingly sounded like a small boy bursting with a secret, asked in a stage whisper, "Unless, given the situation here, you feel like lending a hand?"

CHAPTER 8

*T*ony looked at Kate. After their long sojourn in the country, anything, even another dog-napping, would've tempted him. And this was murder.

"I thought we were having dinner at the Ivory." Kate, not looking at him, was stepping into her trousers. He couldn't tell if her tone was teasing or not.

"It's only five o'clock. There's still time."

"And then there's Winter Wonderland," she continued, digging in her handbag and producing a hairbrush. "There's sure to be queues there, and if we don't arrive early, it may be too chaotic to enjoy."

"I can promise you," Paul declared over speakerphone, "this scene has all the drama of Winter Wonderland. And possibly as many spectators."

Tony suffered a pang of guilt at the mention of Winter Wonderland. That yearly festival of outdoor Christmas lights, food, drink, and music was the sort of thing newlyweds did, but he and Kate had never experienced. Working on a murder squad was more than just the excitement and drama of the scene itself. It was weeks of follow-up paperwork, investigatory reviews, and court appearances. He owed her a little year-end romance. Moreover, the very fact Kate wanted to put herself out there, to participate in a busy holiday outing surrounded by strangers, was a sign of progress. Could he really squander that opportunity simply to play detective again?

"Look, if it's dinner you're after, I promise to buy you a meal as soon as we wrap for the evening," Paul said, exhorting them via iPhone speaker like an old-fashioned preacher thundering from the pulpit. "And I'm not kidding when I say we're shorthanded. In the old days, we'd have twice the manpower. The Chief is down with flu. I'm the senior man. Even the M.E. is a little boy. Ever since Garrett retired, they send us nothing but temps seconded from the Midlands or newly-qualified kiddies. I'm not messing you about. I'm completely sincere."

"You're the boy who cried sincere," Kate called from the en suite bathroom, where she was applying lipstick in front of the lighted mirror. "What a coincidence, that you have a big murder case and you're desperately in need of aid the second we arrive."

"You're right," Paul said. "You've winkled it out of me. I killed the poor blighter myself, brought in a cast of interlopers to muddy the waters, and rigged up the most bizarre murder weapon you've ever seen, all to—"

"Bizarre?" Tony interrupted. It fell upon him to remind Paul and Kate he was part of the conversation; otherwise, the two of them might bicker all night as he silently held the mobile. "What do you mean?"

"I'm not going to tell you," Paul announced, again sounding like a little boy. "If Miss High and Mighty would rather go peer at an old tree encircled by a couple of blinking lights, by all means, take her. Later, after you've read the details, or seen them reenacted in one of those crime documentaries, you can both take comfort in the fact you disbelieved me."

"You are the limit," Kate snapped, marching out of the bathroom with her hair up. The unruly blonde mop was longer and thicker after months of being allowed to do as it pleased beneath a wide-brimmed straw hat. Now it was twisted into a bristly updo, the ends fanned out like the crest of a rooster. That was Kate's investigatory hair, and while it wasn't especially pretty, the sight made Tony realize he'd missed it like crazy.

Plucking the phone from his hands, she barked, "Where are you?"

"Knightsbridge. 17 Holywell. Follow the flashing lights."

"Fine." Stabbing the mobile with a vengeful finger, Kate disconnected, then tossed the iPhone at Tony's lap. As he was stark naked, he hastened to block the missile, catching it just in time.

"Don't just stare at me," Kate admonished him. She stepped into her kitten-heeled shoes, the right built up taller than the left. "Get dressed. Let's go before I change my mind."

CHAPTER 9

I'm not afraid of you, Kate silently told the broad patrician face of 17 Holywell as she and Tony approached the crime scene on foot. *I'm game, I am.*

Her family of origin, the Wakefields, prized the quality known as "game" above all else. As her mum, frequently on the wrong side of the law, once said, "I was banged up over the weekend, but I laughed when those tossers put on the cuffs. You know me, love. I'm game, I am. Not afraid of the nick." It was a sentiment Kate had leaned on heavily during her early career, reminding herself that she, too, was game, no matter what kind of static she faced.

The scooter thief who shouted "Oi, it's Lizzie the Bizzie!" and cackled hysterically as she cuffed him, as if being arrested by a woman was an example of fate taking the piss? She was game.

The suffering looks passed from man to man in the precinct bullpen when she eschewed the preferred feminine silence? When she persisted in asking questions, interjecting theories, and arguing her point? When she refused to behave as though she was there only through the goodness of male hearts, and there-

37

fore owed it to everyone to keep her bloody mouth shut? She was game.

The very first time she'd stepped into Scotland Yard as a qualified DC, no T for "trainee" before the title Detective Constable, only to hear "Oi, it's Lizzie the Bizzie!" from a cluster of suits near the lifts. That had been her welcome to the Yard from the elder statesmen, every one of them hailing from those days when the top brass were indistinguishable from Great War generals. Yet that was their public greeting for her, same as a street thug's jeer. It hadn't fazed her. She was game, game, game.

For real, then. For real again, before I know it, Kate thought. It had to be true.

They'd taken a cab from Strange Mews to Knightsbridge. As expected, the police barriers, patrol cars with flashing lights, and uniformed officers waving off the curious made getting dropped off difficult, so Tony asked the cabbie to let them out at the next street over. Approaching 17 Holywell from the adjacent street, Sacristan Road, revealed a line of back gardens with low stone walls and well-trimmed shrubbery.

"A friendly zone for neighbors," Tony observed.

"And burglars." Kate tried one of the gates, which had no chain and padlock. It swung wide on well-oiled hinges.

"Don't see any dogs about," Tony said. "Nor officers, for that matter. I'm rather surprised not to spy at least one. That's the backside of number 17, just there."

"From the rear, it looks like a shack." Kate glanced around for CCTV cameras. She counted at least two, mounted by the neighboring homes' back doors. 17 Holywell merely had a light that wasn't burning, despite the deepening twilight. Though it was half-five, darkness was almost complete. Through the front window of Sacristan Road's biggest house, a glittering Christmas tree began on the ground floor and reached its peak twelve feet up, a golden star twinkling in the terrace windows.

They cut across the garden with the welcoming gate, only to

find themselves temporarily stymied when they reached the property in question. 17 Holywell's back garden had no entrance, except from inside the house. The gate had been removed, leaving a gap someone had bricked in. The stone walls were only four feet high, which certainly would have been manageable, except for a crowning insult: large pointed shards of glass, thick and dark, as if gathered from shattered beer bottles.

Kate had seen this before, a thick layer of concrete with the jagged glass set into it. As she saw it, a no-nonsense trespasser would simply pulverize the shards with a hammer, then hop the wall. To dissuade most intruders, tall iron spikes would be needed. But that term that had first come to her mind, "crowning insult," seemed very much the point. Decorating the wall with shards of glass wasn't about sleeping safe at night. It was that old vulgar hand gesture, two fingers up, telling anyone who viewed the barrier: Get stuffed.

"If our victim did this, I'm thinking he or she had a charming personality," Kate said.

"Or a reason to anticipate the worst. Perhaps both," Tony said. "If we push through that row of boxwoods, we should be able to follow that path to the other side of the house."

The front half of 17 Holywell was more of a chaotic scene that Kate or Tony usually found in attractive, well-manicured neighborhoods. Up and down the street, porches were lit up. Onlookers paced with phones, or pretended to walk their dogs, or found excuses to go out to the boot of their car and root around. From time to time, a PC asked someone to step back, or stop filming with their mobile and go about their business. The neighbors answered politely, but generally didn't comply. If not for the blue-and-white crime scene tape, which really did have a remarkable effect on the public, Kate had no doubt there would be neighbors crowding 17 Holywell's porch and pounding on the door.

"None of them seem terribly upset," she murmured to Tony.

EMMA JAMESON

"Agreed. That man walking the pair of Yorkies looks positively overjoyed."

"Where'd you two come from?" a PC shouted. A handheld torch flashed in their eyes.

"CID," Tony answered, voice ringing with authority, as Kate, with a tingle of the old excitement, reached for her warrant card.

CHAPTER 10

"*L*ook at you!" Kate barely had time to register Paul's presence in 17 Holywell's front room before she found herself seized and hugged. When he finally released her, he looked her up and down, shaking his head in amazement.

"I mean, really. Just look at you. I've never seen you in a puffer coat. You're like a gender-swapped Michelin man. It *is* just you in there, isn't it?" He grabbed her sleeve, pretending to peer up into it, then went for the hem of the big coat, which fell to her ankles. "Henry! Ritchie! Are you stuffed in there with her, lads? Sing out if you need rescue!"

She kicked him away. "It's a coat. For heaven's sake. Some of us fancy warmth."

He poked one of the coat's many rounded coils. They did look a bit like the body of the Michelin man, Kate realized. Not the old, bulging one of her childhood, but the slimmed-down mascot of the current age, when even cartoons had to be svelte, lest someone accuse the company of setting an unhealthy example

"Oh, it looks warm," Paul agreed. "It also looks like it was last worn by a six-foot, sixteen stone Swede named Bjorn. Guv, you didn't engineer this unisex new look for her, did you?"

Tony, no fool, declined to answer. For his part, Paul looked exactly like he always did—natty for a bloke on a first date, overdressed and overgroomed for a DI on a case. Since his promotion, he'd expanded his already excessive wardrobe. He'd even gone to Paris on a mini-break to shop *Galeries Lafayette Homme*.

"Anyway, now you're back in the real world, where you belong, and I couldn't be happier to see you." Paul turned to Tony, shaking his hand as if it had been decades. "Barely holding it together, aren't you, old man? If I'm being honest, you look like a corpse. One that's been dug up, brushed off, and stuck in an Italian suit."

Tony absorbed this abuse serenely. Kate, well versed in the rules of male engagement, understood that bantering insults meant all was well. Months ago, when Tony had been hospitalized with a battered face, one eye temporarily blinded and turned to the wall, every male visitor, including Paul, had greeted him with a hushed, "My goodness, you look well."

"So glad you two could take time out from the bustle of Devon," Paul continued, sounding as if six months' bottled witticisms and provocations was about to be uncorked all at once. "Any *Hound of the Baskervilles* situations there need sorting? Bit of *Agatha Raisin* in the picturesque cottages?"

"I expected dinner at the Ivory, followed by a leisurely stroll through Winter Wonderland," Tony said with a trace of his old Chief Superintendent persona. "Instead, I was urged to come to this house, at this hour, or forfeit participation in an extraordinary case." He spread his hands. "I see nothing extraordinary thus far. Except, I suppose, a rather Spartan lifestyle for a part of London that generally lives far better."

Kate, who'd been focused on Paul, looked around 17 Holywell's front room and agreed. The back of the house hadn't really resembled a "shack," as she'd claimed when crossing through the neighbors' back gardens, but it had been entirely neglected, without a single flourish or iota of pride. The shutters were beat-up, and some were missing. There was no sitting area, no potted plants, not even a stone birdbath. The front of 17 Holywell had been a little better, with all the shutters in place and what looked like brand-new house numbers affixed over the door, but it was still unadorned. The foyer, through which PCs had led her and Tony to Paul, was completely empty, apart from a coat rack. This front room, although physically large, nevertheless gave the impression of smallness and meanness.

"That sofa looks like it might have come from Oxfam," she said. It had a wooden frame and chintz cushions, dark with age and overuse. "Lord knows the rug's seen better days. Who lives here?"

"Barnaby Galen." Paul looked at Tony. "Heard of him?"

"No. I take it, I should have?"

"Maybe. Still waiting for details on family connections, but according to that lot in the kitchen, he was a multimillionaire. Possibly even a billionaire."

"That lot in the kitchen?" Kate repeated, and then remembered. "Did you say a group of neighbors found him?"

"Sort of. When we get upstairs, I'll clarify," Paul said, glancing toward a pair of uniformed officers guarding the door that apparently led to the kitchen. Holding up his mobile, which as usual was attached to his right hand, he added, "It may take a couple of days for the Met to confirm it, but according to Officer Google, Barnaby Galen was indeed a very rich man. No title, no celebrity connections, and no charities, but loads of filthy *lucre*."

"It doesn't smell like a rich man's house," Kate said. "Ever been called out to a Council house where the plumbing's failed, the parents are junkies, and all the kids get removed and placed in care? That's what this smells like." She wasn't exaggerating. The moment she'd entered the front room, the sour odor had smacked her across the face, like the glove of a nobleman demanding a duel.

"Some of it may be this rug." Tony ran the toe of his wingtip

43

over the pile. Once, it had probably been red with repeating black flourishes. Now it was brownish, and those flourishes had aged into wiggly Rorschach prints, each one suggesting murder. "There's also a bit of a nasty squish beneath my feet. Like rising damp." He bounced slightly, and the floorboards squeaked.

"Why aren't those lights on?" Kate asked, meaning the wall sconces.

"They don't work," Paul said. "That's the only one with electric current." He pointed at the dirty little lamp to one side of the Oxfam sofa. The shade was gray with dust. Kate thought it was so long neglected, any attempt to clean it would probably dissolve the fabric.

The walls were bare, and looked as if they'd always been so. No mirrors, framed art, or vases. Just a coffee table, plain and sturdy, with deep scrapes across the top. It could have been one of her mum's old sticks of furniture—the sort that Lolo Wakefield routinely left behind when changing houses in the middle of the night. Clearly, Barnaby Galen had believed in using a thing till it was used up.

"You mentioned upstairs," Tony said to Paul. "Is the body still there?"

"Yes. The CSI companies are functioning at low strength, too. At present they're massing for a big response. This scene will be a challenge," Paul said. "Not just because of the neighbors who trooped up the stairs, through the master bedroom where the dead man is, and back down again. Because of the general poor hygiene. Kate's sniffer nailed it. There's no running water or functioning toilet in this house."

Kate groaned. She glanced at Tony. He shut his eyes briefly and shook his head.

"Doesn't bode well for all the drips pans here and there, now does it?"

He meant the various pots and pans, everything from copper roasters to humble stainless-steel saucepans, situated on the floor in various spots in Galen's front room. The practice was common enough in old houses to pass without comment. At Briarshaw, the housekeeper called the roof's leaky areas "vulnerabilities," and kept a close eye on the weather report. She had a collection of chipped or ugly pots that served no purpose other than catching drips.

"Don't worry, the pans on this level seem to hold nothing but rainwater," Paul said. "The ground floor toilet only failed last week, according to the neighbors. It's grimy and in need of demolition, but the bog flushed until recently. Upstairs is a different matter. Watch where you step. The first PC on the scene accidentally kicked over a drips pan. Ruined his sock and shoe."

"And further contaminated the scene," Tony said.

Paul shrugged. "Really, it's the end of the world up there, either way. The bog and bathtub have been backed up so long, it's sort of a mummified hellscape. But instead of getting it repaired, it looks like Galen just kept improvising. Filling up new pots and forgetting to empty out of the old ones."

"Let me go out on a limb. Mr. Galen was unmarried?" Kate asked.

"Yes. Never married, if my research pros agree with the sage wisdom of Officer Google," Paul said. He grinned at Tony. "See what fate you saved yourself from by getting married? Kate will never let you subsist like Ebenezer Scrooge, on nothing but money and meanness.

"Did you notice there wasn't even a TV in the front room? There's not one in the house," Paul continued, as if this was a sin beyond using crockery as urinals. "My team found a laptop, which was in good working order, and an old PC that was dead as a doornail. Like Jacob Marley," he added suddenly, apparently remembering that line from the familiar Christmas tale. "No books or magazines. A liquor trolley, heavy on the Scottish single malt. Not sure if his only hobby at home was lifting glasses, but like I say, my team has the laptop, and they'll inform me directly if anything interesting comes up."

My team, Kate thought, suffering a little stab of jealousy. While she'd been in Devon, Paul had been working non-stop, covering for her. The detective shortage written up by the *Telegraph* and other newspapers was quite real; years of austerity had hit the Met hard, putting them far behind in recruitment. It took a special person to join the Met and stick, despite media criticism, inadequate pay rises, and a mirror-maze of policies and political hoops that often made police officers feel like they were criminals. Paul, though still a couple of years shy of forty, was now the equivalent of a grizzled veteran. Of course he had a team.

"So, no wife. No children, at least according to the Internet, I assume," Kate said. "Was Mr. Galen a sort of neighborhood project, then? Someone they looked in on, since he had trouble caring for himself?"

A devilish light glinted in Paul's eyes. "Before we know it, a caravan of CSIs will descend on this house and kick us out without so much as a 'Hate it for you,'" he said. "Let's see the body first, and answer questions later."

CHAPTER 11

efore they went upstairs, Tony and Kate suited up according to Met guidelines—blue overalls, blue nitrile gloves, and filmy blue booties to cover their shoes. For the first time since exiting Strange Mews, Kate was obliged to give up her enormous silver puffer coat, which really did look like it belonged to a towering Swede three times her size. Tony despised the coat, but it didn't take a qualified therapist to realize Kate had selected it as a form of protection. Whether she realized it or not, it was her armor, now that she was back in the city.

Despite his rising excitement to be back in the action, he reminded himself that his first duty was to Kate. Thus far, she'd pleasantly surprised him, first with a positive reaction to the mews house, then by agreeing to forgo their plans in favor of police work. As a DI, Paul had the right to call upon a consultant, so Tony's spur-of-the-moment involvement wouldn't raise any eyebrows. Kate, on the other hand, was opening herself up to another visit from AC Deaver. They were eager for her to recommit, and would see her appearance tonight as an indication she was ready to return.

I'll keep an eye on her, he vowed to himself. *If she goes wobbly about the knees, I'll pull the plug. Even if the scene lives up to Paul's hype.*

As they ascended the stairs, the stench worsened. For a moment, Tony wondered how his old friend, Divisional Surgeon Peter Garrett, was bearing up as he awaited the CSIs. The man had a nose like a bloodhound. Then he remembered that Garrett, who was roughly Tony's age, give or take a year, had announced his surprise retirement over the summer.

As far as Tony knew, Garrett was now at home, attended by hospice workers as he died of liver cancer. The only thing more depressing than that grim mental picture was the fact Garrett had refused to receive any visitors from his professional life. Tony had sent him a card, naturally, but it had not been answered, nor had Tony expected it to be. Garrett didn't want to be gawked at, or bombarded with mawkish sentiment. Such desires, Tony fully understood. But it was still hard to take, knowing that his contemporary, a man he considered a friend, was bowing out while the world of sirens and blue-and-white crime tape spun on without him.

"Did you say something about a medical examiner?" he asked Paul.

"That's me," a thin, almost childish voice piped from the end of the hall. "In the master bedroom. Are you coming in?"

"Yes, it's DI Bhar," Paul returned. "With colleagues."

"Prepare yourself," the young man with the reedy voice said. "Be warned."

Tony shot a look at Kate. From Peter Garrett, who viewed every corpse as a teaching opportunity, and welcomed police into each crime scene as if it were his own dynamic classroom, to this? What sounded like one of Henry's little friends, bleating over a make-believe peril?

They entered the master bedroom, Paul in the lead, Tony and Kate just behind him. As Tony had feared, the stench was worse. Partly it was rotting fibers—curtains, carpets, and upholstery befouled by years of neglect. But mostly it was bodily fluids. Tony had also expected the tang of copper; given the young M.E.'s warning, it was surely a bloody death, perhaps even a dismemberment. Then he saw the scene, and stopped in his tracks.

He couldn't take it in. Beside him, Kate cried out softly. Paul chuckled as if he'd pulled off a particularly impish practical joke.

"Never heard you gasp like that, guv," he said, elbowing Tony's ribs.

"It's not real," Tony muttered.

"Oh, I assure you, it is," a little man Tony had never met declared earnestly. "The first police to arrive thought it was a prank, too. I suppose it's possible that it was intended to be one, but I very much doubt it."

Tony nodded, barely sparing a glance for the M.E., who was blond, perhaps 5'4", and startlingly young. It was the bed, the corpse, and what he could only presume was the murder weapon that captivated him, drawing him closer as if by magic. Dimly he noticed that Kate didn't shy away—on the contrary, she was a step ahead of him, also pulled by the same macabre magnet. He was grateful, because if she'd chosen that moment to "go wobbly at the knees," as he'd put it, he might have found it impossible to turn away.

Barnaby Galen's bed was crowded against the wall, accessible from only one side. It was a four-poster, the type with a canopy frame so the bed could, if the sleeper wished, be entirely shrouded in thick tapestry curtains. In the nineteenth century, when miasma theory posited that bad air, especially night air, caused disease in otherwise healthy people (as opposed to bad food, bad water, and an overall dearth of hygiene), the upper classes had slept behind curtains meant to keep out bad air the way mosquito nets kept out bugs. Either Galen didn't care to sleep that way, or the four-poster's canopy had fallen to pieces quicker than the curtains. The canopy frame above the bed was naked, like an exposed ribcage, and as was the case with many antique beds, the mattress stood high off the floor, necessitating a wooden step stool.

The old man had died sitting up, back against the headboard, as if trying to push his body through it. One hand was pressed to his chest. The other was stuffed in his mouth. Directly opposite him, seemingly staring into the dead man's face, a yellowish skeleton had reared up, apparently from under the bed. One skeletal hand was pointing at Galen. The other hand clutched at the old man's bare foot.

"We're *certain* this is real?" Kate demanded.

"It's not a prank, although I suppose it could have been intended as one," the M.E. said for the second time. He was smiling gently, as if to signal his willingness to cheerfully repeat the facts as often as necessary. "This is a *bona fide* crime scene. Mr. Galen's personal assistant discovered his employer like this approximately three hours ago, around three o'clock this afternoon."

"Personal assistant," Tony repeated on autopilot. The skeleton was wearing a plastic rain bonnet. It was the sort once adopted by many women, back in the days of stiff Aqua Net bouffants that couldn't survive a cloudburst. Such plastic rain bonnets, unfussy and foldable, had been carried in change purses and film canisters, tucked into a lady's handbag. When the weather got woolly, the bonnets were shaken out and tied under the chin. Tony thought perhaps he'd seen the Queen in one, or perhaps Princess Anne, but he couldn't be sure. Finding it on this aged human skeleton—as he moved closer, he decided it almost certainly *was* a genuine human skeleton, based on the bones' irregular coloring, as well as its crumbling teeth—made him suddenly wonder if he was dreaming.

"The assistant's name is Oliver Vine-Jones," Paul said, snapping out the details as he'd once done as Tony's subordinate. "He's not part of that lot in the kitchen. After he discovered the body, he rang 999 but didn't wait for the officers. And since he left the front door ajar, one of the neighbors wandered in. That stupid bugger called in all the rest of them."

"Vine-Jones," Tony murmured. The plastic rain bonnet had yellow ducks printed on it. They were cracked and partially rubbed off, as if the bonnet were very old. "Under arrest, then?"

"Being interviewed at home," the M.E. said.

"What?" With an effort, Tony tore his gaze away from the yellow ducks. "He fled the scene after the emergency dispatcher no doubt instructed him to remain, but you're permitting him the tea-and-biscuits interview snug at home?"

Paul cleared his throat. "It's all under control, guv. A misunderstanding. Naturally, Mr. Vine-Jones is a person of interest, but DC Gulls and DC Kincaid dropped into his place straightaway and found nothing too alarming. I'll explain more in a moment."

"Fine," Tony muttered, returning to the victim, a corpse, and the murder weapon, also a corpse, which was a combination he'd never before encountered. Kate knelt by the foot of the bed, examining where the skeleton's body abruptly terminated. It was actually only half a person. The pelvis and legs were missing; the spinal column seemed to be fused to some kind of metal device.

"This thing wasn't just placed here. It was installed," Kate said. "There's an entire contraption screwed into the bed frame."

"I think there's a remote-control aspect," Paul said cheerfully. "When the CSIs disassemble it, I'll bet there's a Bluetooth trigger that made it deploy."

"Can I touch it?" Kate asked Paul. The M.E. answered.

"Yes, but take care. I accidentally brushed it when I made my initial examination. It shrieked like a banshee. Almost wet myself."

"Brace yourself, then." With a nitrile-clad finger, Tony touched the skull. Nothing happened. From up close, he could see the metal pins and wires holding the old bones together. Surely real human skeletons for science and anatomy students had been done away with decades ago. But there might be a few of them still in circulation, in smaller colleges or private collections. Certainly, the sale of human bones, even those once used for educational purposes, was illegal in most of the western world. Tony knew that the auction giant eBay refused to deal in human remains, so the person that set up this particular murderous prank had needed access to an unusual prop.

He touched the skull again. Nothing happened.

"Where did you brush against it?" Even as he asked the M.E. the question, Tony noticed additional wiring on the skeleton's right hand. Painted roughly the same hue as the phalanges, those wires ran along the wrist, thumb, and fingers. And there was something more: a tiny box with an electronic eye, affixed to the metacarpals. Tony touched it, and the skeleton screamed.

The scream rang through the bedroom, echoing off the cobwebby ceiling and the drab, papered walls. Steeled though he was, Tony jumped. So did Kate, Paul, and the M.E., all of them grinning. From out in the hall, the PCs assigned to guard the scene made noises that could only be described as nervous giggles. It would have been an unforgivable show of callous disregard—a man was dead, his remains in the very room with them—but under the circumstances, Tony didn't know what else they could do.

"Laughing makes me feel like a right monster, but I can't help it," Kate said. "This whole set-up is diabolical. Maybe the sickest thing I've ever seen."

Tony, remembering his promise, looked at her anxiously, but she didn't seem distressed. Her eyes shone and her color was up. It seemed that six months amid the lush green hills and black-faced sheep of Devon hadn't swept away her love of the job. She reminded him of their first joint investigation, when he'd been the cool, unapproachable guv and she'd blazed with the determination to prove herself. Even in the presence of death, seeing Kate back to her old self made his heart turn over.

He glanced at Paul. They'd worked together for years before Kate came along, and the channels of rapid, silent communication were still open. A flick of his eyes told Paul, "Thanks for that." And a slight pull at the side of Paul's mouth replied, "You're welcome."

"Well, don't be shy. Come closer," Kate snapped, motioning Tony and Paul over. The M.E. came too, looking absurdly happy to be there. Tony suddenly suspected this was the young man's inaugural murder scene. Talk about drawing an inside straight the first time you sat down to play poker.

"I don't recommend lying down on the floor," Kate said, doing so nonetheless. "This carpet's sticky-gummy. I don't even want to think about with what," she added, using her mobile to take photos of the skeleton-device's under-bed mechanism. "There are tracks under here. I can smell the oil. I guess the old man went to sleep and the killer triggered the device. The cart rolled up on the tracks and pushed Granny into view. Her hand reached out, maybe touched his foot...."

"And when the hand touched something, that deafening scream rang out," Tony said. "I don't mind saying, if that particular noise had awakened me from a sound sleep... and I sat up to see *that* thing...."

"Granny," Kate put in. "The rain bonnet makes it a her. And a granny."

"Granny," Tony agreed, fighting down wild, inappropriate laughter. "Well, if I'm being honest, I'd probably have a heart attack."

"That's what happened to Mr. Galen," the M.E. said, clearly sensing his moment had come. "I can't confirm it beyond doubt until I perform the post-mortem. I estimate his age as between sixty-five and seventy. I'm not sure I'd call him well-nourished; he looks a bit underweight. He died with his hand to his heart, mouth open, eyes open, and cadaveric spasm froze him in that position. It happens sometimes, when one suffers a violent shock at the moment of demise," he said, sounding intelligent and thoroughly professional, even if he looked like a jumped-up tween masquerading as a grown man. "Usually rigor mortis sets in later, and helps us fix a reasonably accurate time of death. With cadaveric spasm, I may not be able to offer you much."

"Shocked," Paul muttered with cheerful sarcasm. "Utterly shocked."

"So this Granny is the murder weapon? Full stop?" Tony asked.

"There could be additional contributing factors," the M.E. continued. "Mr. Galen's manner of living suggests he may have suffered from the early stages of cognitive decline. Of course, choosing to live in an unhygienic manner could merely indicate bloody-mindedness, rather than mental illness. I'm sure you noted the prescriptions on the bedside table."

Tony was surprised to realize he hadn't. It was difficult to be a good detective in the presence of Granny. He started to address a question to the young M.E., and realized he had no idea what the man was called.

"Forgive me. From the moment I entered this room, I seem to have forgotten my manners. I'm Tony Hetheridge." He put out his hand.

The M.E. shook it, brightening into a smile only a Grinch could have resisted. "Yes, I know. It's a pleasure to meet you at last, Lord Hetheridge. I'm Trevor Stepp."

"Have you worked with the Met for long?" Tony asked. A polite follow-up question was in his DNA, an imperative he found impossible to resist, even in a room with a skeleton dressed in her jaunty cartoon duck rain bonnet.

"I was recruited last month," Trevor said. "I've performed several post-mortems for the MPS, but this is my first call to a crime scene."

"Well. I don't know quite what to say to that. Except—welcome," Tony said. Trevor grinned. Fair-haired and impossibly wide-eyed, he was a tiny Christmas elf of a man in the house of horrors. Once more, Tony had the suspicion he would soon awaken beside Kate in bed at Strange Mews, amazed by the lunatic concoctions of his dreaming mind.

"What are the drugs prescribed for?" he asked Trevor.

"Most commonly, hypertension and hypercholesterolemia. At this stage, I'm not ruling out natural causes. But I'll be very surprised if my post-mortem doesn't reveal a massive myocardial infarction brought on by sudden, overwhelming terror."

Tony looked over the corpse of Barnaby Galen more carefully. He should have been a figure of pity; every murder victim should be, at least on principle. Kate was right; his manner of exiting this world was nothing short of diabolical. But there was something unwholesome about Galen, something craven and ugly, sitting under his canopy frame-ribcage, occupying gray sheets that hadn't been white for a very long time. His sparse hair, grown out several inches on one side, was swept over the top of his pate in a thin, hopeless comb over. His eyes protruded, the corneas exposed to the air for so long, they'd become twin snow globes. The old man's flared nostrils, jutting cheekbones, and corded throat made him seem well on his way to Granny's state of being. For Tony, something about this face-off between man and specter made sense. Death itself, demanding the skull beneath the skin.

"Murder by Granny." Paul gave a low whistle. "I've seen overkill. I've seen victims stabbed so often, they've become human pincushions."

"Or hit in the face so many times, their own mother wouldn't recognize them," Kate said.

"Or dismantled like a collapsible object," Tony said. "But I've never seen a murderer work this hard to shock and horrify as well as kill. If Galen had survived, he would have been locked in a secure hospital ward eating soft foods for the rest of his life."

"I wonder if that wasn't the real aim," Paul said.

No one spoke as they contemplated that possibility.

"At any rate, just think of the time and effort that went into this contraption," Kate said. Rising, she smoothed her blue overalls, frowning at the spots left by contact with the greasy carpet. "Imagine the access necessary to install it. He—or she—would've been in or out several times, measuring and planning. When you look at the tracks, the sensors, the rig to make the hand grasp, we're not just talking about murder. We're talking about sadism. And obsession."

"Oh!" Paul held up his phone. "I'm vibrating. Give me a minute." He listened briefly to what the caller had to say, then thanked them and rang off. "That was my heads-up from PC Wheatley. She's stationed by the barriers. The CSI caravan is on the move. We need to finish up and leg it, before they fling us into the street."

"Caravan?" Kate repeated, but Paul's mobile was summoning him yet again, this time in the form of texts he read aloud. It seemed the MPS had requested technical support from three separate companies. They would work the scene in concert, then divide the collected materials for processing. Even with the extra help, the state of the crime scene suggested a long processing time.

"I think I've seen enough," Tony said, glancing at Kate to see if she agreed. "I'd very much like to know a bit about the neighbors discovered wandering about the scene, if there's time. But before we go, does anyone object if I trigger Granny's scream again?"

This time, Paul gave the PCs in the hall a warning. Then Tony contemplated Granny's wired hand. On closer examination, those bones looked robust and regular, especially compared to the pointing hand, which seemed on the verge of crumbling. Was the wired hand from a gag skeleton, or perhaps from an artificial model meant for a Biology class? Either way, it lay close to Galen's foot. The foot protruded from under the duvet, his toenails hoary and jagged, his toes greenish-white. Wasn't that the universal fear? That if one's foot slips from beneath the covers, something terrible is waiting to take hold of it?

With his gloved fingertip, Tony brushed Granny's hand. On second hearing, the scream, louder than a human's, seemed overlaid with audio effects—scrapes, rattles, the crash of breaking glass. It seemed to emanate from the wall behind Granny.

"I wonder if the speaker is hidden behind that painting," Tony said. "Kate, bring your camera."

The framed still life—a bowl of fruit depicted in oils—suited the master bedroom perfectly; old, ugly, and probably antique. The whole thing was clotted with dust, giving the impression of a picture that hadn't been cleaned in ages. Nevertheless, the frame was plastic, with small, regular holes drilled into it. It was some sort of variation on a Bluetooth speaker.

"Is there such a thing as decorative dust?" Tony wondered aloud as Kate took pictures. The CSIs would do all of that, naturally, and do it better. But Kate liked her own photos to study while she awaited the formal report.

"Decorative dust?" Paul repeated.

"To make something look old and untouched. In a spray can, perhaps, for haunted houses?"

Before Paul could answer, his mobile thrummed again. This time he replied in the crisp, respectful tones of a man answering a superior officer.

"DI Bhar. Yes. I understand. No, we're in booties and gloves. No. No. I assure you, ma'am, no one's more committed to a uncontaminated scene than me. I know that. Fine. We're buggering off now. Yes. Buggering even as I speak. Happy Christmas. Buggering. Goodbye."

CHAPTER 12

$\mathcal{K}$ ate was eager to meet "the kitchen lot," as Paul called them, but understood that the imminent arrival of the CSI caravan would permit only the briefest of introductions. In the old days, Kate and Paul would've been expected to process them one by one, saving anyone particularly suspicious or intriguing for Tony. Now Paul's team—*team*, she thought again, still so bloody envious she could scream—had already done the initial processing, and was on point of releasing the kitchen lot back to their homes, on the understanding that follow-up interviews were likely.

DC Gulls, a petite woman with a round face, curly brown hair, and a deceptively sweet manner, squealed to see Kate again, hugging her twice as Tony and Paul went off to make a last sweep of 17 Holywell's ground floor. Granny's complexity as a murder weapon rendered the idea of a spur-of-the-moment killing moot, but that didn't necessarily mean the murderer had achieved access to Galen's home with the dead man's blessing. Noting the state of the windows and doors was essential, and was the sort of detail Tony couldn't bear entrusting to anyone else. There were many kinds of evidence he was willing to absorb from a report as factual and true, but whether the scene was an easy mark for intruders wasn't one of them.

Their reunion accomplished, Gulls led Kate to Galen's dirty, depressing kitchen, where she proceeded to issue a Who's Who among the detained neighbors. In the thick of them stood DC Kincaid, a miserable expression on his handsome and usually genial face as he checked his notes. Kate, who'd been in his shoes many times, felt for him—a solitary officer, doggedly following procedure while beset on all sides. The kitchen lot, probably tired and frustrated by their confinement in such an unhygienic place, seemed about two clicks from turning into what Kate considered the worst type of angry mob—a rich, entitled one.

An elderly woman with close-cropped hair, makeup applied by the trowel-full, and a portable oxygen delivery system worn over her shoulder like a handbag, was demanding to know why Kincaid wanted her address and phone number repeated. Was he mentally defective? Hard of hearing?

"That's Mrs. Selma Harwood," Gulls told Kate quietly. "Queen Bee of Holywell Street, I reckon."

The man beside her, at least six-foot-four, was wearing a thin robe of forest green with ivory tufts at the cuffs, collar, and hem. His bald head was so close to the kitchen's pendant light, it reflected the glow the way the moon reflects the sun. As Kincaid mumbled apologies to Selma Harwood, the tall man informed him that they, as taxpayers, supplied his salary, and weren't receiving a satisfactory return on investment.

"Who's Father Christmas? Her husband?"

"Boyfriend," Gulls replied. "Cyril Smythe. They live across the street. He was returning from a pageant rehearsal at the church hall when he saw Mr. Galen's front door ajar. So he came in, discovered the body—which had already been discovered and called in, though he wasn't to know that—and fetched Mrs. Harwood in for a look. Before long the other neighbors joined them, although there's not much clarity as to which order."

"And I suppose they all called 999 individually?" Kate said, pitying the poor operators.

Gull shook her head. "Not one of them," she whispered, staring meaningfully back at Kate.

This intriguing tidbit made Kate take a second look at the kitchen lot. Besides Selma and Cyril, there was a smartly dressed woman of perhaps forty, with light brown hair and tortoiseshell specs. Arms crossed over her chest, she glared at Kincaid. Even the pointed toes of her red pumps looked angry.

"Who's that?" Kate asked.

"Leona... oh, I've forgotten. Brown-thingie. Or thingie-Brown. I always fumble the hyphenated names," Gulls said. "I'll get you Kincaid's report by nine o'clock tomorrow, I promise. She's new to Holywell Street, and has no profession. Resistant to giving details."

Observing Leona's stony face, Kate wasn't surprised. By comparison, the woman beside her, heavyset and red-faced, seemed almost friendly. Her frizzy blonde hair looked as if it had been processed to the brink of destruction, virtually destroyed by a cycle of coloring, perming, and blow-drying. Kate fixed her age at around fifty.

"The big lady is Jacinda Cox," Gulls said, as if following Kate's gaze. "She actually isn't a neighbor. She's a friend of Galen's P.A. The man who first discovered the body."

"And fled the scene. You talked to him, didn't you?"

"I did. He only fled in the technical sense," Gulls replied. "There were extenuating circumstances. It'll all be in the report. He's distraught over the murder, by the way. He called Ms. Cox for support, and she took it upon herself to come here."

"Here? Not to the P.A.'s house?" Kate blew out her breath. Who did that? Heard their mate discovered his employer dead and rushed over—not to comfort the mate, but to see the corpse for themselves?

"Last, but not least, there's Adrian Poe," Gulls said, meaning the final member of the kitchen lot. He appeared to be the youngest neighbor, in the twenty-five to thirty zone, with a baby face and bright blue hair. He also had a nose ring, an eyebrow ring, and a variety of earrings in both ears. Without them, Kate might have guessed his age to be eighteen or less.

"You can't convince me he owns a house on this street. He must be someone's layabout kid," she told Gulls.

"Top marks. His parents own the house next door—15 Holywell. The Poes are out of the country since last week, and won't return until January. Adrian's home alone."

"He's the kind of neighbor I'd expect to wander into a crime scene," Kate said. "Given the hair and the piercings, I'm surprised these seniors haven't accused him of killing Galen."

"This lot? They adore Mr. Poe. Look on him as a bit of a mascot, I think," Gulls said. "It's the victim they hated. And not one of them was shy about saying so."

"Including…." Kate groped for the name she'd been given, and was gratified when it came to her. "Jacinda? The P.A.'s friend?"

Gulls nodded. "Hated Mr. Galen on her friend's account. Said he was a slave driver and a tight-fisted old screw."

Kate took that in. "You know what? I'm looking forward to nine o'clock tomorrow morning."

Gulls smiled. "I thought you might, ma'am."

CHAPTER 13

$\mathcal{T}$he CSI caravan arrived. Technicians in protective garb —yellow for one company, white for the other two— descended on 17 Holywell with unhurried, regimented precision. Kate respected the painstaking, by-the-book mentality that allowed the crime techs to accurately collect and process evidence; respected it, but couldn't understand it. Specifically, how they had the bloody patience to go so slowly, to deliberately backtrack, to check and cross-check one another's methods. In general, CSIs took one look at her, or Paul, or Tony—especially Tony, who'd come of age long before nitrile gloves and shoe covers—and saw walking, talking clouds of contamination. They were like Charlie Brown's friend Pigpen, followed everywhere by billowing filth. And CSIs weren't wrong. So once they assumed custody of the scene, there was nothing for it but to go away.

"Ugh. I told you that carpet was foul." Wadding up her soiled overalls, Kate pitched them into the red bag held open for her by a tired-looking PC. As Tony and Paul followed suit, Kate went round to the uniformed officer who'd gathered their personal items in his patrol car's boot. After signing the form on his clip-

EMMA JAMESON

board, she received her handbag and silver puffer coat. The man
grinned at her while passing it over.

"If that doesn't keep you toasty, nothing will, eh?"

Kate regarded the coat as if it belonged to someone else. No
doubt about it, the thing was overlarge and very heavy. While the
December breeze was brisk, her adrenaline was up. At most, she
wanted a windcheater, not a parka.

What was I thinking when I bought....

The golden bubble popped. For about an hour, give or take,
she'd transcended the world of before what happened on the
rooftop, and after what happened on the rooftop. She'd forgotten
her personal obsession with alarms, high walls, and electronic
sensors. She'd been a free agent again, unfettered, thinking of
nothing except the evidence. But now it was upon her again—if
not the fears, precisely, then an awareness that the fears weren't
truly vanquished. That they could, in fact, return at any moment.

"That breeze is going down a treat," Tony said, draping his
coat over his arm. "Quite nice to breathe freely again, after
choking on those fumes."

"Agreed." Paul hooked his coat over his shoulder. "So am I
forgiven? For interrupting the very first day of your holiday love
nest? Do you concede that I was morally obligated, one detective
to another, to drag you onto this scene by any means necessary?"

"Excuse me, sir." A PC approached him, frowning apologetically. "The CSI manager has asked me to move my vehicle. They
want to line up the evidence vans nose to tail. Anyone not on the
forensics team is asked to make way. And, er, vacate the
premises."

"I know when I'm not wanted," Paul said, grinning at the PC
to show there were no hard feelings. "I'm not bothered. Besides, I
promised to buy you two dinner. What do you say? Fancy some
pub grub? Packet of pig snacks and one of those local ales with a
name like Angry Pickle or Got Your Knickers?"

Kate, back in her puffer coat, thought wistfully of the days when she, Tony, and Paul had worked cases from the back of a pub, downing pints as they bounced theories off the walls, and each other. But on a Friday night, any pub within walking distance of Holywell Street would be packed. In some of the hot spots, it might be standing room only, with temporarily liberated workers roaring as they lifted their glasses in celebration.

"What do you think, love?" Tony asked. It didn't take a mind reader to know that he very much wanted to spend the next hour or two hashing out the case. If they parted company with Paul, Tony would quite likely be up all night, making notes and pacing restlessly around the mews house. Nevertheless, his gaze told her that she was in control. If she wanted them to bid Paul farewell and head back to Strange Mews, that's what they would do.

"I'm not sure I can handle a noisy pub," she admitted. "Thirty people is full capacity for our local in Shawbridge, and believe it or not, that gives me hives. And our holiday let is too far away." It wasn't, not by a long shot. But Kate felt strongly that she ought to preserve a safe place, a sanctuary, untouched by the dangers of police work. Paul was her best mate, and she trusted him absolutely. But if she invited him into Strange Mews, wasn't she inviting all of it in—good and bad?

"Let me check my mobile," she said. "I could murder a plate of spaghetti. There's sure to be a trattoria within walking distance."

CHAPTER 14

$\mathcal{L}$ucia's Pie and Prosecco was done up for Christmas in the Italian style: glittering balls, golden ribbons, and miniature trees decorated with white and gold ornaments. The nativity in the restaurant's front window was the biggest and most expansive Kate had ever seen. It was more than the traditional figures of Mary, Joseph, the Christ child, and the Three Wise Men; it went beyond a cutaway stable with lambs and shepherds looking on. This nativity was a six-tier diorama encompassing all sorts of peasants performing everyday tasks, camels laden with packs, lovers kissing, children playing, a king on his throne, the rich feasting, the poor in the fields. Kate had never seen a nativity that enlarged the focus so far beyond the story of a babe in the manger to include, somehow, the entire world.

"It's *il presepe*," said their server, Gianna. She spoke with such a thick accent, Kate needed an extra second after each sentence to decode what she'd just heard. "An Italian creche. The nativity. My mother brought it with her from Naples," she said proudly. "Like the Murano balls." She pointed to the fireplace where blown glass ornaments, each embellished with swirls, nestled among the fresh-cut cedar piled atop the mantle.

"What's that broom all about? Is it a leftover from Halloween?" Paul asked. He meant the decorative straw broom standing beside the tree.

Giana looked appalled by his ignorance. "That belongs to La Befana, you naughty boy."

Paul leaned back in his chair, going into full flirt mode. "Who's that? Your great-grandmother the witch?"

"La Befana is the old woman who delivers gifts to children," Tony said. "On Epiphany night. That's the fifth of January, if memory serves."

"Very good." Giana beamed at Tony, seemingly more interested in conversing with him. "Will you start with a bottle of Prosecco?"

"Three lagers, I think."

"The fifth of January?" Paul repeated, wresting Giana's attention back to him. "The good little children of England are better off. They're visited by Santa Claus two weeks earlier, you know."

"Don't you mean Father Christmas?"

"Six of one, half dozen of another."

Giana turned to Tony. "Is that right?"

"Father Christmas is more like Jack Frost. The spirit of Christmas, as Jack Frost is the spirit of winter," Tony said, eyes twinkling as he showed Paul up. "Santa Claus is the one who buys off the kiddies each year. He was discovered by the Americans, but he conquered this country soon after."

"In Italy we call him Babbo Natale." Gianna indicated a cartoon image, indistinguishable from the American Santa Claus, hanging on the wall. Apparently remembering Kate existed, she turned to her, teasing demeanor becoming all business. "You will have salad, yes?"

Kate tried not to take the server's suggestion personally. She'd gained a couple of pounds during her Devon sojourn. Apparently, her rehab routine, garden chores, and weekly rambles around the estate hadn't quite offset all the hearty country food, much of it farm to table, served at Briarshaw every night. She didn't know why she cared. Even when she'd met Tony, she belonged to the "bosoms and backsides" club, as Lady Margaret Knolls had put it, rather than the "stick insects." Besides, her monthlies were out of whack again. She always felt as fat as a tick when her period was overdue.

"Salad is good," Giana added, as if worried she'd overstepped. "Very filling. Tonight, it's a warm Castelfranco with vincotto and blue cheese."

"I want pizza. *Quattro Formaggi*." Kate tapped the picture inside the menu so there could be no mistake. Her intention to order spaghetti had faded the moment she smelled pizza. The restaurant, warm and cozy and only half-full, seemed unlikely to trigger her anxieties, but just in case, a prophylactic dose of melted cheese seemed just the thing.

"I'll have the same," Tony said.

"Who am I to disagree? Same." Paul was giving Giana what he no doubt considered a look of smoldering intensity. "So why does Italy need Santa *and* an old witch?"

"I don't have time to explain the world to naughty boys." Turning away from him, Giana beamed at Tony. "I'll be back soon with your pints," she said, and went on to take the next table's order.

"Don't kid yourself. She's smitten," Paul told Kate.

"I don't think your look of *moldering* intensity did anything but repel her."

"Stay up all night thinking up that one, did you?"

"When you're out of my sight, I never think of you at all." Kate giggled. "Besides, if she fancied anyone, it was him." She poked Tony's ribs.

"I don't know about that," Tony demurred in that quiet voice that said yes, it was true, and no, he didn't need to crow about it. "I will say, Paul, I don't think your heart was in it."

Paul looked taken aback. "Is that so? What shall I do when she returns? Sing her an aria? Read her a bit of softcore erotic poetry?"

"It did seem like you were going through the motions," Kate said. "Where do things stand between you and Emmeline these days?" She was a little ashamed that she'd waited so long to ask. For months, she'd been immersed in her own recovery, not to mention other concerns, like formalizing Henry's adoption. She should've inquired about her sleuthing partner's love life, but just hadn't. "I kept thinking you'd bring her round to Briarshaw over the summer."

"She was working," Paul said dully. Instead of meeting Kate's gaze, he consulted his phone, which hadn't pinged or vibrated, as if the device had summoned him telepathically.

"I don't have a dog in this fight. If you two have gone off each other again, just say so."

Paul continued to pretend fascination with his mobile. His reticence on the topic of his love life surprised her. He'd always been eager to discuss it before. As for his relationship with Emmeline Wardle, it had been fraught from day one, prone to blow-ups, fragile reconciliations, and periods when they mutually decided to see other people. Non-exclusive coupling was alien to Kate. Even in her younger days, long before Tony, she'd considered one man at a time trouble enough. Two or more? Lunacy. But perhaps Paul was a volume shopper rather than a value shopper.

"We're not off. We're not on. We're nothing worth talking about if my mum rings you, which she might," Paul said, suddenly looking alarmed as he mentioned the possibility. "Did you post anything on social media about coming back to London?"

"I deleted all my accounts after…." Kate trailed off. They knew.

"Well, surely you're not accusing me of exposing my travel plans on Facebook," Tony said.

"True. True." Paul looked momentarily relieved. "Still, she has your mobile numbers."

"Want us to change ours, then?" Kate teased.

Paul's eyes widened hopefully. "Would you?"

She and Tony exchanged a look.

"I didn't mean it," Paul said hastily. "Really. Forget I said it."

Sipping her water, Kate pretended to look at the Christmas bunting. She'd been the one to say it, but it still amazed her that he would seriously expect them to do such a thing, even for a moment. The "Fan Club," as Scotland Yard's special unit called them, were web-savvy fanatics. They knew Tony not only as a retired Chief Superintendent and MPS consultant, but as Baron Wellegrave, Peer of the Realm, and Kate not only as a Scotland Yard detective, but as Lady Hetheridge. Procuring secure mobiles and numbers known only to a controlled few had been a challenge.

"Anyway, Mum's barking, and she's made me barking," Paul said. "I don't want to talk about women. Let's talk about the case, all right?"

In some venues, that suggestion might have been indiscreet, even dangerously unprofessional. But Lucia's Pie and Prosecco was only half-full, and their corner table was a sufficiently secluded spot to discuss the case.

"About our victim," Tony began. "I've searched my memory, but the name Barnaby Galen doesn't ring any bells."

"Let's return to our old friend, Officer Google." Swiping at his mobile, Paul read off the screen, "'Barnaby Galen, a diversified multimillionaire, made the bulk of his fortune in the payday loan industry. Mr. Galen, 72, has never married. He has no children. He resides in Knightsbridge, London, in a house once owned by Victorian train designer and steam engineer, John Covetly Cooper. In the early 2000s, Mr. Galen's payday loan company, Ye Olde Money Man, was targeted by the pressure group Humanity First. This group alleged that the company had flagrantly predatory lending practices, such as £35 interest per month for every £100 borrowed....'"

Kate made a disgusted sound. "Lord. That ought to be illegal. Isn't it?"

"These days, yes," Tony agreed. "When I was a young man, that sort of naked usury wasn't permitted, either. You know how the cycle goes. The lending industry is regulated, over-regulated, set free to do absolutely anything for a period, and reined in again."

"He picked the right time to profit, I guess. Is there anything else?" Kate asked Paul.

"Not really. His name has appeared on the *Forbes* list at least once, and if you search for the company name, Ye Olde Money Man, it links back to some investigatory journalism and op-eds about income inequality. That's as much as a quick look with Officer Google can reveal. Gulls will dig up plenty more in the next few days, I promise."

"Multimillionaire," Tony repeated. "He must've lived like a hermit. Not on the board of any charities, never seen at gallery openings or political fetes."

"Should I know who John Covetly Cooper is?" Kate asked. She always felt a bit thick when the conversation turned to historical personages she'd never heard of.

Tony shrugged. Paul said, "I don't think he was famous, apart from railway enthusiasts, maybe. But doesn't he sound like a character in a steampunk TV show? Lieutenant Major J.C. Cooper at your service, milady," he said, slipping into his Colonel Blimp voice. "'I can steer this airship and fight duels with my rapier. But alas, my heart is only a cold clockwork mechanism, powered by aether.'"

"Should I call a doctor? Have you taken leave of your senses?" Giana asked, placing Paul's lager before him.

"No, no, just fine," he said, tasting his drink. He didn't even try to catch Giana's eye as she set down Kate and Tony's pints, then retreated. It was true; the earlier flirtation had been an act.

"I got to see the kitchen lot," Kate volunteered, after they'd all had a moment to savor the round. "There was no time for me to talk to any of them, and honestly, they might not have been in a fit state. They were giving poor Kincaid a right royal time. Gulls said the neighbors are quite friendly with one another along Holywell Street. But they weren't fond of Mr. Galen."

"Certainly not," Paul said. "Remember when one of you asked if the old man was a sort of neighborhood project? The sad, lost little pensioner who everyone looks in on? Well, it was just the opposite. They watched out for Galen, the way you watch out for a rabid dog. None of them even pretended to be surprised that someone would murder him."

"What did he do to them?" Kate asked.

"I didn't get the comprehensive list. I imagine Kincaid did, though. But mostly it came down to rudeness," Paul said. "Shouting when a dog was walked past his front garden. Calling the police on harmless parties. Dumping slop-pots in other people's yards."

"Oi," Kate muttered. "Quite the charmer."

"But were they surprised by the method?" Tony asked. "Did any of the neighbors say anything interesting on that score?"

Paul considered the question. "They did... only because they didn't, if you know what I mean. It's hard to be certain. But when I arrived on the scene and saw Granny, I shrieked. And so did you," he told Kate.

"Only a little."

"Even Tony got pale. He said something like, 'It's not real,'" Paul said, imitating Tony as if he, too, were Colonel Blimp. "And poor Trevor, the M.E. who looks like Ronan Farrow—"

"Oh, you're right, he does look like Ronan Farrow," Kate cried.

"I don't sound like Colonel Blimp," Tony said. "Nor do I know who Ronan Farrow is. But do you mean to say, the neighbors were sort of, well, blasé about a human skeleton that rode up from under the bed on miniature train tracks?"

Kate burst out laughing. "It was Lieutenant Major J.C. Cooper's ghost. He did it! Death by a steampunk skeleton."

"Well, that's it. You've cracked it. Time for me to pack it in," Paul said with mock despair. "And I thought Tony was onto something with the kitchen lot. They all thoroughly despised Galen. They didn't need psychiatric triage after taking in a completely bizarre death scene. Maybe because they were all in on it? Meaning we'd finally achieved…." He paused, taking a breath.

"A *Murder on the Orient Express* crime," Kate, Tony, and Paul said in unison. They laughed again, and finished their pints.

"Quattro Formaggi," Giana announced, placing a large pie in the center of the table. The moment Kate laid eyes on it, she realized how very hungry she actually was. She and Tony had grabbed a quick lunch before boarding the train to London, but that had been hours ago. Worries over the scale or her personal numerical value, as determined by the size of her knickers, went up in smoke. She ate with gusto.

"This is amazing. There's no decent pizza in Shawbridge, just the frozen stuff Henry and Ritchie like," Kate said. "I didn't know how much I missed the real thing until I took a bite."

"I didn't realize how much I missed the real thing until I set foot inside it," Tony said.

"To London," Paul said, lifting his glass.

"To London," Kate said.

"To London," Tony said, with feeling. Kate smiled at him, and he patted her thigh under the table.

"So, what did you discover when you made that last circuit around the house," Kate asked, getting back to her pizza. "No security system with motion detectors, I assume?"

"From what the kitchen lot said, Galen was far too frugal for anything like that," Paul replied.

"Even the CCTV cameras mounted beside the front and back doors were fakes," Tony said. "Bad enough when they film night and day, but aren't properly monitored. These are obvious dummies. The flimsy, bargain-bin kind."

"Were any of the doors forced?" Kate asked.

"No," Tony said. "The windows were in good shape, too. I think it's likely someone gained easy access to the house, either with Galen's permission or with a duplicate key."

On that thought, they suspended the conversation until they'd reduced the pizza to a smattering of crumbs on a scarred pie plate. Then came another round of pints and a deeper discussion of what Kate really wanted to focus on: Granny.

"I want you to have a look at my pictures," Kate said, bringing up the images on her iPhone. "I crawled around on that disgusting carpet to get them, so you could study Mr. FX's handiwork."

"Mr. what?" Tony looked blank.

"F." Kate drew the letter in the air. "X. As in the abbreviation for special effects. You know. The cinema."

"Mr. FX. A fitting name," Paul said, leaning back in his chair the way Tony often did when contemplating a case. Paul, however, kept one hand on the table, lest he get wrapped up in his thoughts and overbalance. "You know, I watched a documentary about haunted attractions not long ago. The American kind, with actors in costumes, where they really try to terrify the patrons. Did you know haunted houses were invented in England?"

Tony looked up from his pint to find Paul awaiting an answer. "Why are you staring at me?"

"Oh, I thought you might have attended the opening. The Orton and Spooner Ghost House was wildly popular in 1915."

Tony said nothing. He also forgot nothing, as Paul very well knew. Kate giggled at the face-off. "I suppose it was here in London?"

"No," Paul said. "It was in Liphook. Still is, I reckon. As coincidence would have it—assuming there is such a thing as coincidences in this world—the Orton and Spooner Ghost House was a marvel of steam power. Possibly right up the real John Covetly Cooper's alley, unless he was the dull sort who hates flights of fancy," Paul added. "The floors rocked. The patrons felt ghosts brushing by them. Blasts of steam, actually. The whole place vibrated. And since they walked through it in total darkness, it was just scary enough to be a hit with the general public."

"Sounds like you absolutely devoured this documentary," Kate said.

"It was fun. Really all I remember are two things—the Orton and Spooner Ghost House, and the term, 'startle scare.' That's what Granny looks like to me," Paul said. "When you go through haunted houses, there are usually dark corridors where something brushes against you, like the steam blasts in the Orton House. Then there are tableaus, where you see a terrible scene, vampires feasting or so forth. But what makes a haunted house great are startle scares coming along at deliberate intervals. They usually drop down or spring up."

"I think Granny—the skeleton component, I mean—folded flat while under the bed," Kate said, passing her mobile to Tony and Paul so they could study her image of the under-bed tracks. "Then once she was out, the platform slid backwards, tipping her body upright."

"Diabolical," Tony murmured. "Anyone who could get that sort of access to the man's bedroom could have hidden in one of that house's disused rooms, then come out and strangled him in his sleep. Not to mention the fact Galen kept his essential medications out in plain sight. The killer could've switched the pills and had him dead in a matter of days. Plus, that sort of demise would very likely be written off as natural in a man Galen's age."

For what felt like a long time, no one spoke. Then Kate said, "I suppose we're dealing with a true psychopath. *Another* true psychopath."

"I would've preferred the *Orient Express* scenario, if I'm being honest," Tony said.

Paul began to hum under his breath. The tune "Jingle Bells."

"That's your answer? 'Jingle Bells?'" Kate kicked him under the table.

"Ow! Violence in the workplace! You'll end up in an MPS reeducation camp, and you'll deserve it," Paul said. "I'm caroling because this case is Scrooge all over again."

Tony set down his near-empty pint with a *bump*. "You're right."

Kate didn't see it. "You mean, with Tiny Tim and Bob Cratchit and whatnot?"

"Yes. Think about it," Paul said eagerly. "Galen's a rich old man. He has no family. He has no friends. He got wealthy lending money but he doesn't enjoy his riches. He lives alone in a wreck of a mansion. One night a terrible specter visits him in his bed. Except in this case, he doesn't learn a valuable lesson. He drops dead."

"We don't know that Galen had no friends. Gulls said his P.A. was gutted over the murder. We also don't know that Galen didn't enjoy his money," Kate said reasonably.

"He might have hired a cleaner," Tony said.

"If I've learned one thing from my service on the Toff Squad," Paul said, blazing on as if neither of them had spoken, "it's this. Rich people never go it alone. Not even if they're full-on paranoids and misanthropes. Galen might have been too much of a skinflint to pay for things like cleaners. And plumbers. And authentic CCTV cameras. But I promise you, he had one dogsbody. One miserable, downtrodden, afraid-of-his-own-shadow employee. Enter the P.A."

"His Bob Cratchit," Tony said. "You're probably right."

"I am," Paul said breezily, signaling Giana for the check. "Now we just need to find out who in Galen's life fancied playing the Spirit of Christmas Yet to Come, and we'll have the case wrapped in time for Christmas lunch."

CHAPTER 15

*I*t had filled up and grown hot inside Lucia's Pie and Prosecco. Giana was clearly overwhelmed by too many tables requiring refills, split checks, and special requests, so Paul had offered to hover beside the bar until he could settle their bill. That freed Tony and Kate to pop out for some air.

The street was relatively quiet. Traffic was light, with only a few knots of weekend revelers making their way along the sidewalk, some quiet, some chatting and laughing. By long habit, Tony scanned the area—rooftops, shop fronts, open restaurants, dark side streets—and found nothing to concern himself. Statistically, anyone could be mugged, of course. London's knife crime numbers were nothing to be waved away. But Knightsbridge was as safe as any part of the city, and Tony felt confident that his situational awareness was appropriate, rather than paranoid.

He chanced a look at Kate to gauge how she was doing. He was ready to play it off if she caught him in the act, either by stroking her hair or giving her a quick kiss. Neither was necessary. She appeared engrossed by Lucia's front window, which featured a bevy of Italian Christmas glitz. A Murano glass Christmas tree with red and green swirls; a Babbo Natale doll, a

79

twin to Santa Claus apart from his basket of traditional loaves; a magnificent pandoro star cake, iced and sprinkled with cranberries. This last had no doubt been varnished to permit long-term display, an idea that struck Tony as tragic, since he'd always been particularly fond of pandoro.

"I can feel you looking at me," Kate said, without taking her eyes off the expansive village scene. "I can't help it, I'm floored by the Italian nativity. Look at all the tiny details. The little boy catching a fish. The sheep with silver bells around their necks. The sprinkles of gold dust on the cotton wool clouds. Somebody put their heart and soul into this."

Tony made a sound of agreement. He was more interested in the delight in Kate's voice, and how remarkably well she'd seemed all evening. Many times in Devon, especially during the autumn, he'd worried that she wouldn't turn the corner. Or that perhaps her doctors had overlooked some internal injury. A man who's bored of the countryside and has no intellectual work to perform begins to invent terrible scenarios. Health sites on the Internet didn't help. Suppose Kate had a nick to her spleen? Or an incipient hernia? According to various terrifying online doctors, even the best hospital occasionally missed a subtle but troublesome ailment. Especially when it was camouflaged by bigger concerns, like Kate's smashed right kneecap.

October had been the worst. For most of the month, Kate had been moody, disinterested in food, and down with a stomach bug, or so she claimed. Had she actually been too anxious to keep food down? Henry had remained healthy, and there had never been a germ or virus that got within a hundred yards of Henry Hetheridge that didn't immediately turn him poorly, often for days at a time.

But in November, things had turned around. She'd accepted his therapy challenge. It was probably no coincidence that she'd resumed eating properly around the same time. Of course, now she was complaining that the earth trembled when she walked.

He ignored all that. If anything, she looked more beautiful than ever, and tonight, she seemed genuinely happy.

"I wonder if I ought to come back in the daylight. Snap some close-ups of the nativity village for Henry to show Ritchie," Kate said. "It's a sort of layer cake community. He might like that. Stacking different kinds of people and activities on top of one another, I mean."

"I had no idea he ever created anything with people in it." Tony was developing an appreciation for his brother-in-law's LEGO creations, some of which had appeared in a gallery show-casing submissions by mentally challenged artists. He didn't understand it, but in point of fact, he didn't understand much art beyond approximately 1960. Nevertheless, Ritchie's bold, asymmetrical constructions provoked emotion, and according to Lady Margaret Knolls, a longtime patron of painters and sculptors, "If it makes you feel something, it's art."

"He used to play around with LEGO people when I was a kid," Kate said, examining a trio of angels surrounded by cotton-wool snow. "I love Christmas decorations." She shot a look at him over her shoulder. "But you don't go in for any of this, do you?"

"That's a baseless accusation."

"Harvey told me he's been in charge of all your holiday décor since the day you hired him. That until he came along, you didn't even bother."

"In those days bachelors didn't bother with trees. That's how you lured women into your home, by appearing in desperate need of help with such things."

"Name one Christmas decoration you like. One that makes you come over positively aglow with the Christmas spirit," Kate said, pretending to shiver, as if buffeted by a magical peppermint wind.

Tony laughed.

"I'm quite serious!"

"I have no idea. If you like, I suppose I could list the things that strangle the Christmas spirit. Starting with the commercials."

"I like some of the commercials. Excitable Edgar in the John Lewis advert is my favorite. Admit it, Tony. You're a Scrooge."

"Oh, very well. If I have to choose one thing, well—I quite like a nativity scene. Not the Italian sort," he clarified, indicating the exquisitely detailed *presage* in Lucia's window. "Not even the tabletop stables with farm animals and drummer boys and Wise Men on camels, looking on. Just the trio: Mary, Joseph, and the baby in his creche."

Kate looked surprised. "I'd never have guessed. You always say you're not religious."

"I'm not. Occupational hazard of a life spent on murder squads. But you asked my idea of the Christmas spirit," Tony said. "The nativity—well, that's it, isn't it? The miracle. The human miracle. Man, woman, and child. New life, and the continuation of life, in spite of everything."

Behind him, the bell over Lucia's door jangled. Out came Paul, fanning his face. "Too hot in there, and too spendy. But you'll be pleased to hear, the Yard picked up most of the tab. And no one can say we weren't working. The case of Scrooge vs. Granny is off to a brilliant start," he said. "Of course, tomorrow is Saturday, and we don't have a prayer of any preliminary research or forensic data before Monday noon."

"We might if Galen had any posh relations breathing down the top brass' necks," Kate said.

"Right. But since he was all alone in the world, it might take even longer. What do you say we meet up around ten o'clock on Monday?" Paul asked. "At that little bakery down from the Yard? The one on the Embankment that does the mini doughnuts Kate fancies?"

"Do me a favor," Kate barked. "You want me back at work on Monday? I'm here on holiday, ain't I?"

Tony secretly found Kate's response encouraging. He'd

endured the entire train ride from Devon to London steeled for the moment she turned to him and announced she couldn't go on. That she'd never set foot in the city again. And look at her now, not the least bit frightened by Paul's presumption. In fact, in spite of her vigorous denial, he rather thought she was excited by the notion of continuing with the case.

"It's fate!" Paul told her. "Fate brought you here. This week. Tonight. To give me a break because I bloody well deserve it. And it's a Christmas case, isn't it? Scrooge himself, frightened to death in his own bed by a spirit uninterested in redemption."

"Speaking only for myself," Tony said, unable to stop himself, "It's been too long since I had a case. I'm in, Paul. I'll meet you on the Embankment around ten Monday."

"Will Jackson be there?" Kate asked.

Paul shrugged. "Only if the flu lets up. Poor sod. He went on a get-in-shape kick while you were away. Seems like it might be the death of him. Why?"

"No reason. Only... I was wondering how he would feel about Gulls and Kincaid giving the P.A. a pass. I forget his name. Your Bob Cratchit, who found the body, called 999, and legged it. Gulls said something about extenuating circumstances."

"If she said it, I'm sure she's correct," Paul said, with a casual wave of the hand that surprised Tony. It seemed his former protégé had mastered the art of delegation.

"Don't look at me like that," Paul continued, apparently reading a challenge in Kate's face. "Gulls is many things, but sloppy isn't one of them. If she interviewed the P.A. and decided he didn't abandon the scene maliciously, she's probably right. And Kincaid was there. He's not as meticulous about the rules as Gulls, but he's no rubber stamp. He gives me a bell whenever there's a serious disagreement."

"I'm just curious to find out what constitutes a good reason for running off," Kate said. "Did he want to wash his hands? Burn his clothes? Hide something incriminating, maybe, before facing the rozzers?"

Paul folded his arms across his chest. "I refuse to continue this conversation with you here. If you want to know more, be on the Embankment Monday."

"Fine. I'll be there." Kate shrugged into her puffer coat. Pulling a long cobalt blue muffler from a pocket, she wound it around her neck. In Tony's opinion, it was the perfect color for her, setting off her blonde hair and pink cheeks.

"But when I say I've had enough, we go back to the mews together, Tony. Got it?" she said. "Otherwise we'll get sucked into the Yard's vortex and be there all night."

"Got it," Tony said mildly. "Jingle Bells" came suddenly into his mind, but he restrained himself from humming it.

CHAPTER 16

*R*ather than take the tube back, which could sometimes get loud and rowdy on a Friday night, Tony hailed their third Black cab of the day, and they rode back to Strange Mews in comfort. Along the way, Kate's mobile chimed. It wasn't the specific ring she'd chosen for Henry, Maura, or the staff at Briarshaw. When Kate looked at the screen, she laughed.

"It's Sharada Bhar. Should I answer it?"

"I wish you wouldn't. I'd like to get to sleep before two A.M.," Tony said. "She called me last week to ask what I thought about a new installment of her 'Lordly Detective' series in which the PM has been assassinated. Her hero realizes a paid actor is carrying on in the PM's place."

"What tips him off? Does the actor accidentally speak the truth and behave rationally?"

Tony chuckled. "It's not a contemporary story. It's set in the time of Gladstone and Disraeli. Neither of them deserves quite *that* level of censure. Anyway, I told her in the kindest way possible that as a bestselling author, her instincts will serve her better than mine ever could. Then I pretended Ritchie had set something else on fire and rang off."

"Maybe we *should* change our numbers," Kate said as her phone dinged again, this time signaling that a voicemail was being received. Slipping her mobile in her bag, and cuddled up to him with what sounded like a happy sigh.

CHAPTER 17

$\mathcal{K}$ ate fell asleep easily, nestled in Tony's arms, but woke up long before first light and couldn't get back to sleep. It wasn't the return of the zombie stomach bug, as she'd called it; her immune system had apparently won that battle after a ridiculously long engagement. Nor was she troubled by bad dreams.

She *did* dream about the events of that night sometimes. Sometimes she dreamed about the lift ride that preceded the violence. In reality, of course, she'd been blissfully unaware of what awaited her, and the trip had been entirely commonplace. In dreams, however, that ride in the lift car was clotted with horror, like a wound that might split open and pour out fresh blood at any moment. The horror was in knowing, *knowing*, that death waited for her, and for Tony.

Other times, Kate dreamed she was back in the hospital. It was after her emergency surgery, when she'd first come around, nauseated and disoriented. In reality, Paul and Maura had been there to reassure her that everyone was okay. In the dream, they were both shattered with grief, weeping helplessly until finally someone blurted out the unbearable news: Henry and Ritchie had been found dead, slaughtered by the same madman who'd nearly killed Kate and Tony. That dream always ended with Kate sitting up in bed, heart thumping, slick with a cold sweat. However, since discussing the helpless terror of these dreams with her therapist, Alix, Kate had slept better, without a recurrence.

So it wasn't a nightmare that disturbed Kate's slumber; she simply woke up and couldn't get back to sleep. Perhaps it was only excitement. Not every murder case was interesting. Many were heartbreaking in their sheer banality; the neighbor killed for playing the TV too loud, the food vendor knifed for telling a mouthy customer to shut it. The three most common weapons? Knives, hands, and whatever could be used as a bludgeon. Maybe Paul was right. It was fate. A murder weapon like Granny came along once in a lifetime.

Maybe it's excitement. But I never used to wake up in the middle of the night, unless it was because of Ritchie. Or Henry. Or the Yard, Kate thought, slipping quietly out of bed and into her satin robe. *Everything's different now.*

Her therapist, Alix, had made those three words into a mantra. "Say it with me, Kate. Everything's different now. It's a cliché because it's an inescapable fact. Even when it happens too slowly to perceive, everything's changing every day. Every minute. But most of the time we're too busy with our jobs and our families to focus on the changes. Then the sky falls and the earth opens up and we finally stop. Look around. Take it all in. That's when we demand to know why everything's suddenly different now. That's when we want things to return to the old state of being, which was probably imaginary."

This speech from Alix had come near the end of Kate's first session. Now it echoed in her ears as she padded down the spiral staircase, enjoying the feel of the cool, nubby treads under her bare feet. Alix, a sturdy fireplug of a woman with two round black moles, one on her left cheek and the other beside her right eye, spoke in a brisk, dictating manner that reminded Kate of Paul's mum, Sharada. Alix tended to punctuate her remarks by waving her hands, like a magician's flourish. A sort of "Presto! Now you feel good!" gesture, Kate had thought at the time.

Because she'd arrived at therapy for no reason other than Tony's insistence, Kate had initially felt a fair bit of hostility toward Alix. Her short, bristly dark hair, for one thing. It had a central white streak, not unlike a badger. The sleeveless waist-coats Alix favored had also bugged Kate. Why did she always wear them with her blouses and skirts? The wretched things did nothing but emphasize the rolls around her midsection. Those moles, for a third thing. Even the spelling of her name. Wasn't A-L-I-X a bit precious for a fifty-something therapeutic badger, who ought to at least be called something serious, like Margaret or Agnes?

In the kitchen, Kate flicked on the recessed lights, which glowed discreetly around the countertops and appliances. The mews house was rather like a smart hotel. And how lovely to spend a few days in a living space without encroachment from Henry and Ritchie. No half-finished juice boxes left here and there. No jar of peanut butter stuck inside the refrigerator, lid missing. No mysterious puddle of water spread across the floor tiles, a slippery place just waiting for a foot.

I was such a witch to her at first. Maybe Alix is used to that sort of thing.

She recalled how she'd responded to the therapist's claim that the old status quo Kate longed for was probably imaginary: with heat, and at some volume.

"Is that the tinned revelation you serve up to new clients?" Kate had demanded, suddenly furious. "Off with the lid, warm it over, and there it is. 'Things change. Too bloody bad.' Well, I'm not here because I found a gray hair or I'm no longer happy in my work or I think I missed my calling as a ballerina. I almost died. My whole family was almost annihilated. I don't know what to do with that!" she'd screamed, voice breaking. "I don't know what to do!"

After that outburst, the silence had felt enormous; the stillness inside an empty cathedral, perhaps, or a cavern buried beneath the earth. Kate, who'd worked so hard to maintain her composure around Tony, Henry, and Ritchie, had dissolved into sobs. That was the worst part, breaking down in front of a stranger. As she fought to regain control, she'd expected Alix to clear her throat and murmur something about how sometimes the match between therapist and client doesn't work out. Then she would be escorted back to the front desk, where the receptionist could offer her the names of other psychologists to try. Instead, Alix had shifted from her armchair to the sofa cushion next to Kate. Gently putting her arms around her, she'd said,

"I'm so sorry. Of course you don't know. It's too big right now. It must seem overwhelming. But we'll get it sorted. If we put our heads together, I promise you, we'll get it sorted."

Kate had melted. Maybe the quick turnaround was predictable. After all, Alix was something Kate had nowhere else in her life: a person who would listen to her rage, whinge, and bleat without becoming frightened or taking it all too seriously.

At home at Briarshaw, everyone was fighting their own battles. Ritchie, who hated change, was reacquainting himself with Maura, learning to trust her guidance as he trusted Kate's. Henry, clever and anxious by nature, was dealing with his brush with mortality, blaming himself for a mistake any child might have made. Maura, of course, was abstaining from alcohol and drugs one day at a time, with some days clearly tougher than others. As for Tony … well. Tony was determined to maintain the façade that he fought no internal battles whatever.

Kate knew better. After the first death threat they'd received from those serial killer groupies, the Fan Club, Tony had reminded everyone that these things happened to public figures. The rooftop affair had caused a sensation, not only in the U.K., but in the western world. Moreover, members of the British aristocracy sometimes attracted stalkers. As a family, they couldn't go to pieces over every minor unpleasantness.

That speech had worked wonders on Kate, Henry, Maura, Mrs. Snell, and the household staff. After giving it, Tony had retreated to his exercise room, locked the door, and not come out for three hours. At the time, Kate had suspected her husband of suffering a full-blown panic attack. Having experienced several herself, she knew the signs. But he'd refused to admit it, at least until the day he proposed they both enter therapy. That episode was something he'd said he'd like to address.

Kate suspected he'd already worked through it himself, somehow. She knew that years before, he'd dealt with a similar incident after a brush with death on the job. Yet he'd insisted he needed help.

Because he knew I did.

She'd come downstairs to peek in the fridge, a stainless-steel Samsung, surely the crown jewel of kitchen mod-cons. But now that it stood before her, guilt crept in.

I should wait for breakfast. I can't keep telling myself I'm making up for the zombie stomach bug. That was almost two months ago.

It wasn't as if slimming was unknown to her. She'd been doing it, on and off, for half her life. Only just lately, she'd become especially defiant about resuming the process. When packing for London, she'd even made the sad concession of purchasing new knickers and jeans in first-ever sizes she didn't want to think about.

Maybe I'll call December a lost cause, she thought. *Make getting healthy my New Year's resolution.*

She peeked inside the Samsung refrigerator, expecting to find nothing but bottled water. Instead, she found the basics: eggs, butter, cream, a hunk of cheddar, prewashed salad (spinach and wild rocket, her favorite), balsamic dressing, minced beef, marinara sauce, and one of those health-conscious foods to which she occasionally subjected Tony, "courgetti," which was courgettes sliced into pasta-like strips.

Kimchi. The thought popped into Kate's head from absolutely nowhere. Suddenly she could taste it, fermented and ultra-sour, filling some void she'd never registered until that moment. The fridge held no bottled kimchi, of course, which was just as well; when it came to Korean food, she preferred fresh. That was the beauty of being back in London. Any culinary desire, no matter how capricious, could be fulfilled, often in under an hour.

Tony seems so happy to be back. Getting within a stone's throw of the Yard tomorrow should make him even happier.

Kate *did* feel a little worried about Monday, though she had no intention of telling her husband. How would she do out there by the Thames, getting blasted by cold winds off the river as they ate doughnuts at one of the Embankment's many wrought iron tables? Scotland Yard was, after all, one of England's top terror targets.

Maybe it would be like Lucia's Pie and Prosecco. During dinner she'd had the occasional wobbly moment. Once, she'd glimpsed a face in the crowd that reminded her of *him.* Of course, it wasn't; that vicious sod was dead and buried. Another time, a muffled bang from Lucia's kitchen had almost sounded like suppressed gunfire. Those brief moments had come and gone without Tony or Paul being any the wiser. According to Alix, each time Kate successfully waited out a panicked moment, she increased the likelihood of waiting out the next one. And being less paralyzed by fear of a recurrence.

Like one of Pavlov's dogs, thinking of the Embankment at mid-morning made Kate almost slaver at the memory of mini-doughnuts. How long till breakfast?

She checked her phone's clock. She'd carried it down with her from the bedroom, because, well such was the curse of modern life. She didn't feel guilty over screen usage, because she wasn't addicted to Twitter or online shopping. She had a son roughly a hundred and seventy-five miles away, and she needed to stay in touch.

The iPhone's clock read 3:47 A.M. According to the gnawing in her stomach, Quattro Formaggi, split three ways, was only a distant memory.

Kate decided to check the cupboard. Inside, she discovered a cache of guilty pleasures: Walkers Ready Salted Crisps, Cadbury Dairy Milk "Pots of Joy," and a couple of cherry Bakewell tarts.

Someone squealed with joy. That same someone unwrapped a tart, popped it on a plate, and took a fork to it. At the halfway point, Kate came to her senses. Recalling the size of her brand-new jeans, she searched until she found some tin foil and wrapped up the remaining pastry. Over breakfast, she'd entice Tony into eating it. Then they'd be equally guilty and the cosmos would be balanced again.

She rechecked her phone. 4:15 A.M. She still felt wide awake. There was nothing for it but to put the kettle on.

CHAPTER 18

*C*arrying the mug and her phone into the living room, Kate plopped down on the long white Chesterfield, arranged the faux-fur throw over her legs, and even switched on the gas fireplace. The first five minutes were supremely relaxing. Then her mind began to creep.

Was Henry coping all right? Was Ritchie taking advantage of Maura, who had yet to memorize the complete Ritchie Wakefield playbook?

She caught herself worrying about them so often, it was becoming a source of guilt. Ritchie might be immune to such obsessing, but Kate thought Henry was capable of sensing and internalizing her fears, which wouldn't be good. The kid was already highly risk averse and prone to overthinking almost everything. She wanted to encourage his confidence, not smother him with her own anxieties.

The topic had come up during her last in-office session with Alix. Kate had admitted, "I just want to make a deal with God. I have the wording planned, I could draw up the contract right now. If God Almighty will promise not to let the Fan Club hurt

Henry and Ritchie, then I, Kate, will promise to take whatever violence would have come their way. That's reasonable, isn't it?"

Alix hadn't replied.

"I'm quite serious. If I could just get that deal signed, a commitment from God that Henry and Ritchie will be spared, I think I'd be in a much better frame of mind, moving forward." Speaking this aloud had energized Kate so much, she'd popped up from her chair and begun pacing around Alix's office. "It's more than generous. No protection for me. Not even for Tony. We're coppers. We chose a dangerous life and we can face the consequences. How hard would it be for God to commit to simply protecting Henry and Ritchie?"

"Classic bargaining." Alix had sounded bored.

"But that's from the stages of grief."

"Yes. Shock. Denial. Bargaining. Depression and finally, acceptance."

Kate, whose jaunt around the room had brought her back to the sofa, dropped down again. "But I'm here because I don't know how to stop being freaked out all the time. Not because I'm grieving."

Alix had only stared back at her, her expression clearly saying, *You sure about that, girlie?*

"I mean, I guess if you want to stretch the definition of grieving," Kate had said doubtfully. "But this is specific to Henry and Ritchie. It's not that they were a hundred percent safe back then. It's just that I never worried about them this way. The idea of them being killed wasn't quite real to me, so it had no effect."

"If I were you, I'd grieve the loss of that outlook," Alix had said. "I'd much rather have the contract you described. Counter-signed by the archangel Michael, one hopes." Alix had smiled at Kate. "Say it with me. Everything's different now. Part of truly accepting that is grieving for the past. You said it yourself, Henry and Ritchie have never led charmed lives. They've always been in some sort of danger, like every person alive. But you once had the illusion it wasn't so, and grieving for the loss of that illusion is perfectly natural. One might even say, essential."

As Kate finished her tea, it occurred to her that she'd promised to send Alix a short progress report each day. Not by text; Alix didn't accept texts from clients, which was a reasonable boundary to safeguard her privacy. In the event of an emergency, Kate had been directed to call the office and leave a message with the service. Otherwise, she was supposed to email Alix's professional account.

While poised to open her email app, Kate noticed an unheard voicemail. Henry *had* been a touch clingy when they said goodbye at the station. And heaven knew Ritchie had all sorts of tricks when it came to mealtimes and bedtimes.

She opened the message, which turned out to be from Sharada Bhar. It was the call she'd ignored on the cab ride home. Despite a valiant effort, her phone's transcription feature had failed to make much sense of Sharada's heavily-accented speech. The transcribed paragraphs were mostly word salads. In those salads, one word that came up over and over was "the pall." Kate had recently learned "pall" not only meant a dark cloud, but literally referred to the dark cloth draped over a coffin. It was reasonable to assume Sharada was actually saying "Deepal," not "the pall," but either way, Kate had a feeling the message wasn't sunshine and daisies.

She listened to the message with the mobile held a couple of inches away from her ear. It wasn't on speakerphone. Nevertheless, Sharada Bhar was a forceful orator who could've thundered down mountains, had she so chosen.

"Hallo, Kate! A little bird told me you and your handsome husband are back in London. I'll bet you're glad to be back. I can't imagine spending so much time in the country. If I married Mr. Darcy, I would say to him, 'Oh, I love you, Fitzwilliam, and Pemberley is beautiful, but if you don't take me to London for the season, I will set myself on fire.' Is it true that when Deepal visited you last June, you let him try to climb a tree? I think you know that boy was never meant for dangerous things like that. I don't let Deepal climb so much as a stepladder. But what's done is done. I need to talk to you about what Deepal's doing now."

Sharada took an audible breath. The line went silent for a couple of seconds. The woman sounded like she was on the brink of tears, but Kate didn't find that alarming. According to Paul, his mum always worked herself up to the brink of emotional disintegration before asking a favor.

"First, let me remind you, Kate, I don't hold what happened against you. You are not to blame. But ever since Paul saved your life, and Lord Hetheridge's life, he's changed. I thought it would be wonderful for my son to be a hero. But he's breaking my heart."

Kate paused the voicemail. She didn't want to overreact to the message. Sharada was more than her best mate's mum, she was a family friend. She'd even given Kate some valuable advice, back in the day; the sort of advice only a woman with an unshakable faith in romantic love could provide. Also, it was fair to say that Paul had saved a lot of lives during the rooftop incident, including possibly Kate's and Tony's. But they'd fought the personal battle, and fought it to the death. Sharada, who saw the world through Paul-colored glasses, refused to acknowledge anyone else's contribution.

Taking a deep breath, Kate restarted the message. Sharada continued,

"I didn't want Deepal to take his own flat, but I allowed it. This is what mothers do. Permit learning experiences. Maybe Deepal is the big man at Scotland Yard, but let him run out of socks and underpants. Then you tell me who's the big man?"

Kate giggled. Sharada was offering brickbats she could lob at Paul for years to come.

"So, I allowed the flat business to teach him a lesson," Sharada said. "He started working even more, and as I said, I don't blame you, Kate. Even though I kept thinking, any day now, Kate will return. Then Deepal can catch his breath and spend five minutes with his mother. But you didn't come back and Deepal was always working, working, working. Finally, one Saturday afternoon I filled up a hamper with all the foods he likes and took it to his flat. So we might have a lovely picnic!" Sharada's voice rose. If she was exaggerating the depth of her emotion, she deserved the BAFTA. "And do you know what I found?"

"No," Kate mouthed at her mobile.

"He moved houses," Sharada screeched. "My Deepal moved houses! And he didn't tell me."

Kate clapped a hand over her mouth. Her instinct was to scream with laughter, but she didn't want to wake Tony.

"Naturally, I confronted him. And do you know what Deepal did? He told me it was none of my business where he lives. Can you believe that? He refused to tell me," Sharada wailed. She paused, audibly choking back tears.

Kate felt guilty for almost laughing. The woman sounded gutted.

"Anyway," Sharada said at last. "I know this message is too long. Soon it will cut me off. Please find out where my Deepal lives. I'll call you tomorrow."

CHAPTER 19

On Monday morning, Paul Bhar arrived at Victoria's Embankment, home of what he called the *new* New Scotland Yard, at seven o' clock. The sky was still dark. Along the river, ornate nineteenth-century lamps shone, their lights softened by patches of mist off the Thames. A tugboat blatted its horn as a larger vessel chugged past, the tug's headlights bouncing off the bigger ship's riveted hull. Here and there, red ribbons and evergreen wreaths were visible on shop windows and doors. Even the Yard was tastefully adorned for the season, crowned with white fairy lights.

Inside the fortress of glass and steel, a uniformed guard stood next to the security array. For a thickset bull of a young man, he had an unusually prominent Adam's apple. Situated as it was beneath heavily-lidded eyes, broad cheeks, and a double chin, his neck should have been an afterthought. Perhaps even indistinguishable from what was stacked on top. Instead, the guard's Adam's apple bulged above his collar, as if he'd swallowed part of a Terry's Chocolate Orange in one gulp.

Note to self. Pick up a Terry's Chocolate Orange on the way home, Paul thought, loading his leather hold-all, a very nice Perry Ellis number, originally £600, that he'd located on eBay for £300, onto the moving belt. By long habit, he'd already freed his phone and computer from the hold-all, which he loaded behind the Perry Ellis bag in separate plastic bins.

"Hiya," he told the security guard.

"Charmed, I'm sure," the guard replied in a dead voice. "Place all electronic devices, including laptops and mobiles, onto the belt in separate containers."

"I just did that. You watched me. Er, Carbuncle." He squinted to make sure he'd read the guard's name correctly off his identity badge.

"I stand in awe. Wait, please." With a glacial slowness that couldn't possibly be genuine, the guard examined the x-rays of Paul's belongings. He didn't appear to be studying them, or zoom in for a closer look. He simply stared, unblinking, at the screen for at least thirty seconds.

"Do me a—"

Paul never got the word "favor" out. "Right," Officer Carbuncle announced in an ominous tone. "Step forward for additional screening."

Paul stood with his arms out as the guard waved the handheld detector around him. Carbuncle wanded his legs and rear so slowly, he might have been measuring Paul for new trousers.

"You realize my ID says DI, don't you?" Paul asked. "As in, Detective Inspector?"

"Go through," the guard said in his dead tone.

Reclaiming his phone, laptop, and hold-all, Paul decided to overlook the unnecessary rigmarole. He even gave the guard a smile, hoping it might throw him off his sour game. "Cheers, mate."

"Double check the belt. We are not responsible for possessions left behind."

Paul's smile faded. "C'mon. Really. That belt is empty. I'm holding my things. You watched me pick them up."

Carbuncle began examining his manicure.

Resisting the temptation to shout, "My ID says DI," which would sound completely impotent at this point, Paul decided to push on. Before long, Kate and Tony would be expecting him at the Embankment's bakery. He needed the quiet early-morning time to check his electronic inbox and read over any preliminary materials his team had compiled. This was also the moment he'd set aside to finally open and read the letter his mum had posted to his office address, if he could stomach it.

Early Monday mornings at the Yard were often subdued, but never deserted. He was alone in the lift, but its doors opened onto a floor already lit up. The scent of brewing coffee was in the air. Heading toward his desk, he overheard someone around the corner, speaking low and persuasively into a telephone. A copper assuring a grass they could count on his discretion, probably. Or a detective making the early rounds with his snouts in the press, scrounging for leads. As Paul passed the bullpen, one of the new DCs who sometimes assisted the Toff Squad gave him a wave before returning to her PowerPoint presentation. Judging by the density of the charts, it concerned money laundering, one of her specialties. There was something reassuring about the sight of evidence being assembled. Crime never stopped, but neither did the MPS.

At the coffee station, DCI Vic Jackson's perennially positive administrative assistant, Joy, was loading up a mug. She winked at him.

"I spoke to the Chief over the weekend. Told him you lot have a corker."

"How did he sound?"

"Anxious to get back. But still rather pitiful. I think he needs a few more days in bed. Is it true DI Hetheridge is back? And her husband's consulting?"

Paul glanced around to see if anyone had overheard. "Yes, my old guv's on board. But I'm not a hundred percent sure about Kate. You heard that from Jackson?" he asked, amazed.

"I heard it from half a dozen people, including the Chief. Word gets around," Joy said. "By the way, he asked me to tell you to be careful with the press. He said, keep everything about the murder weapon out of the papers. Have reporters already contacted you?"

"No," Paul said. "But there were some gathered outside the crime scene last night, hanging around the barriers, as usual. They shouted questions, but we ignored them. When the CSI caravan rolled up, it was like the circus coming to town. I think they were shocked speechless."

"Well, that won't last. Let me know if I can help." Joy tasted her coffee, beamed approval, and headed back to her desk, a cheerful realm decorated with yellow smiley faces and inspirational mottos. After months of working with her, Paul still had no idea if she was completely on the level. Because she was black, heavyset, and a woman, three types of people DCI Jackson had frequently offended during his drinking days, there had long been a rumor going around that Joy was actually a plant from the Met's HR department. As the theory went, she was waiting for Jackson to say something cataclysmically offensive, while he, shrewder and less bloody-minded when sober, was doing his level best to adhere to workplace best practices. It was an ongoing mystery that Paul had yet to make any headway with.

Paul hung up his coat, a Perry Ellis he'd paid the full £900 for, and his umbrella, a £50 item from the Sharper Image. Dropping into his swivel chair with a sigh, he contemplated the sealed envelope sitting in his inbox. At first glance, it had seemed innocent. But the directions were written in a heavy, right-slanting hand he would've recognized anywhere.

His mum wasn't backing off. Although he'd stopped short of changing his mobile number—suppose she had a true emergency?—his original plan, to keep calls between them brief and informative, had gone up in smoke. Sharada refused to back off, or even take it down a notch. She'd started leaving him long, accusatory messages, undeterred by the one-minute limit he'd set; she simply called over and over, feeding him her aggrieved speeches in mini-bites. As for his personal email account, he'd had no choice but to change it, because Sharada was a bestselling novelist. She could compose screeds the way spiders spun webs. Since he wouldn't answer her calls and her emails kept bouncing back, she'd posted a screed to Scotland Yard.

He picked up the envelope. She'd stuck on an extra stamp, which was wise, given the letter's heft. It was stiff, as if there was an enclosure. Other coppers might worry about opening a letter stuffed with anthrax powder or grains of ricin. He feared family photos, or perhaps one of his baby-curls, tied with a pale blue ribbon. Emotional anthrax, as it were.

Why did I ever think I could pull this off? he wondered for the thousandth time.

Because there was no other choice.

His back was against the wall. No matter what path he chose, there would be screeds, and tears, and bad feelings. At least this way, he could sidestep most of it. If that sounded cowardly, that's because it was. His career was back on track. He'd received a promotion, a medal for valor, and even brief acclaim in the media. But in his personal life, he was doing anything but covering himself in glory.

He decided his best course was to check his electronic inbox. Hiding his mum's letter under some interoffice memos, he downloaded the preliminary profile on Barnaby Galen and started to read.

CHAPTER 20

$\mathscr{B}$y ten o'clock, the mist above the Thames was gone. The river was its usual lusty brown with plenty of shipping traffic motoring along. Near the London Eye, a red double-decker New Routemaster was unloading tourists. Near the snug bakery with its daily special on mini donuts, Paul glimpsed the pale winter sun glinting off something silver. Either a blonde Michelin woman was milling about, taking the air, or that was Kate in her silver puffer coat.

Last night, she seemed game, he thought. Paul very much hoped the return to London had snapped Kate back to her old self. But he couldn't shake the feeling she was only putting a brave face on it, and would crack under the first real strain.

It's that barmy coat, he thought, waving at Kate and presumably Tony, almost invisible at a distance because he was dressed like a normal human being. Paul closed the distance as quick as he could.

"Good morning! God, I miss the old days," he added, with a look at the bakery's queue, which was well into the double digits. "Remember those breakfast buffets at the old HQ? Coming in late and hungover. Walking smack into a potted plant while trying to avoid Mrs. Snell's glare?"

"Good times," Kate giggled. Massive puffer coat or no, she looked very well. Her eyes were bright and her cheeks glowed pink.

"We had autonomy in those days," Paul continued as the three of them glommed onto the queue. "Now I have to pass a security shakedown just to get through the door. I'm stuck in a ruddy bullpen where the juniors feel free to borrow my desk the moment I stand up, and if I want anything more than a cup of coffee, it requires an expedition down the street. In the old days, I might go twenty-four hours without answering to anyone other than the guv here. Now I get ten messages a day asking where I am and what I'm doing."

"I don't miss the old days." The twinkle in Tony's light eyes suggested he was telling the truth. "I was beginning to feel boxed in. I suppose the whole point of mentoring you and Kate was to see you promoted, which I have done. Consulting with the Yard between my own private clients is my idea of heaven."

Many in the bakery queue were ordering simple drinks, like tall whites, so the line moved fast. Within five minutes, they were carrying their cups, plus a seductively greasy bag filled with mini doughnuts, to one of the sturdy sets of tables and chairs scattered along the riverside. The day was more windy than cold, but Paul wasn't worried about his look; he'd put enough product in his hair to ensure the designer cut kept its shape. Kate wore a bun, and Tony's thick, steel-gray hair ruffled evenly, despite the gusts barreling off the river. Perhaps a baron's hair knew its duty, and resisted untidy configurations.

"Ooh. Hot," Kate said, after a sip of coffee. "You, too, Paul. I meant to say so last night."

"I'm hot?"

"Yeah. Pains me to admit it." She grinned. "But there's something different since I saw you last. Go in for some weekend plastic surgery? Bit of Botox?"

"Is she buttering me up?" Paul asked Tony.

He shrugged.

"I thought maybe," Kate said carefully, drawing the word out, "you've been happier, since you've put up a hard boundary between you and Sharada. I don't blame you. But…."

Paul groaned.

"But she's taking it so hard. She's going to pieces. Did you really move houses without telling her where?"

He looked at Tony for help, but his old guv was studying the boat traffic on the Thames as if captivated.

"It's complicated," he said, digging in the greasy bag for a doughnut. To buy himself time, he ate it, then bolted down a mouthful of coffee. It was so hot, he almost gagged.

"I did warn you," Kate said. "Anyway. Full disclosure, since you're my mate and I'm on your side. Sharada left me a long message begging me to find out where you live. She said she'd ring me today to see what I found out. Do you want me to ignore the call?"

"Please," he said. Unable to withstand her gaze, he dug out a second doughnut. Mercifully, Tony came to his rescue at last.

"I was thinking about the case this morning. I always like to start with the person who discovered the body," Tony said. "Kate got a peek at the neighbors, and I agree that if all of them entered the house but not one of them bothered to ring 999, that's provocatively odd behavior. Still, the person who claims to have found the victim very often has something to do with his death."

"Our Bob Cratchit," Paul agreed, relieved to switch gears. "His name's Oliver Vine-Jones. I thought the three of us might interview him together, if you're up for it. Since you're already set up as a consultant," he told Tony, "I have the authority to include you. But Kate, you're more of a question mark. I don't think AC Deaver will declare that if you help out, you're back on the job, sabbatical finished, but he might. You'll certainly be leaving yourself open to more obligations. Sworn affidavits and court appearances."

"I know," Kate said. "If I hadn't seen Granny, I'd probably be content to loll around the holiday let while you and Tony work the case. But now that I've had a taste of it, I want to see it through."

"Excellent," Paul said. "Now here's what we know about Barnaby Galen. It's incomplete, obviously, but a little bit of background will give us a framework when we interview his P.A.

"Galen turned seventy-two last week. He was born in a Yorkshire village called Bernsley. When he was nineteen, he received a surprise inheritance from a distant relative. Someone in America he'd never met chose to bequeath twenty thousand pounds on him because he was the last male Galen, or some such nonsense. He didn't stick around Bernsley after that. He relocated to Manchester."

"This was forty or fifty years ago?" Tony asked.

"Fifty," Paul agreed. "Apparently while he was in Manchester, he started a business with a friend. Let me check my notes…."

Withdrawing his leather-bound notebook from his inside coat pocket, Paul consulted the notes he'd jotted. Even when he had digital copies of reports, he still liked to jot the salient details into his notebook. It made him feel in command of the facts, being able to flip back the book's leather cover and reel them off at a moment's notice.

"Here's his name. Philip Montgomery. Mind you, this bloke had a rap sheet. Oh, and he was born in Bernsley as well, so perhaps they grew up together. Anyway, he was cautioned as a juvenile for breaking and entering. Banged up at age eighteen for petty theft. Went by 'Monty.'

"So, Galen and his school chum Monty landed in Manchester with twenty thousand pounds to play with," Paul continued. "Galen's story is, he wanted to use his financial stake to start a private equity firm. Of course, Monty was a budding criminal, so maybe he steered things wrong. Or maybe Galen was a willing conspirator. Either way, they both wound up indicted and tried for their parts in a fraudulent enterprise. Venture capitalism gone wrong."

"Galen had a rap sheet," Kate said, pouncing on the detail. "Any other brushes with the law?"

"Yes, but don't get ahead of me." Paul tried a second sip of coffee, which fortunately wasn't as scorching as the first. "Anyway, Galen was young, only twenty-two, and a nice-looking kid, so the court went easy on him. He was found only partially at fault. Sentenced to a year's probation. But his mate Monty got the book thrown at him."

"Disgruntled ex-partner," Kate called, as a pensioner might call "Bingo!"

"It was fifty years ago, but yes," Tony said, looking equally interested.

"Monty was twenty-four, which isn't much older, but apparently the court didn't find him nearly as sympathetic. He had those priors. Here's his mug shot. Looked a bit like Lurch, didn't he? Not sure his barrister tried very hard, either. So the court decided he bore the lion's share of the blame, and sentenced him to fifteen years."

"What happened when he got out? Did he get himself sent down again?" Kate asked. Like all coppers, she was fatalistic when it came to the rehab potential of career criminals.

"No. He died," Paul said. "Got released a bit early for good behavior. And to facilitate his cancer treatment. Testicular," he added, and shuddered. "Died at age thirty-seven."

"What was the nature of their fraud scheme?" Tony asked.

"The readout just said 'venture capital scheme,'" Paul said. "I have Kincaid on it. I told him I want everything he can unearth on Galen."

"So, after his year of probation, what did he do?" Kate asked.

"Nothing specific. We know he lived in Manchester for another fifteen years. Then he lived in America for a time on a business visa. It was while he was in New York City that he became associated with the payday loan industry. Then he came back to the UK and started Ye Olde Money Man."

"I remember those ads," Kate said. "Skeevy, with a side of slimy. There was this cartoon family, all grinning from ear to ear, catching pound notes that fell from the sky."

"I could imagine your mum using Ye Olde Money Man," Paul said.

"Shows what you know," Kate returned with a grin. "My mum didn't get regular paydays. Just money under the table. She never punched a time clock in her life. But some of our neighbors relied on payday loans. Getting the cash was always a godsend, but repaying the loans put them farther and farther behind. One step forward, two steps back."

"But business was good for Galen," Tony said.

"Very good," Paul agreed. "Ye Olde Money Man might not have been the sole source of his millions, but it was the cornerstone of his empire. He never married, or had any kids. Didn't have a conspicuous lifestyle. When he turned sixty-two, he sold it all off. Washed his hands of everything but some London real estate. He owns a nice chunk of Hackney."

"Slums?" Kate asked.

"Maybe not technically. But judging by the addresses, I wouldn't care to live in them. Mind you, I'm getting Gulls to check Galen's portfolio. If she finds anything different, I'll update you."

"You mentioned other brushes with the law?" Tony said.

"Oh. I did, didn't I?" Paul consulted his notes. "Yes, he appeared in court three times last year on harassment charges. It was settled with a fine. Kincaid's meant to get the details from the woman who sued Galen and won."

"That woke me up. Either that, or my coffee's kicking in," Kate said, diving into the greasy bag for what had to be her fifth mini doughnut. "Did we go over why Bob Cratchit—Galen's P.A., I mean—did a runner instead of staying inside 17 Holywell as instructed?"

"Something about childcare," Paul said. "He found the body, called 999, then called his wife. That's when he realized his youngest children were home alone, trying to make their own dinner on a dodgy cooker. He said he rushed home to sort things and just never got back."

"Before a certain someone joined my team," Tony said archly, "I would've found that excuse outrageous. Now I have to admit, it sounds plausible."

"Maybe," Kate said. "I'd like to hear the story from his own lips. So does the P.A. manage all Galen's properties?"

"I don't know," Paul admitted. Smiling, he looked from Kate to Tony. "Shall we go find out?"

CHAPTER 21

Oliver Vine-Jones wasn't only an employee of the slumlord Barnaby Galen, he was also a tenant. He lived in Verbena Road, Hackney, in a long row of terraced houses that scowled at the passersby like wartime wives, queued up to swap ration coupons for meat. The peaked roofs were the wives' kerchiefs; the white doors were their pinafores, the black steps their boots. They were a grim reminder of the era of mend or make do.

Or do without, Kate thought. Living without certain things most people took for granted was the key to survival in places like Verbena Road. Although the Wakefields never dwelt in this particular neighborhood, Kate still felt a kinship. As her mother Lolo's fortunes rose and fell, the Wakefields had moved houses many times, often in the middle of the night. Some of the Council estates they'd lived on were nicer than these crumbling rental flats on Verbena Road.

A Black cab dropped them off by the Vine-Jones residence, Number 9. Such a relatively luxurious mode of travel was becoming commonplace for them, at least during the holiday season. Kate knew that Paul and Tony would have been just as happy taking the tube or a bus. Certainly either choice might have been faster. But Kate was fighting minor anxieties, trying to reacclimate herself to the metropolitan lifestyle she'd avoided for so long. With the tube in particular, she didn't think she could bear the crowds.

"Watch yourselves, madam and sirs," the cabbie said as they alighted. "I realize it's broad daylight, but sometimes the wrong element comes out early. Tis the season to snatch bags and steal watches."

"Thanks, but we're CID," Paul replied with a studied careless-ness Kate found hilarious. He was cruising into sight of the big four-oh. Yet in her opinion, he still expended far too much mental energy worrying over what people, even strangers, thought of him. He'd spent half the cab ride bleating about the infuriating attitude of someone named Carbuncle. As if being cursed with such a name wouldn't make anyone obstinate.

"CID? Well, that's all right, then," the cabbie said, pretending to be impressed. "But don't be too hard on the proles, hey, guv'ner? On this patch, some of them have been on the back foot since Maggie Thatcher got in." Having got the last word, he drove away.

That 9 Verbena Road was a household with small children was obvious at a glance. The front step was decorated with scrawls in blue, yellow, and pink chalk. A broken truck, down on its axels as if stripped by a chop shop, was abandoned on the sidewalk. Nearby, Kate spied a semi-deflated rubber bouncer and a cheap doll of the Poundland variety she'd once played with. These dolls didn't receive individual names like "Sindy" or "Tressie." The box they came in only said, "Fashion Girl."

The front windows were closed, but the sounds of kids play-ing, arguing, or some combination of the two penetrated the glass nonetheless.

"You're dead!" a little boy cried.

A girl shrieked.

"You're dead, dead, dead!"

Paul looked horrified. "Good Lord. Listen to that. You have to wonder why blokes ever sign up for it. At least on purpose."

Kate gave him a sharp poke in the ribs. "Quiet, you. Henry's only a few years older, and you like talking to him."

"Henry's all right," Paul agreed reluctantly. "Kind of suspect he's an aberration, though. And that lot screaming blue murder is the rule."

Kate tried the bell. It didn't work. She rapped smartly on the house's door, which had looked white from the street, but up close was more of a neglected gray. It needed a fresh coat of paint, just as the terraced row's stonework needed a thorough pressure washing.

The knock temporarily silenced the children. For a couple of beats, nothing happened. Then the little boy shouted, "Didn't I tell you? They've come to kill you!"

The little girl shrieked again. Paul, wincing, shrank slightly inside his natty Perry Ellis coat.

"Just a tick," a woman called from inside the house.

Kate, Paul, and Tony waited for what felt like ages. The shouty kids kept up their act, growing louder every few seconds, yet still the door remained closed. Kate knocked again.

"Terribly sorry! Half a minute," the woman called.

"Yay, parenthood." Paul gave a mock cheer.

As Kate raised her fist a third time, the door was opened by her idea of a remarkably pretty woman. She had dark brown skin, long-lashed brown eyes, and black hair gathered in a high ponytail. Tiny studs shone in her earlobes. She wore no makeup, and her frock was the sort of housedress Kate hadn't seen for years: sleeveless with a cinched waist and a full A-line skirt. It was so simply tailored, it might have been homemade.

"You must be the police," she said. Her smile turned her pretty face into a beautiful one, if only for one radiant moment. "The constable told us to expect a follow-up visit, but we didn't look for it so soon."

"It's the filth. You're nicked!" cried a small boy, popping up from behind the sofa and grinning like a fiend. His sister, a pink-ribboned, skirted version of him, shrieked on cue. Kate thought suddenly of Granny's scream. This child's wasn't as loud, and didn't have the creepy sound effects overlaid, but there was still a similarity.

"I'm DI Kate Hetheridge," Kate said, raising her voice to be heard above the din. "This is my partner, DI Paul Bhar. And that's Tony Hetheridge, a consultant in partnership with Scotland Yard." She grinned at Tony. The introductions no longer tripped lightly off the tongue.

"I'm Priya Vine-Jones. But wait. Are you both named Hetheridge?" She looked the trio over, brightening as recognition dawned. "You are, aren't you? And didn't I see you on *Good Morning Britain?*" she asked Paul, looking as excited as if she'd run into a real celeb, like Mary Berry or Jeremy Clarkson.

Before Paul could reply, Priya continued, "It was you, wasn't it? My goodness. It was so terrible, that whole affair, and it would have been so much worse without your heroism. I can't believe it's really you—all of you—here on my doorstep." She paused, happiness sliding off her face as she slowly cottoned on. "Ollie's in trouble for leaving Mr. Galen's house, isn't he?"

"Not necessarily," Tony cut in, using his most reassuring voice. "We just want to ask him some questions. Never fear, interviews are routine after a suspicious death, Mrs. Vine-Jones. May we come in?"

"Yes, please. Where are my manners? Do come in, of course, of course." Priya stepped back so they could come through. As she closed the door behind them, she became aware of her beribboned little girl standing on the sofa.

"Reena! What have I told you about doing that with your shoes on?"

"Sorry, Mum," the little girl chirped. She hopped off.

"Riteish, how are you coming on that picture for Daddy?"

"I can't draw anything good. I need a big box of crayons with more colors," the boy declared. "I need Laser Lemon. I need Bluebell."

"You do beautiful work with eight colors. *Blend*," Mrs. Vine-Jones exhorted her son. "Now go upstairs and get to work. Daddy needs cheering up. Draw something that will make him smile."

As Riteish trudged up the stairs, casting poor-me glances at Kate, Tony, and Paul as he went, Priya turned to the girl. "Reena, have you practiced your violin today? I haven't heard a note."

"I can't. Amara's in bed. She said she'll *die* if she has to listen to 'Ode to Joy' again."

"Practice in the kitchen, then. That way, Amara can sleep and Mrs. Kinsey won't pound on the walls." Priya shot an apologetic look at Kate. "Sorry, we're at sixes and sevens. My oldest girl, Amara, has come down with something. That makes finding space to practice difficult. These walls are like rice paper. And our neighbor, I'm sorry to say, isn't a music lover. Anyway. If you'll just have a seat." She brushed at the sofa cushion her child had trod on in her scuffed Mary Janes. "I'll go wake up Ollie. He was up most of the night, poor thing. Now he's having a nap with the baby."

Soon after Priya had climbed the stairs, a thin, grating noise came from the kitchen. Reena was tuning up on the violin. It sounded like an alien life form being tortured with an eggbeater.

"*Four* children," Paul whispered to Kate. He looked utterly appalled. "A boy, two girls, and a baby. Why would anyone have four? It's mental."

Kate ignored that. The Vine-Jones's living room brought her right back to her childhood. The family's telly was ancient, at

119

least by current standards. On the shelf under the TV was a VCR and a few beat-up VHS tapes. They still bore price stickers from their point of origin, a boot sale or church fête. There was nothing decorating the walls, apart from a few school awards. Plenty of family photos, though, in inexpensive plastic frames. Kate noticed one that looked like a snap of Ollie and Priya outside the Registry Office on their wedding day. They appeared quite happy. Catching herself smiling at the image, Kate realized she was already disposed to like this couple. So much for investigatory agnosticism, a virtue she'd always preached.

"Five children," she murmured to Paul.

"What?"

"Read the name on those school awards. Best Science Fair Entry, Year Five: Nathan Vine-Jones. Robotics and STEM Camp Merit Award: Nathan Vine-Jones. If Reena and Riteish are twins, Amara is asleep and the baby is with dad, then Nathan makes five. He's probably the first born."

"And perhaps this is his handiwork," Tony said, picking up what Kate thought was a robot constructed from Erector set parts. Its eyes were fairy light bulbs; its mouth was a perforated disc, the holes suggesting it could speak. It had been so skillfully crafted, it almost looked like a storebought toy, apart from mismatched joints and a few blobs of paint, here and there.

"Maybe that, too," Paul said, pointing at a large rectangular object bolted to the wall. Entirely metal, it seemed to have multiple elements—panels, bars, hinges, and something like a mesh cage. The whole thing was painted bright pink.

Above them, Priya and her husband were having a discussion. It was rising in volume. Kate clearly heard Priya say, "But they're top people. That means we're in trouble, doesn't it?"

Ollie's answer was too soft to make out. Kate swapped looks with Tony and Paul. Then footsteps sounded on the stairs, and the couple came down, both wearing smiles. Neither matched the genuine emotion captured in that joyous wedding snap.

"This is Ollie," his wife said, pushing her gangly, red-haired husband toward Kate, Paul, and Tony as if he were an especially large, reluctant child. "You get started. I'll put the kettle on and see if my friend Delia can spare any fancy biscuits."

Ollie approached Kate first. "Hallo," he said, with a touch of a posh accent. "How do you do?"

He shook her hand, just once and just right. "How do you do?" he said to Paul, ducking his head a little as he spoke, like many self-consciously tall men. "How do you do?" he said to Tony, delivering one last correct shake.

Kate had replied, "Hi," and Paul had come back with his usual, "Hiya." By contrast, Tony had looked Oliver Vine-Jones in the eye, shook his hand firmly, and said, "How do you do?"

There it was, like the click of magnets with opposite poles sticking together. We share this; we are of the same class.

"Forgive me," Ollie told Tony. "My wife *did* tell me your name, but it's been a mad couple of days, and I'm afraid I forgot. Is it—?"

"Hetheridge. Anthony, though I prefer Tony. Lord Leo Hetheridge was my father. My mother was Lady Patricia," Tony said, reciting his pedigree with the sort of easy manners Kate longed to replicate. He was giving these family details as breadcrumbs to aid Ollie, not outgun him socially. Kate had seen her husband take both tacks, as the situation dictated.

"Lady Patricia," Ollie said, brightening. "Of course. My Aunt Barbara was a friend of Lady Patricia's. When I was seven, I think I might have been a colossal pest at one of your mother's garden parties. Tossed out, if I remember rightly."

His upper-crust pronunciation was quite noticeable now, Kate thought. It wasn't quite the Received Pronunciation that had spread throughout the nation via radio and television. It was more of a drawl, both intimidating and amusing. When Tony slipped into it, she sometimes tried to imitate him. That meant saying complete sentences without moving her upper lip.

"Yes, well, if you disrupted one of my mother's parties, you and I have something in common," Tony said. "I was banned at age nine on charges of unsuitability for general human contact. Only your name, Vine-Jones is so familiar to me. I can't quite place...."

"My father is the Baron Gilbert's younger brother. Charles Vine-Jones III. My mother, Lady Helen, was the Honorable Helen Burney before she married."

Kate exchanged a glance with Paul. Moments like these were why the Toff Squad existed—to provide a liaison between the world of Met inquiries and the upper classes, which tended to retreat into the still highly-relevant "old boy" network at the first hint of trouble. In such cases, what was needed was a superintendent who could follow upper class witnesses and suspects into that network, and draw them out again.

Until the powers that be, in their perverse desire to fix everything that wasn't broken, had forced Tony out, Kate thought. Now she was expected to step into the breach. But how could she? It was that mutual background, the click of magnets coming together, that mattered. She was a commoner who'd married into a courtesy title. In this case, it was pure luck Tony had involved himself. Who would've expected Ollie Vine-Jones of 9 Verbena Road to unveil connections to a baron and an earl? While his wife was out begging fancy biscuits from a neighbor, no less?

"Do you know, I saw Lady Helen last January, at the steering committee of that children's education charity," Tony said.

"Education." Ollie cringed. "Story of my life, worrying about children's education. But never mind that. Soldiering on."

"I imagine so. How is Lady Helen these days? And your father, of course."

"No idea. Sorry. We don't speak." Ollie clearly meant to sound flippant, but his head drooped. Kate suspected he found the topic mortifying. Heaven knew he didn't live in a style commensurate with his upbringing. Had he been disowned?

"Ah. Well. Never mind," Tony said. "And on behalf of the Met, we're grateful to you for helping us with our inquiries today."

Once again, Kate wondered if she would ever develop the same aplomb. Tony was made for moments like that. When Ollie said he and his parents no longer spoke, Tony's response had been cool and almost relieved, as if he was grateful to escape the obligation to discuss Charles and Helen Vine-Jones, anyway. Whenever Kate stepped in it, conversationally speaking, and accidently caused mutual embarrassment, her usual course was to stumble around verbally, laugh at an odd moment, and in sum, make an uncomfortable moment worse.

"Shall we all sit?" Ollie asked. Perhaps it was just the mention of his parents, but he looked uncomfortable. Twice he'd regarded Paul warily, as if he might spring forward at any moment with handcuffs.

"Sure, but first—may I ask what this is?" Kate pointed to the bright pink metal jumble bolted to the wall.

Ollie brightened. "That just happens to be my son Nathan's invention. As you've no doubt noticed, space in our front room and dining nook is obviously at a premium. Enter the space saver. Observe."

Ollie unfolded the device's front panel. "What's this? It's a changing board for nappies."

Lifting the board, he rotated it to the right, where it rested with its bottom edge on the floor. That exposed the second wing, a short ladder with four rungs. "This is a drying rack for baby clothes. Or women's underthings."

Lifting the rack, he rotated it to the left, resting it against the floor. That exposed a third rack, a metal rectangle covered in plastic mesh. "Another rack, but for jumpers that have to dry flat." Lifting it, he rotated it a hundred and eighty degrees, resting its bottom edge on the floor. The three panels, combined with the wall, created an open-topped box. Arranging the panels in this position caused a thin, square creche mattress to fall from its slot, creating the box's padded floor.

"And there you have it. Ta-da! A playpen," Ollie concluded.

Kate applauded. "So clever."

"Well done," Paul said, sounding a wee bit grudging.

"Yes, well done," Tony agreed. "I couldn't help but notice that your son Nathan has received several awards at school. Did he design that project at science camp?"

Ollie looked as proud as a peacock with LED tail feathers. "He made this design when he was four years old."

"You're kidding," Kate said. Henry was bright, and had hit all his milestones early. But at four years old, his biggest creative accomplishment had been coloring inside the lines.

"We'd just had another baby," Ollie said. "Our first girl, Amara. So we asked Nathan to take his responsibilities as big brother seriously and help out around the place. We didn't expect anything special. We only wanted him to feel protective toward his little sister. But he sat down and drew this. Not just the idea of a collapsible playpen, or the uses of the individual elements. He told me how he wanted the pieces to rotate and reorient. I went to the hardware store and chose the materials. I couldn't have assembled it without his direction. He told me how to arrange it all so it functioned. He also chose the color in honor of Amara: pink."

"Top marks," Tony said.

"Your boy's a genius," Kate burst out. "I mean, literally."

Ollie nodded. Pride made his cheeks bloom. He wasn't a good-looking man; his face was too long, his eyes deeply recessed, his chin weak. His red hair was thinning and losing color, not going white so much as going translucent. But when he heard his child's genius acknowledged, Ollie became comely in a way no surgeon could bestow.

Everyone took a seat. Kate, Paul, and Tony returned to their places on the sofa; Ollie went to the dining nook and selected a chair. The dining table was deeply scarred, probably an Oxfam or church fête find. Only four of the six chairs matched. Apart from a sprinkling of stray toys, however, the dining area was clean and presentable. That was more than Kate could say for most of the rooms she'd grown up in.

Placing his chair in their midst, Ollie sat down, drawing his long legs up awkwardly because the coffee table prevented him from stretching them out. He began, "I suppose I ought to start by apologizing...."

"Said every Englishman ever," Paul said.

"Yes. Precisely," he chuckled. "I'm most comfortable when I'm apologizing, and I often start before it's warranted, if you want the truth. But I do hope you'll forgive me for leaving the scene yesterday, in spite of being instructed not to go. I never meant to leave the door ajar, and I certainly didn't expect Cy—Selma's better half—to wander inside. But they're both a bit... aggressive when it comes to knowing what's happening in the neighborhood."

"What happened to make you leave?" Kate asked.

"After I called 999, I told the operator I couldn't remain on the line with her. I had to reach my wife, Priya, and tell her I wouldn't be home for hours. It was about three o'clock. I knew the kids would be home soon. I wanted Priya to leave her job early and look after them in my place. That was one of the upsides of working for Mr. Galen. He liked an early start and an early finish, so we didn't need sitters very often."

"Where does your wife work?" Paul asked, leather notebook open and pen poised.

"Helping Hands UK. It's a non-profit. Anyway," Ollie said, "what I didn't know was that Priya had already left work, because Amara's school had informed her Amara was poorly. Vomiting, with a fever. Priya took her straight to the urgent care center. As you can imagine, there was quite a wait. She tried to text me that the twins would be home alone if I didn't get back by half-three.

But the message didn't go through. Her phone's rubbish, one of those no-contract things." He sighed, waving that away. "So I rang the house, expecting to get Priya, and Riteish answered. He said Mummy wasn't home, and he and Reena were making grilled cheese sandwiches. Only the cooker was smoking and the house smelled bad…." He stopped, regarding them sheepishly. "Maybe you don't want every detail."

"Actually, we do," Kate said pleasantly. "I must admit, I turned up prepared to give you a stern lecture about obeying lawful commands from 999 officers. But given the situation, I would've done the same."

"Thanks. I don't know what got into the twins, trying to do a fry-up," Ollie said. "They're not even allowed to use the microwave."

"How's the sick kiddie?" Paul asked.

"Better. Fever's down with paracetamol. No vomiting today. Of course, when you have a big family, it's like dominoes. All of us will probably come down with it eventually."

"Your wife mentioned you didn't sleep well last night," Kate said. "Are you feeling ill?"

Ollie looked blank. "What? Oh. No. Last night I was just going over accounts. I worked for Mr. Galen for almost twelve years. He owns—owned—this house. Now I'll need a new job, and quite likely a new home. At a typical London rent," he added. "Living here was part of my salary." He cleared his throat. "About finding Mr. Galen—where should I start?"

"What time did you arrive at 17 Holywell?" Kate asked, also taking notes, although unlike Paul, she preferred her mobile. The latest app gave her a screen like a blank sheet of paper. She scribbled notes on the white screen with her stylus, and the app turned those handwritten words into a typed draft.

"Half-two, I think. Or a quarter to three. I can't say for sure, because I turned up on a whim," Ollie said. "Perhaps temptation is a better word. I thought I'd turned the page, but habit drove me back again."

"Turn the page?" Paul asked.

"The job was over. Mr. Galen sacked me on Wednesday," Ollie said. "When I went to his house yesterday afternoon, I was going to beg for my job back.

CHAPTER 22

This poor bugger, Paul thought. He hoped it didn't show on his face. But it seemed to Paul that Ollie Vine-Jones had been down on his luck for the whole of his adult life, or at least the last decade.

"For now, let's put aside what happened regarding your employment," Paul said. "You said you went by Mr. Galen's at approximately a quarter to three. Did you have reason to believe anything was amiss?"

"No. I hadn't heard from him, which was disappointing. He's sacked me three times before, you know," Ollie said, again with that sheepish look. He ducked his head, as if even while sitting down, he might be too easy a target with his back straight and his head held high. "So when he sacked me on Wednesday, I didn't come over in hives or rush off to consult a job placement service. I thought, fine, I'll have Thursday morning off, and then Mr. Galen will call and shout at me a bit more and everything will be right as rain."

"He was intemperate in everything?" Tony asked.

Ollie actually grinned. "Intemperate. Now that's a lovely word. He was barmy, if you want the truth. Hard, stubborn, and a

129

bit cruel, if I'm being honest. He liked to hold the whip hand over you. He wanted you to know that whatever he'd given you could be taken away, should you ever displease him."

"I'd rather dig ditches than work for someone like that," Paul blurted. Then he added more reasonably, "Of course, if I had a big family to provide for, I'm sure I'd look at things differently."

"Too right," Ollie said. "Anyway, Thursday came and went. Mr. Galen stopped by the property—there's an eviction pending —but he didn't come by or give me a bell. I started to wonder if this time, he'd really sacked me for good and all."

"Did you notice anything suspicious as you approached his home?" Kate asked. "I take it there's no security system, just a few dummy CCTV cameras?"

"Yes. Mr. Galen thought security systems were subscription rackets. You pay and pay, and the fees go up every year, but you get little or nothing in return. He bought those dummy cams from a Chinese novelty company. That's why they look like toys. But no, I didn't notice anything odd. His front garden always looked sad and unkempt.

"Mr. Galen was getting a bit hard of hearing, so his doorbell is rigged up very loud," Ollie continued. "My boy did it for him. Nathan's quite good with wiring. All our lamps have homemade dimmer switches, thanks to him. I rang three times, and the bell echoed like a ruddy gong. But there was no answer. I told myself, that's that. I meant to go home. Only—I still had my key. And I needed my job back."

"Key," Kate repeated. "How long have you possessed a key to Galen's home?"

"Four or five years."

"Why did he give it to you? Did working as his P.A. extend to duties inside his house?"

Ollie looked horrified. "No, thank goodness. He really only slept there. You've seen the state of the plumbing. The last couple of months, he'd been showering in unlet units and eating all three meals out. If I'd been obligated to spend much time inside that house, I would've needed hazard pay."

"Then why the key?" Tony asked.

"For Nathan. As I've said, Mr. Galen was tight-fisted. He didn't care to hire proper companies or insure things. So when he had problems around the house, he liked to pick tenants who were behind in their rent, or desperate to earn extra money, and get them to do the work for a fraction of the cost," Ollie said. "By the time Nathan was eight, he could do small electrical and plumbing jobs as well as any amateur. So, once a week, Mr. Galen had Nathan come by to work on this or that. The jobs kept Nathan in pocket money. It wasn't much, but given our family's budget, every little bit helps."

"So you entered by using the key?" Paul asked.

Ollie nodded. "Everything looked just the same. Which is to say, terrible. Nothing gave me the impression someone had intruded, or that anything was amiss. But again, the house was always jumbled and smelled like death." He shrugged.

"You described Mr. Galen's personality as difficult," Tony said. "That he was miserly and refused to pay for the sort of expenses most homeowners consider inevitable. Are you aware he was a very rich man?"

"Course I was. He bragged about it whenever anyone got under his skin. Source of all his power."

"Would you care to speculate on why he chose to live so uncomfortably?"

Ollie had an answer ready. His reply was so elegant, Paul suspected he'd formulated it some time ago, and had given it often, when people asked about his employer's strange behavior.

"People always think that no matter what the question is, the answer is money, and plenty of it," Ollie said. "And they're right in this sense: money is the answer to some questions. Food, clothes, shelter—just ask Priya, she's worked for non-profits all her life. You need money for those things, and money can turn around a deadly situation in the wink of an eye.

"But there comes a point when it loses its power. You can't buy good health, or true friends. You can't correct the past with money, either," he continued. "Twenty or thirty years ago, Mr. Galen reached the point where money was no object for him, and would never be again. But just amassing cash didn't change what was between his ears. Inside, he was a skint coal miner's son from the North, and always would be. An object of pity and contempt."

Paul didn't interrupt. Neither did Kate or Tony. Ollie, gathering strength, went on.

"Sometimes, he talked to me about it. Not because he wanted to make a connection. Mr. Galen couldn't do that. He had to be on top, the king, the emperor, with everyone else looking up to him. But once in awhile he'd tell me about his childhood. Maybe he thought it excused how cruel he'd become. He told me how he'd gone to bed hungry most nights. That his school clothes and books were provided by a church charity. Everyone in the village knew his dad drank most of what he earned. Their family slept in a cottage with no heat, apart from a cast iron stove. No plumbing, either, just a pump, an outhouse, and a pot under the bed. The one bed he shared with his dad, mum, and two little sisters, mind you."

"In his final years, he didn't mind living that way again, with makeshift chamber pots and no running water," Paul said. "Even as a multimillionaire."

"I reckon he amassed the fortune to feel safe," Ollie said. "And spending the money—any money—threatened that feeling of safety."

Someone pounded on the front door. At the same time, a male voice boomed, "Knock, knock, Vine-Jones family! Knock, knock!"

Ollie closed his eyes briefly. "It's Cy. Cyril Smythe. Mr. Galen's neighbor. Shall I answer?" he asked Paul and Kate.

"Please do." Paul had no worries about interviewing two witnesses at once. If they started to feed off one another's stories, or one seemed to exert influence over the other, he'd split them up and handle both with increased suspicion.

When Ollie opened the door, one of the Holywell Street neighbors formerly known as the kitchen lot entered. For a moment, Paul didn't remember him. Then the man's height, well over six feet, and his shiny bald pate struck a chord. As if sensing that he might not be recognized, Cy proclaimed,

"It's me! Father Christmas! Out of my green robe and going about incognito to check on the behavior of all little boys and girls."

"You're not Father Christmas," Riteish said from the top of the stairs. Paul spied the little boy's round, impudent face grinning down at them, and something stirred in his ribcage. It might have been emotion, or it might have been his cardiovascular system, trying to cope with doughnuts and coffee laced with heavy cream. He preferred to assume the latter.

"Riteish! Upstairs," Ollie called.

"We want Santa Claus," Riteish told Cy. "He's an American, and he's rich."

"Ho, ho, ho," Cy boomed, seeming to enjoy the kid's cheek. "Obey your old dad or it's nothing but coal for you, come Christmas."

As Riteish dragged himself back to eight-crayon exile, Cy took in Paul, Kate, and Tony as a group. "Now this is a fine bunch of coppers. Scotland Yard, am I right? Don't go too hard on Vine-Jones for leaving the scene yesterday, please. He has a load of responsibilities. And it's my fault for seeing the open door and going in for a peek."

Paul couldn't place Cy's accent. It wasn't quite RP, but it didn't sound like any particular region. He looked somewhere between seventy and eighty, slim and wiry, with big, snow white false teeth that matched his lightweight tracksuit. His windcheater, made by the same designer, was white with neon green accents. It matched his trainers, also white with reflective green stripes.

"Surely you weren't jogging in the neighborhood," Ollie said, hovering by the front door as if hoping to show Cy out again.

"No. And I don't jog. Joints can't take it. Lift weights sometimes. Done it since my twenties. And I power walk," Cy said. "Twice a day, up and down Holywell, plus rambles nearby. You wouldn't believe the things you notice, walking about in midday, when most people are at work and no one pays an old man any mind."

Without being invited, Cy marched to the dining nook, grabbed a chair, and planted himself just behind Ollie. Kate shifted uncomfortably. Paul wasn't surprised. Yet another tall man, loud and somewhat overbearing, made it seem like the incredible shrinking living room.

Ollie said, "I'm, er, not sure if these detectives want...."

"To gaze upon my ugly mug? Not likely, I'll grant you," Cy said, clapping Ollie on the back as if he'd said something hilarious. Though by no means conventionally attractive, Cy wasn't a horror show. His nose was overlarge, his ears stuck out, and his ersatz teeth were startling, but none of those things made him hard to look at.

"I came by for two reasons. No, three reasons," Cy continued. "First, to apologize again for bringing Selma—that's my lady friend—and the rest of the Holywell mafia into Galen's house. It was foolish, and selfish. But we meant no harm. We were only curious," he said, spreading his arms as if to emphasize the frailty of human nature. "Galen's been a right bastard to all of us—sorry, I know it's Christmas, but this is a time of year to be truthful, and that's a home truth, hand to God. Selma used to say how unfair it was that a cruel old rotter like him would outlive her. There's something almost comforting in seeing him go first."

"Is that so?" Kate asked, in a neutral voice that signaled her interest, at least to Paul's ears.

"Oh, yes," Cy replied. "Selma has what they call COPD. Can't get her breath. At first, she just needed supplemental oxygen for outings, or to sleep at night. Now she has to carry an oxygen generator with her everywhere. Does breathing treatments twice a week at the pulmonary clinic." He shook his head. "If any of you lot still smoke, I urge you to give it up for New Year's. If Selma sees another Christmas after this one, it will be a miracle.

"Second reason I came by, to tell my mate Vine-Jones here, I might have a line on a job for him. Old man Galen wasn't the only game in town," Cy continued.

"What sort of work do you do?" Paul asked, aiming for good manners, though he thought Cy must surely be retired.

"Carrying Selma's handbag, sorting her pills, and giving her a cuddle on a long winter's night," Cy said, flashing those big white choppers again. "I'm a kept man. You think I have money, living the flash life on Holywell Street, with my designer trackies and whatnot?" He shook his head. "Not a chance. I've worked since I was fifteen. I was still working two years ago, when Selma hired me to trim her rose bushes. We hit it off famously. Pretty soon I packed my suitcase and came to stay. If not for my gracious lady, I'd probably be living in one of Galen's overpriced flats, always teetering on the brink of eviction."

During this speech, delivered with the unselfconscious air of a man who sees no reason to apologize for his life choices, Paul again detected a faint accent that wasn't London. But each time it started to veer, Cy course-corrected back to the Received Pronunciation of the Beeb and other media presenters.

"How long have you lived in London?" Paul asked.

"Oh, my, look at that, why don't you," Cy said, giving Ollie a conspiratorial wink. "That's how they do it on *Luther*, don't they? Segue into questioning. I suppose I've earned it. Left my fingerprints on the door knob, no doubt." He patted his bald head. "No hairs, though. Take that, *CSI*. And to answer your question, I was born in Wales, my gentle lad. But my mum married a Londoner and our family moved to Cheapside when I was nine. I've always tried to talk in a way that keeps 'em guessing. Opens more doors, I find."

"What sort of job do you propose for Mr. Vine-Jones?" Kate asked.

"Nothing, posh, milady," he said with a touch of flirtation. "I have a friend who works in SoHo. She's a high muckety-muck with a company called Fantastic Flights. They do special effects for the cinema. You've seen *Star Wars*?"

"Of course," Paul and Kate said.

"Well, Fantastic Flights didn't do *Star Wars*, but they've done movies that are sort of *Star Wars*-lite," Cy said. "Most of what they do is computer graphics, which is coding and art design and stuff. But the execs need personal assistants who can fetch lunches, book flights, field phone calls, and so on. Leona admitted the exec she has in mind is a beast," he told Ollie as an aside. "But if you can last over a decade with Barnaby Galen, you can handle some cinema tosser."

"Leona," Paul said, seizing on the name. "Is that one of your neighborhood mafia, as you put it? Leona Brown-Bell?"

"Yes, indeed. Another survivor of the killer kitchen caper," Cy said. "We were held captive in there for almost three hours. I'm still having flashbacks. Leona was a bit salty throughout, so if you tried to interview her, I apologize. She's a self-made woman. Grew up in Bristol, I think. Top marks in school, a star at Uni, and now she's the number two woman at Fantastic Flights. She doesn't take kindly to being told what to do, or asked the same question twice."

"Even when one of her neighbors has clearly been murdered?" Tony asked. "I'm given to understand your neighborhood mafia wandered around, inspecting what was clearly a crime scene, but not one of you bothered to ring 999. Why was that?"

Paul bit back a smile. He enjoyed it when Tony played bad cop; it made his role so much easier.

"Oh, come on, now, guv, it wasn't like that," Cy said. He didn't sound put on his guard; to the contrary, he sounded like he was enjoying himself. "I was out getting my afternoon power walk. Walking west, I saw young Ollie on Galen's doorstep, ringing the bell. When I returned, walking east, I saw him dash out like a shot. Didn't notice me waving at him. Left the door ajar. I thought the mean old screw had gone too far." Cy grinned. "I decided to go in and tell Galen he couldn't go on that way. He was abusive to Selma. He was outrageous to poor Adrian and Leona, his closest neighbors. And he was an absolute swine to Jacinda. So I went in planning to give him both barrels. Instead, I found him dead."

"I can see how the sight might have scrambled your thoughts," Ollie put in. "I think I screamed. I found myself on the floor, on my knees, shaking all over and asking myself if it was even real. I pinched myself, and I haven't done that since I was a boy."

"Let Cy tell the story," Kate suggested. "If you tell it together, you might accidentally embellish one another's memory."

"But he's got it exactly right, all of it," Cy said. "Next thing I knew, I was ringing up Selma. I told her to get over to Galen's. She was with Adrian, working on the Fash Freaks. They're posh dolls. It's a daft hobby," he added, dismissing that avenue with a wave of the hand. "They came over. I'm not sure who tipped off Leona. As for Jacinda…."

"That was my fault," Ollie said. "I went home in a state of panic. Of course, the kids were all right and the place wasn't on fire, though their fry-up was burned black and the kitchen was full of smoke. I couldn't get Priya on the phone and I didn't know why Amara wasn't home yet. So I called my mate Jacinda. I met her through Humans Need Houses, of all things. They're a pressure group that helps tenants who feel they're being evicted unfairly. Mr. Galen was always on the wrong side of them. I wanted her to come here, but I must've given her the impression I was returning to 17 Holywell. She went there instead."

"And found herself imprisoned in the world's foulest kitchen with me and mine," Cy said heartily. "So, yes, we were all in the house and we didn't ring 999. By my best guess, we were there less than ten minutes before the first patrol cars arrived. Had the response time been longer," he concluded, looking Tony in the eye, "I'm quite sure one of us would have remembered our duty."

The large rectangle in his jacket pocket buzzed loudly. Withdrawing a mobile, Cy looked at the message on the screen and stood up. "Sorry, all. Milady calls with an urgent request. Takeaway curry and a foot massage. I *am* free to leave, hey, guv?" he asked, looking pointedly at Tony. "Not under forty-eight hour hold so I might help you with your inquiries?"

"Free to go," Tony replied. "You forgot to tell us your third reason for coming by, though."

"Beg pardon?"

"When you arrived. You said you had two, make that three, reasons for dropping in," Tony said.

"Oh! Bless my soul. Quite right," Cy declared. "And ta for the reminder. Only I was concerned about your Nathan," he told Ollie. "Did he ever find his red toolkit?"

Ollie blinked. "He told you it was missing?"

"Of course. He was frantic to locate it," Cy said.

"Did he call you?"

Cy cleared his throat and shuffled his feet. "He, er, actually came round the neighborhood, checking the places he'd been before. Now it comes to it, he asked me to keep schtum on the matter, because his mum said Holywell Street was out of bounds. I shouldn't have opened my great gob."

"It's all right," Ollie replied unconvincingly. "And thank you for asking, but I'm afraid the kit's still missing. We'll have to find a way to replace it in the new year."

"See that you do. A boy needs tools. Especially that boy. Well, duty calls. I'm off to rub milady's feet. Happy Christmas to you all. Ho, ho, ho," he called, and departed.

CHAPTER 23

*L*ess than a minute after Cy Smythe departed, Priya came through from the kitchen. Spread across the tray in her hands was a teapot, five cups, and a plate of Mr. Kipling Viennese Whirls. Paul's stomach rumbled appreciatively. Apparently, his cardiovascular system had successfully neutralized the morning's fat and sugar, and was ready for onslaught number two.

"Sorry it took me so long." Smiling apologetically, Priya placed the tray on the coffee table and sat down in Cy's abandoned chair.

"You were hiding, admit it," Ollie said, going straight for a biscuit.

"I was. I don't like that man. And did I hear him asking about Nathan?"

"The red toolkit," Ollie said. "He knew it went missing. Wanted to know if it had been found. Oh, and he claimed he might know of a job for me."

Priya, who'd began pouring for everyone, sighed. "Talk about a quandary. Ordinarily I'd say that nothing good could come from his suggestions. But as long as the job isn't actually on Holywell Street, perhaps you should give it a look, my love."

"I realize this might not be part of the inquiry," Paul said, accepting a cup of tea. "But may I ask why you don't care for Mr. Smythe?"

"Other than the fact that he's loud, overbearing, and a bit vulgar," Kate said, smiling. "I feel comfortable making those accusations because I've been told off for being all three, from time to time."

"I can't quite say," Priya demurred, though her tone suggested she had the words, and only wanted to water them down a bit before sharing. "Ollie's probably told you our eldest, Nathan, does odd jobs here and there for pocket money. For the last few years, he's done this and that at Mr. Galen's place. Nothing major, just enough to keep him in prawn crisps and fizzy drinks. Then Cy started, I don't know, trying to befriend him. He's seventy-five years old if he's a day, and Nathan's eleven. It didn't feel right."

"We're not making an allegation," Ollie hastened to add. "Isn't that right, Priya? We're not trying to give Scotland Yard the impression Cy is the type who interferes with boys."

Priya shrugged. "I said what I said. He's too old, in my opinion, to befriend an eleven-year-old. Mr. Galen certainly didn't. He was as rude to Nathan as he was to poor Ollie. It was just a job, and I thought if Nathan was willing to take a few lumps to earn pocket money, then good for him. But Cy? Cy shouldn't even know where we live, as far as I'm concerned. He's the reason I forbid Nathan to go back to Holywell Street, or do any more jobs for Mr. Galen. Which is probably why the house's plumbing failed. It might even have something to do with Ollie getting sacked."

"Losing Nathan as his handyman annoyed him, but that wasn't why," Ollie said.

"What reason did he give?" Tony asked, accepting his cup from Priya.

"It all started with the audit." Having demolished his fancy biscuit, Ollie sipped his tea. "Mr. Galen was spun up over the financials, as usual. He'd sacked his accountant. Said he had proof the man was cheating him. I think it was pure paranoia. But when Mr. Galen convinced himself something was true, nothing could change his mind. And he thought he could prepare for the audit himself. Not just by gathering the documentation, you understand. He was trying to, er, optimize the books, if you take my meaning."

"Trying to strongarm my husband into going along with his blatantly unscrupulous business practices," Priya said with feeling. "As if working for him wasn't bad enough."

"Did you tell him you wanted no part of it?" Paul asked. The Mr. Kipling Viennese Whirl was as tasty as he remembered.

"I don't know if you've noticed, but I'm not exactly the confrontational sort," Ollie said. "I made excuses. After all, I'm not a qualified accountant. I never even finished Uni. I told him he'd be flirting with prison if he asked me to tidy his books."

"You may not be obnoxious, but you stand up for what you believe in," Priya contradicted him. She'd served everyone except herself, Paul noticed. She'd taken no biscuit, left her teacup empty, and seemed chiefly concerned with speaking up for her husband. "And it's not as if you weren't clever enough to complete your education. Only... life got in the way."

"All for the best, my love," he said, smiling at her. Then to Paul, Kate, and Tony, he explained, "When I was twenty-two, I decided to take a gap year and join the Peace Corps. I'd never been anywhere or done anything, apart from the things my family decided for me. The Peace Corps' mission excited me, so I decided to go for it. In those days, it seemed to me that the world was getting more dangerous and desperate all the time. I wanted to make some small contribution in the other direction."

"Would I be rash in assuming your parents weren't best pleased?" Tony asked with a smile.

"They were incandescent with anger." Ollie shrugged. "Every child has to rebel. I waited until I was an adult, and threw everyone for a loop. Still, the Peace Corps was only a one-year commitment. Afterwards, I was supposed to return to Uni and finish my degree in Business Administration, of all things." He rolled his eyes. "Instead, I met Priya and fell in love. I took a job in London to be near her. We married, and had Nathan a year later, and we've never looked back."

"So your refusal to help cook the books caused Mr. Galen to sack you?" Paul asked.

"That was part of it. But remember how I told you, he always had to hold the whip hand?" Ollie asked. "When you said no to him, there was always a new demand. Usually a bigger demand. He had to feel like he'd ultimately prevailed. He knew it was no use trying to bully me into faking financial documents. So he thought up a bigger demand, something I theoretically had to agree to, no matter how much it hurt.

"He said he was worried about his other big property, the terraced houses on Hyacinth Street. It's here in Hackney, less than a quarter mile away, as the crow flies," Ollie said. "Mr. Galen ordered me to move out of this house and into an empty unit on Hyacinth."

"Uproot your family on a whim?" Paul asked.

"Not my family. Just me."

Priya sighed. "This is the sort of man who was murdered. A tyrant."

"Sweetheart," Ollie reproved.

"I said what I said," Priya repeated stubbornly. Paul grinned at her. Maybe Ollie hadn't been on a decade-long run of rotten luck after all.

"Mr. Galen had lots of trouble with tenants on Hyacinth. He thought a mole in the building would do the trick. So in addition to my other duties as his P.A., he wanted me to move into Hyacinth and keep tabs on the tenants without their knowledge." Ollie sighed. "I tried to reason with him. That I was needed at home, and what's more, I wanted to be at home. But he kept banging on that it wouldn't be very different. Hyacinth Street is within walking distance, so I could pop in here from time to time. Simple. Bob's your uncle."

"Of course you said no. Ridiculous," Kate said.

"Only I didn't just say no. I lost control," Ollie said quietly. "I told Mr. Galen what I really thought of him. That he was cruel. Inhuman. That he had no regard for anything except holding power over other people and extracting money from them."

Paul thought Ollie was telling the truth, but his demeanor was atypical. Usually when witnesses recounted an argument, they relived it to some degree, voice rising and color heightening. Looking back on his moment of overt rebellion, Ollie didn't seem triumphant. He was shame-faced.

"How did Mr. Galen react?" Paul asked.

"I've never seen him so angry. For a moment, I thought he might fall down with a heart attack, or stroke," Ollie said. "Then he told me to go, pack my things, and take my family to a homeless shelter."

"This house is why Ollie put up with that man for all those years," Priya said. "It's my fault, really. I didn't go to Uni. The only work I know how to do is service work—helping people fill in forms, and apply for the right program, or get matched with charities that can get them through the winter. When I'm not at the non-profit, I'm busy with the kids. I always wanted to be a mum, so I'm not complaining. I wouldn't have it any other way. But that left Ollie in the position of breadwinner, and his family wouldn't even speak to him. Again, because of me."

"Their loss," Ollie said stoutly. "And I accepted the position with Mr. Galen with open eyes. He advertised for someone willing to go above and beyond without hesitation. I took the job, the salary, and this house, knowing it was far from perfect. But it's allowed me and Priya to raise a family, and we've been happy here. Happier on our very worst day, I think, than poor Mr. Galen ever was in the whole of his life."

"Is this the police? Are we being questioned?"

A young man had appeared in the kitchen doorway. He had deep-set eyes, like his father, and dark brown eyes and hair, like his mother. Clearly, this was Nathan, the whiz kid who'd designed a complicated device at age four, and won so many school awards over the years. He seemed younger than eleven, face still pudgy, not yet in his teen growth spurt. Nevertheless, he affected a bored, man-of-the-world air, as if he were twenty-five, and not living at home so much as just passing through.

"Mr. Galen's death is under investigation," Priya said, in the tone of a mum repeating something she'd already said more than once. To Paul, Kate, and Tony, she said, "May I present our eldest, Nathan. What are you doing home so soon?"

"Half-day," Nathan informed her. "Did you know Bill and his parents attended an open house at the Orangery Boys' School last night. He was telling me about the tour. They have a science lab that's state-of-the-art."

"How wonderful for them." Priya looked pained.

"Bill's dad says there's such a thing as scholarships for talent. And bursaries, too, for low-income students."

"I don't know if you should discuss our family finances with Bill's dad," Ollie said.

"There's a thing call a means test," Nathan continued, undeterred. The presence of strangers didn't bother him at all; if anything, he seemed to believe a disinterested audience increased his likelihood of getting a fair hearing. "I'll bet we could pass it, or fail it, however it's reckoned. Then we'll get a bursary and I can go. Bill was a shoo-in because his dad's in the clergy. But I can get in on talent, I know I can."

"Nathan," Priya said sharply. "We're well aware of these

things. If applying for a bursary would make it possible, we'd do it. We've exhausted all the avenues, love. Your father works every hour God sends. If there was a way to send you to the Orangery, or St. Paul's, we'd do it, sweetheart. I promise."

"You haven't really tried," Nathan yelled. Now he seemed as young as Henry Hetheridge, raging at Ritchie over a purloined Cornetto. "I don't want to go to a rubbish school! It's not fair!"

"That's it. Upstairs," Priya demanded, springing to her feet. Nathan had already started up, presumably intending to lock himself in his bedroom. His mother followed, probably biting her tongue in front of guests, Paul thought, but planning to lay into her son more fully when no one outside the family could hear.

"Education," Ollie said, and smiled weakly. "The great leveler of hopes and dreams. If you can't afford it, your opportunities are narrower. That's the way the system's designed, and I'm afraid I don't see it changing in my lifetime. Nathan will accept it, eventually. Only his emotions haven't caught up to his intellect yet."

They finished the tea and biscuits in silence. Making eye contact with Kate and Tony, Paul decided everyone had heard enough for a satisfactory first interview. There was only one question left, but it was of vital importance.

"I think we're on point of wrapping up," Paul told Ollie. "We may call on you again, of course, so please don't leave the city. I would like to know this: Did Mr. Galen have any enemies? You saw the murder weapon. It's nothing short of extraordinary. Is there anyone in his life who might have hated him enough to put in that kind of time and trouble?"

Ollie's face took on a pale, deer-in-the-headlights look. "Oh. Good heavens. Mr. Galen had nothing but enemies. He disliked everyone. And it was mutual, as near as I could tell."

"Some examples?" Kate prompted.

"Very well. Um… let's see. He certainly hated most of the municipal government," Ollie said. "Building inspectors were scum, as he saw it. Magistrates were all corrupt. All against him.

The housing authorities were on the take, he said. And taking too much these days. He had no respect whatsoever for bailiffs. He told them to their faces they were emasculated blobs," Ollie added, shaking his head. "Really, no matter how his individual tenants felt about him, he hated them all, every last one. He wouldn't have spit on them if they were on fire."

CHAPTER 24

"*Madness!* This is glorious madness," Paul whooped for the third time.

After interviewing Ollie and Priya Vine-Jones, Paul had talked Kate and Tony into bringing him to see their holiday let. At first, Kate had seemed a wee bit unwilling, but had clearly decided not to shut him out. He viewed that as a positive sign.

"I usually never like spiral staircases in magazines, but I must admit, this one's quite nice," he called down to them from the landing. Kate was in the kitchen selecting a bottle of wine. Tony was sitting on the white Chesterfield. "It's so big. Four bedrooms?"

"Five," Tony said. Before Paul could ask, he added, "Two and a half baths."

"I demand to know how much you paid for the week."

"Bugger off."

"He won't tell me, either," Kate said. She uncorked a bottle of Riesling.

"I had limited time. Lord knows I had a precise list of requirements," Tony retorted. "In such a case, you take what you can get and don't complain."

"Twenty thousand," Paul accused, watching his old guv's face. No one was more unreadable than Tony, when he chose to be.

"Good grief. Do you think so?" Kate asked. There was a *glug* as she filled a stem glass two-thirds full and sniffed it.

"Not for the week. But I doubt this sort of property lets for a mere seven days at a time. He probably took the whole month. Am I close?"

Tony didn't answer.

"Tell me," Paul said, perching experimentally on the stair's wrought iron bannister. Could he slide all the way to the floor without falling? As a little boy of Riteish's age, he'd been something of a bannister-sliding legend. "Tell me, or I'll slide down in protest."

"Please yourself," Tony said. "But if you break your neck, I won't be held liable. I'll get Dr. Stepp or some other obliging M.E. to rule it suicide."

"Thirty thousand. That's the real price of a month in this upholstered brothel, isn't it?" Paul asked. "You're ashamed to admit it. Come on. Give."

Tony seemed not to hear.

"You leave me no choice." Balancing his rump on the bannister, Paul attempted a slide. It did not end well. He made it only a couple of inches before slipping off the rail, pitching over the side, and landing on the floor. He lay there for a minute with his cheek against the heart-of-pine planks, listening to Kate and Tony's laughter.

"Come on. Up." Tony extended a hand to him.

"I meant to do that," he groaned, allowing himself to be helped to his feet. Catching Kate's eye, he said weakly, "Wine."

Kate brought him a glass. "Taste this. Let me know what you think."

He sipped. "It's perfect, thank you."

Kate looked dubious. "It doesn't smell a little off to you?"

"Nope."

"Tony?"

He sniffed the wine, swirled, and tasted. "Fine."

Kate sniffed her glass again, shook her head, and put the glass on the counter. "One of you can drink that for me. Maybe there's something wrong with my nose. I'll have water."

They settled into the living room. Tony switched on the gas fireplace. As the wine did its work, Paul forgot his tumble off the bannister, and everyone sank into companionable silence. After about five minutes, he asked, "All right, this is lovely, but how long do we have to wait?"

"You're asking me?" Tony asked. "For what?"

"For you to ask for our impressions of the case so far. I'm past ready to hash it all out."

Tony looked amused. "In case you've forgotten, you're the man in charge. I'm merely a consultant."

Paul *had* forgotten, as it happened. For years he'd wanted the Carbuncles of the world to see him as the man in charge, and treat him accordingly. Now it was happening, and some part of him apparently wanted to put up his feet and let his old guv call the tune.

"All right," he said, sitting up straighter and putting on his best tone of authority. "First impressions. Kate."

"We're not short of suspects," she said. "According to Ollie, Barnaby Galen didn't have a friend in the world. He considered everyone an enemy. And to hear Cy Smythe tell it, he'd crossed the line with everyone on Holywell Street."

"Apart from Cy himself," Tony said.

"What do you mean?" Paul asked.

Tony, who rarely took notes, reeled off what Cy had said from memory. "He told us he was out walking when he noticed Ollie on Galen's doorstep. When he reversed directions, he saw Ollie leaving in a hurry. The front door was left open. Cy claimed he jumped to the conclusion that Galen had mistreated Ollie—"

"Which doesn't seem like a stretch," Kate cut in.

"True. Cy seemed to want us to believe Galen had terrorized the neighborhood," Tony said. "He named the next-door neighbors, Adrian and Leona. He named his partner, Selma. He even said Galen had been a swine to Jacinda Cox. Mention of her stood out to me. Jacinda Cox is Ollie's friend, correct? Someone from a homeless advocacy group that he met in the course of his work. She doesn't live on Holywell. She apparently went to the crime scene by mistake, thinking that her friend had experienced a bad shock and needed support. Why should Cy know anything about her, or how Galen treated her?"

"He did say they were all held hostage in Galen's kitchen," Paul pointed out. "For three hours, which sounds about right. I reckon she told him how Galen behaved toward his tenants."

"Fair play," Tony said. "Still, I think it would have been more natural for Cy to tell us what he and Galen had against one another. He left that out entirely. At this point, I suppose we'll have to assume Galen's real animosity was toward Selma, and Cy was simply taking her part."

Paul's glass was already empty. Rising, he made for Kate's wine, abandoned on the kitchen's marble countertop. "Does anyone like Ollie for the murderer?"

"Nope," Kate said.

"No, for all sorts of reasons," Tony said.

"What did you call our suspect?" Paul asked Kate as he returned to his seat with the fresh glass of Riesling. "Mr. FX?"

"Yes. And I did notice," she said with a smile. "My detective muscles haven't completely atrophied from lack of use."

"I presume you refer to the neighbor, Leona Brown-Bell, working in Soho," Tony said. "I looked her up on my mobile during the ride back to Strange Mews. Fantastic Flights is a highly successful special effects company. She's not mentioned by name in any of the promotional material, at least not on a quick search, but that's hardly surprising. Even the most powerful cinema executives rarely become household names."

"Seems a little easy," Paul said.

"I adore easy," Kate retorted. "But yeah, you're right. Besides, Henry has been dragging me to those films and talking my ear off about the visual effects for years. They used to rely heavily on models and puppets. Sometimes they still do, like that baby Yoda creature on telly. But most everything else is CGI. I can't imagine Fantastic Flights does much of anything as old-school as Granny. She looked like something out of a fun fair ride. One of the dark ones, where the car bumps you around corners and scary mannequins pop out."

Paul thought that was a good point. Apparently, so did Tony, who paused to consider it.

"Let's follow that avenue for a moment," he said at last. "To hear him described, Galen was a cruel, miserable old man. He did nothing except make other people unhappy, and live surrounded by his own filth. But surely there must be a personal dimension. In my experience, men of his generation who habitually misuse power don't confine themselves to taking on men. They quite often attack women with even more rancor. Sometimes it takes the form of sexual harassment. Other times it's just pure spite. I wonder why Galen never married. I'd like to know if perhaps he was a serial womanizer. Of the kitchen lot, Leona was the only woman who might be called attractive."

"I didn't know you saw them," Kate said, looking slightly amused.

"You and Paul supplied their names. Google supplied their pictures," Tony said. "Social media is a curse in many ways, but this modern habit people have, uploading selfies to the web, has made our job easier, in my view."

"So, you fancy Leona?" Paul asked. "As Mr., or in this case, Ms. FX?"

"Just a possibility to consider," Tony said neutrally. "Perhaps in the course of tormenting anyone who crossed his path, Galen harmed Leona. Maybe simply by being a bad neighbor. Maybe by making advances or insinuations she found insupportable. In her work, she's exposed to all sorts of fictional narratives. Some of the artists at Fantastic Flights might have started many years ago, when cinema effects were purely props. Leona could have hired someone to make her revenge fantasy come true."

Paul consulted his notebook, flipping through the pages until he found the line he sought. "Cy did say he didn't summon Leona. That he wasn't sure how she knew to come by."

"We'll need to ask her," Kate said. "But it seems like the Holywell neighborhood mafia wasn't shy. If she looked out her window, she might have seen people like Jacinda Cox marching into Galen's house and decided to check out matters herself."

"So no one likes Ollie, the person who arguably suffered the most at Galen's hands, and who just happened to find the body, for his murder?" Paul asked. "No one wants to play devil's advocate and argue that Bob Cratchit might have finally snapped? I agree he's a decent fellow, and Priya is lovely. But we've all worked cases where decent people have killed, after they were pushed too far."

"He said he was up all night looking over his accounts," Kate said. Apparently unsatisfied with only bottled water, she was back in the kitchen again, opening cupboards. "I can believe it. Before I was married, it was just me, Henry, and Ritchie on a good salary in a South London flat. The nicest thing you could call that place was economical. And I still struggled sometimes. Because Galen's dead, Ollie's lost his job and his home. He has *five* kids. And Nathan has his heart set on attending one of those fee-based academies. That family's in real trouble."

"They could go crawling back to Mater and Pater," Paul said, putting on a decent upper crust accent. "And don't forget, Ollie had already been sacked, apparently for good, before Galen was killed. So he was in hot water either way."

"I could see Ollie losing control and bashing Galen over the head," Tony said. He shook his head when Kate, who'd come back to the Chesterfield with a newly-opened box of chocolates, offered him first choice. "I could see him strangling him as he slept. Unpremeditated attacks, in other words. But Granny is the very definition of a premeditated murder. It reminds me of a Sixties film with Vincent Price. I don't suppose either of you recall *The Abominable Doctor Phibes?*"

Paul, selecting a chocolate, shook his head. Kate did the same.

"Well, it's been a dog's age since I saw it. Probably as one of those late movies that used to run on Saturday nights, in the world before satellite television," Tony said. "It was meant to be horrifying, but also sort of darkly comedic. Dr. Phibes didn't just kill his enemies. He destroyed each of them in poetic ways, based on the Biblical plagues of Egypt. Mr. FX did something like that to Galen. He—or she—created a nightmare scenario that goes back to our earliest childhood fears. The monster under the bed that rises up from the darkness and seizes our ankle."

"All true," Paul said. As it turned out, milk chocolate paired well with Riesling. "And setting it up required unlimited access to the Galen house, at least for a week or two. Ollie had a key and admits to using it without permission."

"Think the forensics will come back with a DNA calling card?" Kate asked.

"I'd be surprised," Tony said. "Whoever created Granny surely took the time to wipe her down thoroughly while setting her up. And if one of the kitchen lot, AKA the Holywell mafia, is responsible, they've spread their forensic breadcrumbs all over the residence. If the Met tries to build a case on any one of the neighbors based on, say, a thumbprint recovered from Granny, the defense counsel will simply reveal how many other things they touched while inside.

"Still," he added more thoughtfully, "the fact that Granny is a human skeleton, not a Halloween prop, might provide any number of clues. When your team compiles backgrounds of Galen's neighbors and associates," he told Paul, "it will be interesting to see if anyone is attached to universities or medical colleges."

"Or museums. Or graveyards," Kate said. She bit down experimentally on a chocolate and groaned. "Why do they always put in pistachio?"

"Sadism," Paul said. "Just like Mr. FX."

They settled into companionable silence again. Then Tony said, "I'm waiting for someone to address the elephant in the room."

"If you mean me and the way I'm eating today, you're not wrong," Kate said.

"Here, fishy fish-fish," Paul said in a sing-song voice. "Compliment me, I beg of you!"

"I meant our remaining person of interest. Nathan Vine-Jones," Tony said.

"Pull the other one," Kate barked.

"What she said. And come to think of it, you really are putting it away. If you hate the pistachio ones, why did you finish it?"

"Shut it. Ooh. Caramel."

"I'm not trying to win a popularity contest," Tony said. "But the child created a device at age four that was arguably as complicated as Granny. He won some sort of school prize for robotics. He has a key to Galen's house, which gave him access until his mum forbid him to go back there. And Priya specifically said Galen was no kinder to Nathan than he was to Ollie. Perhaps the boy felt mistreated and decided to strike back. Even a brilliant eleven-year-old might not realize a shock like that could kill an old person. He might have considered it nothing but a prank."

Kate glared at her husband. "That's an awful thought."

"But is it feasible?"

Paul couldn't honestly say it wasn't. Kate clearly wanted to shoot down the theory, but it seemed that none of her arguments were strong enough to present aloud.

"I'm not saying I want it to be so," Tony said. "Ollie truly is the Bob Cratchit of the piece, and Nathan's a bit of a modern Tiny Tim. He needs the best education available, and he won't get it, barring a miracle. Someone with his talents might win the Nobel Prize for science one day, but let's face it, talent is thick on the ground. It's connections that are rare, and priceless."

Paul's mobile trilled. It was Kincaid. Rising, he stepped into the foyer to take the call. The information was necessary, but hardly earth-shattering. Preliminary investigation into the backgrounds of Ollie, Selma, Cy, Adrian, and Leona had revealed no rap sheets or "gotcha" occupations like Human Bone Inspector or Gory Prop Master. Ollie, Adrian, and Leona's public bios were so uncomplicated, they were already complete, apart from the social media deep-dives that had become necessary in the last decade. Selma was twice divorced, and had two middle-aged children living in the United States, which opened up more avenues that had to be checked. Cy's claim about working steadily from age fifteen to his mid-seventies was apparently true. Kincaid reckoned following up on his last ten years' worth of jobs, residences, and contacts might take a week.

There was, however, an interesting ping concerning Ollie's friend, Jacinda Cox. After thanking Kincaid, Paul returned to the living room with a dramatic flourish, announcing solemnly, "I have news." He drained his glass.

"You're secretly married," Kate said. "After you tied the knot, you moved in with your new wife. Now you're scared to death to tell Sharada."

The wine went down wrong. His immediate denial turned into coughs—deep, painful, strangled coughs.

"Sorry! Only kidding. Good lord," Kate cried, hurrying over to take his stem glass before he dropped it.

Tony pounded him on the back as Paul, now mortified as well as shocked, kept right on hacking.

"Is he choking?" Kate asked Tony.

"If he's coughing, he's breathing." Tony maneuvered Paul back to his seat and brought him a glass of water. When he got his breath back and managed to speak again, his voice was feeble.

"My mum guessed, didn't she? She guessed, and told you to accuse me."

"No," Kate said, staring at him. "I was just being awful. As usual. Sorry." She bit her lip. "You're married. For real?"

Paul nodded.

"How'd Emmeline take the news?"

"Em's my wife. We eloped in September."

Kate's mouth opened, then closed again. She turned to Tony. "Did you see this coming?"

"I did not. But if I'm being honest, I think it's high time. Well done, you," he said, shaking Paul's hand. "Congratulations."

"Of course! Congrats! Absolutely." Kate hugged him. "Do I sound a bit mad? I'm just embarrassed. No wonder you're hiding from Sharada. But you've got to come clean eventually. You know that, right? Or Emmeline will feel like she's an embarrassment. And that's no way to kick off a marriage."

"I know," Paul sighed. It took him a moment to remember what he'd even been about to say, before the accidental revelation. "Oh, yes. Remember when we talked about Galen's rap sheet? How he got in a scrape over fraud as a young man, but got off with probation? And stayed on the straight and narrow until last year, when he was taken to court for harassment? Well, the other party wasn't Leona Brown-Bell. It was Jacinda Cox."

"Interesting," Tony said. "Do we know the details?"

"No, but Kincaid's after the court records. There probably isn't a transcript, but we should be able to get a readout of the proceedings," Paul said. His throat hurt from the coughing fit, but he felt a bit relieved, now that the secret was out. "I reckon tomorrow I'll pay her a visit. She lives in Knightsbridge, though not close to Holywell Street. As for tonight—are you up for Winter Wonderland?"

Kate and Tony exchanged glances.

"I know you two were holed up like hermits all weekend. Time to live a little," Paul said. "It just so happens Em and I plan to go around seven. Care to meet up? She's getting impatient for me to introduce her around. And I know she'd love to see you."

"Of course," Kate said.

"We'll be there," Tony said.

CHAPTER 25

*A*t half-six, they took a cab to Hyde Park, alighting at the entrance near Apsley House and Rotten Row. Kate, safely bundled into her puffer coat, the cobalt scarf wrapped around her neck and a matching knit cap on her head, felt overwhelmed by the scope of the festival. As in years past, there was a huge outdoor market, strings of white lights, and a Christmas tree resplendent with blue fairy lights. There was also a seventy-meter observation wheel. Kate's moderate fear of heights, well-controlled before the rooftop incident, made her guts clench at the thought of it. Fortunately, Tony showed no interest in riding.

The evening was pleasantly chilly. Kate felt fine in her quilted armor, but noticed Winter Wonderland's organizers had placed portable heaters here and there; warm zones for anyone who needed to defrost. There was also *glühwein*, or German mulled wine, on offer at various stalls. Kate wasn't in the mood, but hot red wine cooked with sugar, star anise, rum, and cinnamon sticks appeared to be the festival's most popular drink, at least for parents.

Her mobile chimed. It was a text from Paul.

. . .

STOPPED **by HQ and got sucked into the vortex. Gave Em your number. She'll find you in the park. I'll join ASAP.**

KATE AND TONY viewed the exhibits at a leisurely pace, flowing with the crowd, which was mostly inclined to amble. The kids seemed enchanted by everything: food vans, hawkers' carts, shows, and the ice-skating rink. From time to time, someone stumbled into Kate, or accidentally bumped her in the vicinity of her handbag, which she wore crossbody like a tourist. Each time the panic flared, she waited it out, and it passed. It wasn't as bad as she'd feared. By the time she and Tony reached the holiday village's center, where pints as well as hot drinks could be purchased, Kate was starting to enjoy herself.

Her mobile chimed again. This time, the text was from Emmeline.

I SEE YOU! **I'm standing by the giant candy canes.**

KATE, who'd only just glanced over at the twelve-foot, electric red and white candy canes near Santa's grotto, looked again at the woman she'd completely missed the first time. And yes, it was Emmeline Wardle Bhar. Her long blonde hair fell past her shoulders in thick, glossy waves. Instead of a cap, she wore white ear muffs, extra feathery, that were somehow both whimsical and chic. Her pink coat, lipstick and boots gave her ensemble the expertly pulled-together look Kate found so elusive.

No wonder I didn't recognize her. She's put on a few pounds, Kate thought. *We can commiserate over that together.*

Then she looked a third time at Emmeline, and the light dawned.

"Oh, my God!" Kate cried, squeezing Tony's hand. She pulled

him through the crowd to where Paul's new wife stood, waving. "Look at you!"

Emmeline laughed, clearly accustomed to the point-and-shriek reaction. She patted her belly. "I know. I'm five months' gone. Didn't really pop till mid-November. People at my company had been afraid to say anything. They thought I was sneak-eating. When they realized I was up the duff, everyone went mental."

"I can't believe it. I can't believe Paul's going to be a dad," Kate gushed, overcome with genuine feeling. She hadn't been so happy about a pregnancy since her sister Maura's bombshell. A vision came to her of a mini Paul-Em hybrid, done up in designer baby clothes with styling product in its wispy hair, and she actually jumped with joy. Beside her, Tony beamed.

"Heartiest congratulations, my dear," he declared, taking Emmeline's mittened hand in both of his. "I couldn't be happier for the two of you. What a welcome surprise."

Tony's warmth appeared to overwhelm Emmeline. Her brows drew together; she blinked as if fighting back tears. "Thank you. We were both afraid you'd call it a rash decision. Marry in haste and all that."

"Me?" Tony threw back his head and laughed. "Accuse anyone of putting heart over head? I can't believe Paul ever thought such a thing. This is brilliant."

"Thank you," Emmeline repeated. Tiny drops gleamed on her lashes. "Do you know, I've never apologized for the way I spoke to you, the night we met. It was beastly."

"It's forgotten," Tony said with a magnanimity Kate loved and admired. "Now that you've married Paul, you're in the inner circle. And we couldn't be happier to have you."

"Of course we are." Now Kate's eyes were stinging. Apparently, sentimentality was catching at Winter Wonderland. Either that, or she was going gooey-soft in her old age. Time for a diversion.

"Tony, that stall is selling hot chocolates. Would you mind....?"

"Not at all. Seeing as they also sell lager," he added with a smile. "Tell me, Emmeline, will hot chocolate be all right? I could get you a non-alcoholic cider or a bottle of water."

"Hot chocolate would be lovely," Emmeline said.

Tony went off to join the queue, leaving Kate and Emmeline to chat beside the giant candy canes. Standing still wasn't easy. Guests were constantly circling the stalls to discover what was on offer; those who'd made their choices wandered about, hands full of newly-purchased food and drink, searching for someplace to eat. Most of the public tables were loaded with families eating everything from crisps to whole turkey legs. Late-comers wandered in search of somewhere to lean, eyeing Kate and Emmeline with resentment.

"We might be better off waiting between those tents," Emmeline said, leading Kate to a gap between souvenir vendors. One sold glow-in-the-dark Christmas trinkets. The other was flogging perennial tourist grot: Union Jack socks, banks shaped like red phone boxes, and taffy in a cellophane bag proclaiming, "A Gift from England." All of it was made in China, Kate suspected, and marked up five hundred percent.

"This is better, don't you think?" Emmeline asked.

Kate checked her view of Tony in the queue, and decided it was adequate. She turned back to Emmeline. "You really do look wonderful." She started to add, "I'm a bit envious," but stopped herself. Paul had probably mentioned to his new wife that having a baby wasn't in the cards for Kate and Tony. There was no need to bring it up now, just to make Emmeline feel awkward. Besides, Kate reminded herself, she and Tony had only just finalized adopting Henry. They had a son. Grousing to Emmeline about her fertility, or lack thereof, would feel disloyal to a little boy Kate wouldn't trade for the world.

"Yes, well, that's good, because inside I'm falling apart." She fanned her cheeks, which had gone as pink as her coat. "Hormones. I'm up, I'm down, I'm stuffing my face. Just glad the morning sickness is over," she said, looking sidelong as another woman took refuge in the makeshift alley. She was smoking a cigarette, which was prohibited in Royal parks. Kate didn't care, but she was prepared to say something if Emmeline objected.

"The wind's carrying the smoke away from you," the woman told Emmeline in a defiant voice. She moved a few feet away, toward the empty zone behind the vendor's stalls, as if to forestall any complaints.

Emmeline ignored her. "I didn't expect your husband to be so kind," she told Kate. "I just about fell at his feet."

"Tony's wonderful," Kate agreed, so full of love and pride, she thought her heart might burst. "And so is Paul. We're a lucky pair." Kate had never got on well with women, but Emmeline was her junior, approximately ten years younger. Somehow, that made it easier for Kate to guess what the other woman had been going through.

"Your parents," she began, watching Emmeline's face to make sure she wasn't overstepping. "They weren't over the moon, I'm guessing."

"Nope. Thank God they're still in America. Frankly, I hope they never come back," Emmeline said, with a toughness Kate suspected was put on. "They told me off. Said marrying him was the worst mistake I've ever made. They thought I should—well, never mind what they thought. My dad said, 'Bad enough that you're knocked up. Now you want to tie yourself to that wog forever?"

"Ugh." Kate couldn't think of any word that better summed up her feelings.

"Mind you, he said it on my wedding day. Paul and I had just come back from the Registry office. I was dancing on air, and I didn't think it was fair to keep them in the dark any longer, so I gave them a bell," Emmeline said. "I'd convinced myself that when Mum and Dad heard how happy I am, they'd be happy, too.

Instead they went nuclear and I ended up screaming, 'Your grandchild will be a wog! We're calling it Woggie McWogface!' and rang off." She giggled at her own fury.

Kate chuckled, too. "Phone calls like that made me miss the old landlines. When you slammed them down, it seemed like the person on the other end could feel it. As if the slam was transmitted somehow. With mobiles, the call always ends with a gentle *blip*, no matter how cross you are. Someone ought to invent a phone with situational disconnection options. You know. Sound of a car crash. Sound of shattered glass. Or, for lovey-dovey disconnects, tingling bells. Or harp music."

Emmeline seemed to enjoy the idea. "You're all right, Kate. Paul's been lost without you. We're so glad you're—hey," she said sharply as a fourth person, a young man, strode into the vendor-gap, brushing lightly against Kate as he passed. Despite her coat's bulk, the sudden contact with a stranger made the hairs on the back of her neck stand up. Kate's heart kicked into overdrive, bouncing around in her throat.

"Bugger could say 'Excuse me.'" Emmeline shot the young man a look, but he paid no attention. Instead, he approached the woman with the cigarette.

"Don't you know that's a filthy habit?"

"Please. It's one ciggie." The woman regarded him warily, but without surprise. Apparently, they knew one another.

"Maybe we should find another place," Kate told Emmeline. Tony's queue had barely moved. The hot chocolates were coming slowly, and there were several patrons in front of him.

"So you thought you'd just do a legger? Go someplace quiet to suck down acetone and benzene and carbon monoxide?" said the young man, voice rising. He had hollow cheeks and a greasy black shag haircut. To Kate, he looked cast from a familiar mold: English Failed Musician, the sort who was always getting bands together but never playing gigs. His natural habitat was the pub quiz on Tuesday night, where he argued rock n' roll trivia with the quizmaster until the publican asked him to leave.

"It's one ciggie," the smoker said, still defiant. "If you don't like it, you can—"

Failed Musician seized her wrist, squeezing until she dropped the cigarette, which he stomped into the ground.

"Oi! Don't you put your hands on that lady," Emmeline shouted.

Kate went cold. Her heart banged so wildly against her ribs, she thought she might be on the verge of cardiac arrest. It was hard to breathe. An invisible band squeezed her throat, just as Failed Musician squeezed the smoker's wrist.

"Mind your business, porker," Failed Musician shouted at Emmeline. He said something else, but Kate missed those words. All she perceived was a shiny steel blade. It appeared in Failed Musician's right hand, springing out and stabbing the air.

"Oi!" Emmeline cried.

"Don't hurt me!" the smoker screamed.

"Get bent." Failed Musician clouted the smoker across the face. Red blood sprayed out of her nose and down her chin. "Didn't I tell you never to talk back? You think I won't cut you? You stupid, ugly—"

"Oi!" Running straight at Failed Musician, Emmeline whacked him in the head with her handbag. Its strap broke on impact, sending a lipstick and gold-tone compact into the air. Failed Musician roared, slashing his six-inch blade at Emmeline.

"Don't you hurt him," the smoker wailed, turning on Emmeline and shoving her with all her might.

Emmeline hit the dirt. At Uni, she'd been an athlete, but her switch to a career as an estate agent, not to mention her third-trimester pregnancy, had no doubt taken its toll. Once, she might have sprang back to her feet in one smooth movement, or rolled away with catlike grace. Now, she could only shield her face with her arms as Failed Musician slashed at it. The blade snagged her coat, ripping it near the elbow.

"You get bent," Emmeline told him, and brought her knee up into his crotch.

Failed Musician screamed. So did the smoker, who sounded like she'd been staked through the heart. In his agony, Failed Musician had dropped the knife—the better to clap both hands over what doctors sometimes call the affected area—and the smoker dove for it. She might had threatened Emmeline with it, if not for a big man in a flannel coat.

"What's all this then?" he shouted, blocking the smoker's access to the knife. To Emmeline, he said, "Ma'am, are you all right?"

Guests began flooding into the gap between vendors. Failed Musician was still rolling around on the ground, moaning. The smoker was sobbing. The man in the flannel coat, still in custody of the knife, was urging those with mobiles to ring 999. Emmeline was helped up by a pair of solicitous American tourists. They were overjoyed to find that Failed Musician's blade had hardly nicked her, though it had pierced her coat and jumper. Relief transmitted through the onlookers as everyone realized Emmeline was okay.

A man's face suddenly filled Kate's vision. It was round and friendly. "Are you injured? Did he hurt you, miss?" He was black, perhaps thirty-five, and spoke gently.

"I... I...." Kate tried to speak, but each time she opened her mouth, gulping breaths took the place of words. *Was* she hurt? What was she doing on the ground?

"Kate!"

Strong hands grasped her under each arm, pulling her to her feet and holding her there. Gripped by panic at yet another unexpected, overpowering touch, the babble endlessly chasing itself through her mind suddenly became clear:

I can't I can't I can't I can't I can't I can't I can't

A cry escaped her, childlike and without hope—the cry of a small girl who can't find her way clear of the nightmare. The man who'd hauled her to her feet spun her around and shook her.

"Kate! It's me!"

Tony. She tried to say his name, but her mouth opened and closed like a fish, her lungs gulping in air.

"You're all right," he said firmly, looking her straight in the eyes. "You're fine. I'm taking you home. I'm taking you home right now."

But I—but Emmeline—

Some part of her wanted to argue that she couldn't leave the scene, that she was a witness. But Tony, gripping her tight, was already leading her away.

You froze. That was stupid. But you can still give the police a statement. You know the old chestnut—help them with their inquiries.

But maybe none of that mattered. A rising emptiness came over Kate, a vision of the future as empty as a frozen black sunrise.

I'll never be fit for policework again.

CHAPTER 26

"Hiya, Alix. Thanks for answering. Sorry it's so late," Kate said.

The therapist never sat close to her computer's camera. Instead, she leaned back in her chair, allowing Kate to see not just her facial expressions, but her body language as well.

"Half-nine isn't my idea of late."

"You didn't come into the office just for my benefit, did you?"

Alix raised her eyebrows. "Of course not. I was working on a paper when your call came through. Home is too chaotic for me to get anything done at this time of year." She didn't elaborate; keeping mum on the specific details of her personal life was one of the boundaries she'd drawn. "I take it Tony insisted you call?"

Kate nodded. She felt like bursting into tears in front of Alix for the eleventy-millionth time, as Henry would say, and held herself back with effort. "I told him I wanted to go back to Devon. First thing in the morning. He said no. We've never shouted at each other so much. He banged his fist on the table. He said I needed to call you right away."

"Okay," Alix said serenely, as if Kate had just reeled off a string of vacation platitudes: it's lovely, the food is top notch, wish you were here. "Enough preamble. Tell me everything."

Kate told her therapist what had transpired at Winter Wonderland, falling into police-speak a few times as she tried to relay the facts as accurately and objectively as possible. "And then it transpired... Subject produced a bladed weapon... Emmeline struck the assailant below the belt, producing extreme distress...."

"Don't you sound like an officer straight off the telly?" Alix said when Kate had concluded the story. "This Emmeline sounds a bit impulsive. I'm glad she wasn't hurt. And she strikes me as a formidable friend. One you might want to hang on to."

"Yes, of course, but I'm not calling about Emmeline," Kate snapped. "What about me? Freezing solid like a great ninny. Falling to the ground with fear." Choking up again, Kate fought to get the words out. "Tony found me just sitting there, zoned out. It was like my brain had left the building."

"It did," Alix said. "You disassociated from the situation. Most of your higher functions went into lockdown mode as you tried to process the violence. Big deal."

Kate let out her breath in amazement. As she'd awaited Alix's return call via Skype, Kate had imagined many different therapeutic responses. Empathy; reassurance; a stern lecture; medication. Dismissing her breakdown with the phrase "Big deal" hadn't occurred to her.

"Alix! Don't you get it? I froze. I'm a DI. I work on a murder squad. I can't freeze."

Alix shrugged.

"Seriously?" Kate no longer felt like weeping. She felt like throwing her laptop on the floor and jumping up and down on it.

"Untwist your knickers," Alix said. "Something like this was bound to happen. In my view, you can't get well on happy thoughts." She sounded friendly but detached, as if discussing a recipe that had turned out only so-so. "It's a re-acclimation process. And you did leave it rather long, Kate. You crawled into your Briarshaw cocoon, and you stayed, and you stayed, all the while building up the perils of police work in your head. It was brave of you to go out to the festival, knowing it was full of people and noise. That was the right choice, as far as I'm concerned. And seeing that man assault that woman was a genuinely upsetting experience. Anyone would be frightened—"

"No," Kate cut across her. "That's just it. It wouldn't have been a big deal. I could have handled that greasy-haired little wanker, no problem. Even after he pulled out the knife, I could've had him. Dragged him up to the nearest security officer or banged him up myself and laughed about it later."

Alix seemed to consider that. "I must admit, the way you describe yourself before the rooftop incident sounds marvelous. I've always wanted to be that way. Utterly fearless. If I'd been at Winter Wonderland this evening, and witnessed a man getting violent with his girlfriend, only to have my pregnant friend get a knife pulled on her…." Alix shook her head. "Well, I know where I'd be right now. I'd be curled up under my afghan, drinking sherry and watching *Frasier* episodes. I don't blame you for wanting to be fearless again."

"It wasn't that I had no fear," Kate said. "Even when it was low stakes, my heart rate shot up. There was always that surge, that moment of 'Can I do this?' And sometimes I couldn't. I remember once, the bad guy was just a wee drip of a man, and I actually shouted, 'I'll have you!' I thought he'd pull a knife. But he pulled a gun, and I knew I had to run for it. My hands shook for an hour after that."

"I would've been hyperventilating," Alix said.

"I probably did, for a couple of minutes, anyway," Kate said. "You can't fight it. You just have to wait it out."

"Where did you learn that?"

"School," Kate said. "Third form. In those days, I dreamed about taking martial arts. Then I joined the Met and got all the training I ever wanted. That's done now, I reckon. I don't have the balance, even with my corrective heel."

Alix nodded. For a moment, they were silent. Then she said, "There's a secret about the adrenaline surge I'm not sure everyone gets. They think they do—that it's fight or flight."

"Isn't it?"

"It's actually fight, flight, or freeze," Alix said. "And you mentioned the mechanism that governs which option is chosen. It's the question, 'Can I do this?' In the heat of the moment, your brain considers the question, and decides."

"I thought it was pure instinct. Sort of pre-thought," Kate said.

"No, but it feels that way. And it's not even an all-or-nothing decision," Alix said. "When you shouted, 'I'll have you,' you'd assessed the bad guy as small and unthreatening. When he pulled a gun, your brain updated that judgment at once. The chance of getting killed was too high, so you ran. Things usually go that way, so people often speak as if there's only two options, fight or flight. But sometimes, we can't do either.

"Maybe we're injured, in which case, we can't fight. Or trapped, in which case, we can't run," Alix continued. "In that case, we freeze. It's the mind's final defense. To blot out everything that's happening as much as it can and go inert. In some cases, the predator may lose interest. In the rest, we're at least shielded from the terror of our final moments, as much as the mind can permit."

"I understand all that, but the point is, I could've helped Emmeline. I might not be as tough as I used to be, but together we could've put that tosser down hard. Or I could've gone for the closest security guard. It's not as if I couldn't do anything. I could."

"Is that what you told yourself? That you could do either of those things?"

Inside Kate, that terrible emptiness threatened; a cold black sun, rising. She heard it again, a refrain that had been gathering strength for weeks now:

I can't I can't I can't I can't I can't I can't I can't

"No. It was like the rooftop. I blew it up there. I let that evil son of a bitch beat me. If not for Tony, I would've been dead. We all would've been dead."

"Shame he won't forgive you."

Shock burned through Kate, making her forearms come over in gooseflesh.

"Forgive me? He doesn't hold it against me. I know he doesn't!"

"Then who is refusing to forgive you, Kate? And is going back to Devon really going to solve that problem?"

CHAPTER 27

*T*ony was up far later than usual, which was no surprise, considering he hadn't fallen asleep until after four A.M. The immediate crisis was past. Kate's emergency Skype session with Alix had quashed her determination to take the first train back to Briarshaw. They'd cleared the air after the worst row of their short marriage, and by the wee hours, she'd been curled up beside him, peacefully asleep. But Tony's churning emotions hadn't let him rest.

He'd always been like that, prone to delayed emotional reactions. Cool in the moment of truth, doubting himself long after. Finding Kate on the ground at Winter Wonderland, he'd responded sensibly. The revelation that she and Emmeline were physically unharmed should have been a cause for celebration. Instead, when Kate insisted they beat a hasty retreat back to Devon, he'd blown up.

I've been suppressing my own frustrations. Ruthlessly suppressing them, he thought. Despite missing London, his career, and the happy rhythms of his life, he'd held it all in, believing that if he only kept mum, Kate would turn the corner.

After speaking to Alix, Kate had agreed that leaving Strange

Mews before the week was up would only be a step backward. Before her collapse at the festival, Tony had rather hoped they'd spend another day with Paul, consulting on the Galen case. But before going to sleep, Kate had said she needed a quiet day at home. She wanted to soak up a little peace and reflection, she said, before ringing up Emmeline to apologize for abandoning her, and touching base with Paul to make sure he wasn't angry. No matter what Tony said, she remained convinced she'd publicly humiliated herself. Effectively, she was putting herself in timeout, as she might have done with Henry.

In point of fact, Tony had already spoken to Paul and Emmeline at length. Neither blamed Kate for anything, and Paul in particular was eager to have her back on the job. Besides, Paul knew what it was like to freeze. He still bore the scars from one such incident. And who had stepped into the breach to save him? Kate, wielding a cricket bat.

Leaving her alone at Strange Mews felt wrong, but Tony couldn't think of a rational reason why he shouldn't follow up on the Galen case while she stayed behind. The house's security features were top-notch. She had several unread ebooks on her mobile and plenty of restaurants within delivery range. A snatch of verse from Khalil Gibran came back to him: "Let there be spaces in your togetherness." Wise words, and something they'd never had trouble with before.

As for breakfast, he wasn't in the mood for a home fry-up. He wanted a proper meal out, the morning paper, and three cups of coffee. Then he wanted to check in with the M.E., Dr. Trevor Stepp, and hear the conclusions on Galen's post-mortem. And Granny.

CHAPTER 28

The M.E.'s laboratory was as bright and cheery as most such places. The walls were foam green and the overhead fluorescent lights had a burn-through-the-soul quality. The floor appeared to have been varnished while filthy, preserving the filth forever as a sort of decorative pattern. This wasn't true, of course. Tony's sight was more acute after cataract surgery. The implantation of tiny acrylic lenses now focused visual stimuli onto his retinas exactly *so*, permitting him to discern that the tile's pattern was hideous by design. The same trend was popular in industrial-grade carpet: make the design so confused and disordered, no one could be sure if housekeeping had vacuumed lately or not.

The moderately comfortable chair Tony occupied as he waited was upholstered according to the same principle. The fabric was a repeating pattern of indistinct, Daliesque brown hourglasses. One could splash coffee on the cushions, or bleed on them, and no one would be the wiser.

Tuesday was apparently a busy one for interns and residents. They buzzed back and forth, blue scrubs rumpled, lab coats flapping. After about twenty minutes, a stocky black man in the requisite attire came forth. He had booties covering his shoes and a surgical cap covering his short hair.

"Good morning. Or afternoon, very nearly," he said in an accent that suggested the Cayman Islands. He had that affable, haven't-slept-in-weeks-and-mustn't-grumble attitude that many doctors at his stage of training had; eyes heavy-lidded, smile bright. "Are you Lord Hetheridge?"

"Indeed. Dr....?"

"Winston Bodden," he said, shaking hands briskly. "I feel quite lucky Dr. Stepp called me in to coordinate the case. 976 has been an anatomy class, an archaeology project, and a detective novel, rolled into one."

"976? You mean the skeleton contraption that killed Mr. Galen?" Tony asked.

"Yes. That's the last three digits of its evidence number," Dr. Bodden said, swiping his badge at a security checkpoint. A pair of automatic doors opened on another garishly-lit, deserted hall, with two empty gurneys parked beside the sickly green walls. "I understand you CID types call it Granny. Is that on account of the plastic rain bonnet?"

"Yes."

"You know, my own gran had one of those, forty years ago or so. I never knew her, but I saw her wearing it in pictures. The CSIs will make the definitive estimate when we sign it over. But if you ask me, the bonnet on 976 is at least that old."

"The bonnet's here?" Tony was surprised. "I thought they would have collected it with the rest of their samples."

Crime scene investigators, once called scene of crime officers, or SOCOs, were highly protective of evidence that fell within their scope of inquiry. They were keenly aware that a case's evidence could be adulterated or destroyed altogether by witnesses, police officers, or even medical personnel, and strove to photograph, bag, and preemptively collect as much as possible. Any break in the chain of custody would be exploited in court by the defense. Such barristers certainly weren't above suggesting to a jury that if Constable Cockup had breathed on a bloodstain, the DNA in the real killer's blood might have magically transmogrified into that of the poor, innocent man standing in the dock. In murder cases, the Crown was always held to a higher standard than the defense. Over the years, Tony thought that standard had become guilty beyond a shadow of a doubt, as opposed to the intended legal standard, guilty beyond a *reasonable* doubt.

"Oh, they wanted to, according to Dr. Stepp," the med student said, leading Tony to a lift and hitting the button to take them down a floor. "But 976 presented unusual, not to say unique, problems regarding which service had first dibs." He flashed Tony another grin. "The chassis, as it were, and the mechanism were clearly CSI. The bonnet would have been, but it was glued to the skull. And the spinal column was fused to the chassis with plaster and screws. So the decision was made to let the M.E. have the whole thing first. CSI will pick up 976 first thing tomorrow, minus the skull and its two natural teeth."

Tony considered that as the lift deposited them in a darker, more subterranean part of the building. Oddly, it was somewhat less terrible down here, because it was starker; no gurneys left here and there, no Health and Safety posters for the edification of employees, just white walls and a white floor. This seemed like the correct spot for the medical examiner to delve into a murdered body in the service of justice.

In a room like an operating theater, behind a swinging door with a viewing window placed at eye level, Trevor sat on a wheeled stool not far from Barnaby Galen's corpse. His back to the subject, he was dictating his findings into a handheld recording device. As the door swung open, he looked up, saw Tony and Dr. Bodden, and smiled.

"Hullo. Thank you, Winston," Trevor said to the young physician. "Why don't you take the rest of the afternoon off? I'm sure you'd like a nap before cramming for tomorrow's exam."

"Thank you, sir." Nodding to Tony, Winston departed, leaving him and Trevor alone with Barnaby Galen's corpse.

"Post-mortem complete, I see." Tony said. He'd attended many autopsies over the years. At this stage, what most people would consider the worst moments—opening the skull, cutting a Y-suture in the chest, removing and weighing the individual organs —was long past. Restored to a decent semblance of himself, Galen was ready for transfer to a mortuary, where he would be eligible for an open casket. Assuming, of course, that anyone on Earth wanted such a thing, or cared how this man was laid to rest.

"Yes. And my preliminary findings are simple," Trevor said. As fresh and youthful as Tony remembered, the M.E. looked slightly overwhelmed by his long yellow surgical gown, clearly made for taller, wider men. But despite the chirpy sound of his voice, his statements were clear and competent.

"Barnaby Galen was a well-nourished individual of seventy-two years, suffering from high blood pressure and significant arterial blockage, to speak in the vernacular. His heart was mildly enlarged, which is consistent with a history of cigarette smoking, discontinued approximately ten years ago, and a sedentary life-style. Advanced atherosclerosis of the aorta was the secondary cause of death. The first, of course, was the deliberate and excessive shock produced when he was awakened from a sound sleep to a sight—and a sound—that might cause anyone extreme distress. For Mr. Galen, the result was cardiovascular overload, followed by a massive heart attack."

Tony nodded. "Any surprises?"

"Not really," Trevor said. "I did find two dental caries that must have caused him pain, and a moderate hernia, never treated. Either he distrusted doctors, or he considered it normal to go about in pain."

"He was tight-fisted," Tony said, thinking of all the Scrooge-themed films, plays, and TV programs he'd been subjected to over the years. "But the NHS would have cost nothing more than he'd already paid in."

"Yes. One more thing. Mr. Galen seems to have had a highly active youth," Trevor said. "Or an abusive childhood. At this point, I couldn't swear to one over the other. But he had poorly-healed fractures in both legs. Some of his ribs had been broken. Oh, and he'd had two surgeries. A rhinoplasty, and a vasectomy."

Tony took that in. "Do you have all his health records yet?"

Trevor shook his head. "Only from the last few years. I think these surgeries were carried out when Mr. Galen was under forty. They'll be awaiting digital scanning, sitting in their original charts in an archive somewhere."

"It may not be important," Tony said. The vasectomy was no great surprise. A man as miserly as Galen would lie awake at night fearing paternity suits; a vasectomy might have seemed like a necessary step to defend his fortune. As for the rhinoplasty, well, perhaps he'd disliked his looks.

"Anything else? I promise not to hold you to it, if further analysis changes the picture," Tony said.

Trevor smiled. "Nothing in this room. Shall we go next door and look at 976? Or as you call it, Granny?"

CHAPTER 29

*T*he exam room containing EV-892-02-976, AKA 976, AKA Granny the diabolical murder weapon, was situated just next door to the room that housed Barnaby Galen's mortal remains.

Tony, who had a passing familiarity with forensic pathology protocols, wasn't surprised to see the mechanical aspects of the contraption separated from Granny's skeletal components. The "chassis," as the medical student had called the rolling cart that had propelled Granny out from under Galen's bed and into the deepest depths of his soul, was sealed in a transparent bag. So, too, were dozens of other components that had been teased out by this highly atypical post-mortem process. At a glance, Tony saw what might have been a hundred clear baggies of varying sizes, all identified with stick-on barcodes.

"Lots of metal bits used to fasten the bones together," Tony said.

"Yes. At the crime scene, I believe we all had the impression 976 was a DIY job, and we were correct. The mismatched types of wire, screws, and brackets prove it."

Tony inspected the bagged skeletal remains, many of which

were fragmented or crumbling into powder. "Disassembly was difficult, I take it?

"Yes. I did my best not to fracture the bones as I removed the fasteners. But in several cases, the bones crumbled. Naturally, we filmed the entire process and catalogued the pieces, but the CSIs will probably want to burn me in effigy."

Tony had expected to find Granny laid out on a white-draped stainless-steel table, each bone occupying its anatomical place. In previous cases concerning a skeletonized corpse, that had been the procedure, even when only a few bones were recovered. Once, he'd seen a table laid out with a single rib bone, placed carefully where it belonged and leaving the rest of the missing bones to the imagination.

In Granny's case, Trevor had forgone a gurney-length table. Instead, he'd used eight small instrument trays, lined up in a row and covered with separate sterile drapes. On the first tray was Granny's skull, complete with glued-on rain bonnet. Under the exam room's unsparing fluorescent glare, Tony found the bonnet, with its deteriorating pattern of yellow ducks, rather poignant. As Dr. Bodden had mentioned, Granny had only two teeth, both molars. Her mandible, or lower jaw, had apparently come from a different person, and was therefore located on the next table. Now that Tony saw it under fluorescent light, it was clearly older, or at least much darker in color.

On the third table were three loose teeth, all of them molars. On the fourth table, which was rather overloaded, Tony saw the bones of two arms and one hand. Specifically, a left hand, almost destroyed by disassembly. Most of the phalanges were in pieces.

"As I said. Burned in effigy," Trevor said regretfully. "The killer wasn't worried about joining the bones in a way that could be undone."

"None of this strikes me as the work of someone with medical knowledge. Do you agree?" Tony asked.

"Completely."

Table number five contained the discs of a spinal column. Number six and seven had ribs, all stained dark brown. They looked like they might have come from an archaeological dig. Table eight had six more vertebra, each enclosed by a square formed by strips of Transpore medical tape.

"Each bone that's taped off represents an orphan. A duplicate," Trevor said. "When he made Granny's spine, the killer sacrificed anatomical accuracy for stability."

"Where's the right hand?" Tony asked. That had been the key element, the part rigged to clamp onto Galen and trigger an earsplitting alarm.

"Just there. With the other items we determined should go to the CSI crew. They were pre-processed at the scene with latent fingerprint film, but I don't reckon the techs got any joy," Trevor said. "The killer almost certainly used gloves while building and installing Granny.

"Anyway, regarding to right hand, it's the only part of her that's store-bought," Trevor continued. "Replicas are so well-made these days, there's less of a distinction between toys and biology school models than you might think. Nor could I find an item number, manufacturer, or country of origin."

"The store-bought hand is snow white," Tony said. "Anatom-ical models are sort of yellow, aren't they? And so are horror novelties."

"True. So yes, the hand could have been cut off a child's toy," Trevor said. "Any of your suspects have kiddies?"

"Yes," Tony said. "Mind you, we're calling the killer Mr. FX at the moment. While I was at breakfast, I looked up cinema-quality movie props on the web. There are companies that sell life-sized, posable, astonishingly realistic skeletons for around four thou-sand pounds, depending on the vendor."

"Meaning your killer is on a budget?"

"It fits with the amateur nature of the project. Of course," Tony continuing, sliding into devil's advocate mode himself, since he had no other detective present to play it for him, "only a killer who lives alone, and has no prying neighbors or friends, could order a huge parcel from a prop shop, unbox a life-sized skeleton, and go about affixing it to a cart without raising questions. Buying such a thing from a reputable company would create a paper trail as well."

"Granny's such a personal creation," Trevor said thoughtfully. "What's the point of doing it, if you're just going to purchase a spook off the shelf?"

Personal, Tony thought, turning the idea over in his mind.

"Let me know if I have this right," he said, not so much seeking Trevor's approval as wanting to organize his thoughts. "Mr. FX assembled Granny from a variety of bones. All human, apart from the right hand, and in a range of ages?"

Trevor nodded.

"Oldest?"

"It's impossible to be sure. The very oldest might be over a hundred years old. Filched from a museum, perhaps. A definitive answer on that will take weeks."

"Youngest?"

"Also impossible to say with certainty. Maybe fifty years old? If it helps, I don't think any of the bones come from the recently deceased. It's highly unlikely your killer stole bodies from the morgue to get his bones."

Tony lapsed into silence again. He drifted back to the first table, staring down at Granny's skull.

"We had a human anatomy skeleton in my science class at Eton. Back in the mists of time. The professor said it was male, and probably South Asian, from the colonial period. I wonder if many of those vintage skeletons, purchased and used before the laws changed, are still in circulation?"

"Probably not," Trevor said. "Strictly speaking, I think they're meant to be packed up and disposed of. There's probably a Health and Safety subcommittee or a Cabinet Minister in charge of—well, I don't know. Burying the remains? It's hard to say. These days I think people want to do the right thing, but in the case of a hundred-year-old anonymous skeleton, it's easier said than done. At Uni, my anatomy professor said he packed away his real human skeleton, which had been on display in the lecture hall since the Great War. Apparently, it languished in a sub-basement for ages. When storage space ran short, he took it home and displayed it in his own study." Trevor looked suddenly uncomfortable. "Which is against the law."

"Never fear, I shan't bang him up," Tony said. "I do wonder how common it is, for academic scientists to have old bones lying about."

"They don't make good souvenirs. Apart from ethical issues, see how fragile they are?" Trevor indicated the crumbling phalanges. "Artificial bones are far superior from a teaching standpoint. Well, in communicating the basics, at least. If I'm being honest, when it comes to the nuances, authentic bones are more challenging. Like Granny's skull. If it weren't for the bonnet, I doubt many first years would be able to appreciate that she's almost certainly female."

"How do you know? I assume there's no tissue available."

"Quite right," Trevor said. "And I don't claim a hundred percent certainty. But it's my considered opinion this skull belonged to a woman. The eye sockets are rounder. There's no forehead ridge. It's also a bit smaller than what's typical for males."

"I recall the shape of the jaw can be a giveaway, too," Tony said. "But Granny's jaw has been relegated to another table."

"Yes. It's too old, and probably male."

Tony sighed. "I'd be lying if I didn't admit to hoping you might work a bit of DNA magic. But that's out of the question, isn't it?"

"Afraid so."

"You called Granny a very personal murder weapon, and I

agree," Tony said. "I can't help thinking that bonnet is meant to indicate which undead fiend had come for Galen in the dead of night. He'd lived a long, unpleasant life full of enemies, especially toward the end. I think Granny's creator wanted to be sure that when Galen beheld her, he knew her."

Trevor, clearly flattered to find himself used as a detective's sounding board, nodded.

"I mean, a lot of effort went into shoring up that skull," Tony continued. "Mr. FX collected other teeth and stuck them in. He found a mandible and wired it in place. If he had access to so many bones, there were even duplicates available to reinforce the spinal column, why not pick a skull with a jaw and teeth? I wonder if it's a special skull. One with a specific meaning for Galen, and possibly Mr. FX, too."

Trevor remained politely silent. Tony studied the human remains for a little while longer, then said, "Some time ago, I worked on a cold case. A skull was dug up in a man's wine cellar. It had been there for thirty years. Peter Garrett, bless him, created a sculpture of what the deceased probably looked like. Using the skull itself as a base, he covered it over in modeling clay. It took a few weeks, in between his more urgent cases. But the result was an astonishing portrait. It looked very much like the basement owner's lover, who'd gone missing decades before. We won that case. Do you think something similar would be possible with Granny?"

"I don't know," Trevor said. He smiled slyly, like a boy magician about to pull his very first rabbit out of the hat. "The skull itself is evidence. Laboratory guidelines don't allow us to willfully damage or risk damaging it. And the method you describe is generally outsourced. Our medical college works with an art school in New York City, believe it or not. The process requires applying for permission to use the 3-D printer, getting a facsimile made, and shipping it to the dean of the art school in

America. It might be February or later before a student is assigned to reconstruct the face."

"Is that so?" Tony asked, wondering why Trevor seemed so pleased to shoot down the notion.

"Yes," Trevor said, smile widening. "However, this lab recently purchased brand new, state-of-the-art 3-D modeling software. I can scan in Granny, assign some of my med students, and let them go to town. In which case, you might have a digital reconstruction in two or three days."

CHAPTER 30

The morning after Emmeline's disastrous evening at Winter Wonderland, Paul woke to the sound of "Beacon" playing on his iPhone. It was mid-morning. Being the DI while Jackson was out had its advantages. He could stroll into the Yard after lunch and no one was likely to ask where he'd been.

He hadn't slept well, even though the previous night had been exhausting. While he'd been en route to the festival, Emmeline had clashed with the knifeman. Afterward, she'd tried to call him, but his mobile service was spotty that night. His phone didn't register the voicemail until an hour later, and by then, Emmeline was no longer at Hyde Park; she was at the nearest precinct, pressing charges against one Jonah Lee Felt. Disembarking at Hyde Park, Paul arrived, heard the message at last, went slightly mental, rushed about demanding answers, and received three more phone calls. One was from Tony, telling him about Kate. One was from the precinct officer on duty, telling him about Felt. And one was from Emmeline, telling him off for being missing in action.

At least Felt was sorted. He'd resisted arrest, so the MPS responded by banging him up for the night. As for his smoker girlfriend, she'd lied shamelessly about her bloody nose and fat lip, claiming Emmeline punched her. And although several witnesses said otherwise, and Felt's right hand bore a mark where he'd nicked himself on the dozy donkey's front tooth, Emmeline still had to defend herself, and that took time. Eventually her family solicitor, a milquetoasty relation who'd advised her during a certain double murder case, arrived to help. He insisted Emmeline go to the hospital for checks, even though she was manifestly unharmed. Therefore, Paul had taken her, and they'd waited for what felt like forever. Finally, a doctor who looked perhaps sixteen years old had sunnily informed them that Emmeline was the healthiest person he'd seen all day.

While giving evidence at the precinct, Paul had felt like he was taking the incident in stride. During the endless wait at the hospital, however, he'd begun to process the enormity of what happened. Emmeline could have been hurt; the baby could've been hurt.

Emmeline could have died. The baby could have died.

They loved one another, yes, of course they did, but they'd never meant to get pregnant. The news had hit like a thunderbolt. For the first few days, Paul experienced nothing but abject fear. It was like being told an asteroid was careening toward Earth, on course to expunge his life as he knew it. He'd always intended to get married someday. He'd always intended to have children someday. He'd never intended someday to actually arrive.

I ought to sue Boots. Though he wasn't even sure that he'd bought the faulty condoms at Boots. It might have been Rexall. Or Asda, come to think of it. And he'd never been loyal to any particular brand. He only knew that he'd done his part, and yet some shop had sold him a product that failed. Now look at him. Married with a kid on the way.

What if that tosser had stabbed her in the belly? What if he'd sent her into early labor, or injured the baby for life? Injured my *baby for life?*

Those thoughts, which had really only hit him during their interminable spell in the hospital waiting room, had made him go weak at the knees. Was this what fatherhood was going to be like? Responsibility, boredom, and the odd moment of terror?

He silenced his mobile alarm. Beside him, Emmeline slept on, snoring lightly. She, too, had been up most of the night, first with what he thought of as "adrenaline hangover," then with the acid reflux that had begun to plague her as soon as the morning sickness receded.

The snoring had taken some getting used to. But she looked lovely, even with her hair tangled and her mouth open. He resisted the temptation to pat her belly. The last ultrasound had proclaimed the baby healthy and developing properly. They'd declined to be told the child's sex. He was hoping for a boy. Emmeline said it didn't matter to her, but he'd noticed her looking over miniature dresses and lace headbands in Asda's baby section.

On her left arm, a small cut was visible. Paul's jaw tightened at the sight. Yes, it was only a scratch, but Felt's knife had done it. The man was already a convicted domestic abuser. Paul intended to see him prosecuted to the full extent of the law. Felt had been banged up twice for ABH—actual bodily harm. He'd assaulted an aunt on Boxing Day two years ago, and his own mother the previous Christmas Day. Apparently, the holidays had an insalubrious effect on him. But the Magistrate Court, despite finding him guilty both times, had imposed only fines and an anger management course.

When Felt stood in the dock again, Paul would make certain the authorities learned that this time, he'd attacked an expectant mother. Even if it only landed Felt in the nick for six months, that was six months he richly deserved.

After a shower, Paul dressed quickly, choosing his cufflinks and tie with less care than he once would have. He was coming to terms with the fact that his days of spending first and thinking it over later were over. When he'd lived with his mum, he'd helped out, of course, but somehow whenever he overdid it at the men's shops, Sharada waved a magic wand and settled the rest of the month's accounts herself. Living on his own had required actual planning. And now that he lived with Emmeline in her flat, the cost of living had gone up exponentially.

Their flat on Denbigh Street, Pimlico, was the sort of cozy starter home of which young lovers dreamt—until they met an estate agent and received a crash course in what they could actually afford. Being an estate agent herself, and having grown up in what many still unironically called "the right circles," Emmeline had access to early listings, short sales, and so on. She'd latched onto the flat, which had a separate bedroom, a decent living room, and a view, for the price of a gloomy efficiency in Bexley. On cold, bright mornings with only the odd cloud in the sky, Paul sometimes had a pinch-me-I'm-dreaming sensation. Then his brain inevitably dredged up the situation with Sharada, and his feet touched earth again.

I have to fix this. Maybe if Kate and I chew it over, I'll get a brain-wave on what to do.

Kate, of course, was also an issue, though he still had hope things would eventually get back to normal. Tony had seemed very cool and grim when they spoke after the incident. Later, he'd phoned again to say Kate was better, and would be spending a quiet Tuesday at the holiday let. They weren't buying rail tickets back to Devon, thank goodness. But Kate wasn't joining Paul at the Yard, either.

What if she really did mean to pack it in?

CHAPTER 31

On a good day, it was a five-minute trip from the Pimlico tube station to Victoria Embankment. Even when crowds, mechanical issues, or inclement weather caused delays, it was still a trip Paul made on autopilot. A lifelong Londoner, he didn't have to utilize a single one of his "little gray cells," as Hercule Poirot called them, to select the likeliest carriage, wend his way through the crowd, and install himself in the most advantageous position for a rapid exit. When the carriage stopped, he was away like he was shot out of a gun. Behind him, most of his fellow riders were still gathering coats and bags.

That day, he found the Yard was a bit of a madhouse, which either boded well for public safety or badly for it, depending on your viewpoint. His team was eager to touch base. The moment Paul sat down at his desk, he texted DC Kincaid, who turned up on the double.

"Got you those details from the Crown Court at Leeds. HM Prison Wakefield," he said, unzipping the messenger bag that served as his briefcase and flicking through the papers inside. "Here we are."

Flashing a brilliant smile, Kincaid passed the report across the desk. The young detective constable, who was blond-haired, blue-eyed, and as pretty as gilt-edged Irish china, was sometimes hard to like, but Paul did his best. It was pure aggro, working with a man who made women stop in their tracks.

Then again, my single days are done. He still had to remind himself of that sometimes. Usually the thought was accompanied by relief.

"I'll have the digital file for you tomorrow. This is the quick and dirty version," Kincaid began. "Fifty years ago, Barnaby Galen and his business partner, Philip Montgomery, alias Monty Montgomery, first came on Scotland Yard's radar. While living in Manchester, they were tried and convicted of running a confidence scheme. Specifically, wooing upper-middle class types interested in purchasing vacation property.

"Galen and Monty presented themselves as representatives of an English company that was building a resort in Spain. There was no company, beyond the two of them, and there was no resort, but they told buyers a parcel of land in Madrid would soon be the home of a two-hundred suite luxury hotel called *El Santuario*. They pre-sold units to over fifty individuals or couples in Leeds. It was a sophisticated scheme. They had phony blueprints, conceptual paintings, and a big tabletop model of the nonexistent hotel. References in Spain, too, for potential buyers who wanted to do their due diligence. Those phony references included *El Santuario's* manager, the building firm, and the Mayor of Madrid himself."

"Sounds like a pretty solid con, as long as it didn't go on too long," Paul said.

"Exactly. You're meant to fly by night after a week or two," Kincaid said with a grin. "Galen and Monty got greedy. They lingered too long, and a prospective buyer with relatives in Spain smelled a rat and rang up the Yard."

"Did Galen and Monty have co-conspirators in Spain?"

"We'll never know. The moment the Yard made inquiries, the

Spanish side of the operation dried up and blew away. The so-called Mayor of Madrid turned out to be Monty himself, speaking with a put-on Spanish accent. The police tapped his phone, recorded the routine, and played it during the trial. He was sentenced to HM Prison Wakefield and did fifteen years."

"I remember that part," Paul said. "Released early for cancer treatment, right? Where did he die?"

"In Manchester," Kincaid said. "Not sure why he went back. After his release, he spent six months in his home village of Bernsley. Then he returned to Manchester, stayed there less than a week, and dropped dead. No relatives from Bernsley claimed the body. He had a public health burial—in those days, a pauper's funeral."

"I guess Galen didn't show up?"

"No. Near as I can tell, there wasn't a formal ceremony."

Paul sighed. "I have to admit, I was hoping for a girlfriend or kid. The way Galen was murdered… it's just so personal. I feel like the answer has to be in Galen's past. Monty, who he abandoned, would be perfect. But Monty kicked it decades ago."

After Kincaid, it was DC Gulls's turn to report. Although it was one o'clock in the afternoon, she was still bright-eyed and bushy-tailed, like one of those woodland creatures the lazy princesses force to do housekeeping.

"Hiya, guv. Where's DI Hetheridge?"

"I don't know. Maybe in a bubble bath. Her sabbatical isn't finished, you know."

Gulls gave a disappointed huff. Only five-foot-two, with springy curls, merry brown eyes, and an easy smile, she looked more like a kindergarten teacher than a police officer. Her speaking voice was more "Row, Row Your Boat" than "Oi, Sunshine, you're nicked!" Having been forced to accept her presence on Jackson's team, Paul had come to appreciate her work ethic and zeal for research. Moreover, as Tony said, there was a role for a police officer with a nonthreatening aura. It encouraged overconfidence in suspects, and overconfident suspects were a copper's best friend.

"I have a bit more on Barnaby Galen. Want to hear?"

"Off you go."

She opened a folder and read, "Barnaby Galen grew up in a Yorkshire village called Bernsley—"

"Know that."

"Galen's immediate family has been dead for a long time. His father—"

"Know that."

She glared at him. "Did you know he had two living sisters until the Nineties? And they died at the same time, in a car crash?"

"Did the local authorities rule it foul play?"

"No."

"Right. Know it now. Probably don't care."

"You said I should dig deep for extended family," Gulls reminded him, now sounding more saccharine than sweet. "Galen is survived by a brother-in-law, a niece, and three nephews. I gave the brother-in-law a bell. He'd never met Galen or had any contact with him. He said his late wife called him a tearaway."

"Now I know ancient slang for juvenile delinquent. Go on."

"As for education...."

"You mean to tell me the humble village of Barnsley—"

"Bernsley."

"—kept decades of records on elderly students' marks, merits, and demerits?"

"No records, but—"

"Why don't you skip to how Galen fell in with Philip Montgomery? That might be interesting."

"Most of the village hated the Montgomery family. They were considered incorrigible. The police records in Bernsley are good. Scanned into a searchable database. Monty's grandfather was hanged. His father was sent down twice and died in prison. Two of his brothers were Borstal boys, but died or ran away."

Gulls paused, seemingly thrown by her success at uttering a series of sentences without interruption. Then she continued, "Monty's first arrest came at age seventeen. B and E. The officer who wrote the report said Monty had previously been warned off the record for bad behavior, but took no mind. The second time Monty ran afoul of the law, he was twenty-one. In the end, no charges were brought, but he was questioned several times. It was a murder inquiry."

"If poor old Monty were alive, I'd be riveted," Paul said.

"Of course, since charges didn't stick, he and Galen soon relocated to Manchester—"

"Know all about the hotel scam."

"This is about Galen's bequest. The twenty thousand pounds he received upon the death of a distant relative in America."

"It's bollocks, isn't it?"

"I think so, sir. Yesterday, I took the first train to Bernsley. Had a look at the parish records. Then I knocked on doors. I think the dead relative from America's a lie, and so does every pensioner in the village who remembers Galen and Monty."

"Because it sounds too good to be true?" Paul asked.

"Because around the time Galen came into the money, a rich old woman named Seraphina Doughty disappeared and was never seen or heard from again. That's the murder inquiry I mentioned. Monty was a person of interest. Apparently, Galen was too, at first, but he was eliminated. I think Monty would've been charged if the police had found a body, or some other way to make it stick."

Paul leaned forward in his chair. There was rising excitement in Gulls's voice. Until this point, she'd kept herself in check, setting the stage for her revelation. Now she was ready to pop.

"One of Seraphina's cousins had a picture of her framed on

the wall. I scanned the image to include in my findings. Turn the page."

Paul did. The second page of Gull's report was a highly-magnified segment of a 35mm snapshot. Old prints weren't designed to be blown up or zoomed in on. This black and white image of Seraphina Doughty represented only about a fourth of the original print, which had probably featured several people. It didn't reveal hair color or eye color, and it was too blurry to define her facial features. What Paul did see, quite clearly, was Seraphina's plastic rain bonnet. It was decorated with a pattern of jaunty marching ducks.

"Right," he said. "Does this woman have any living relations?"

"Dozens of them. Over twenty in Bernsley alone," Gulls said with a smile. "I'm already tracing them. Searching for London connections."

CHAPTER 32

*K*ate didn't wake up until almost eleven. Her mobile, which she'd uncharacteristically silenced, was overloaded with texts. Tony said he was off to have breakfast, then check the preliminary reports on Galen and Granny. Paul said he was at Scotland Yard and had interesting news courtesy of Gulls, which he'd be holding hostage until she called him back. He'd added an emoticon to the message: a duck. To Kate's surprise, it gave her a little thrill of anticipation. If his team had discovered a link to the plastic rain bonnet, they might be within days of cracking the case.

Ritchie didn't text, but Maura did frequently, often on their brother's behalf. Since Kate and Tony had gone, Ritchie had soured on everything in Devon: the house, the farm, and even the snacks at his Teen and Adult Clubhouse. Henry, also a fan of texting each thought that passed through his head, wanted to know if he'd be back in his London school when the new term began. It seemed like the golden bubble of life at Briarshaw really had popped.

Two more texts awaited Kate. One was from Sharada, stating coldly that she'd expected better than to be ignored after baring her soul and begging for help. The other, from Emmeline, was a cheery invite to lunch. Paul's new wife was apparently determined to make sure the Winter Wonderland incident didn't ruin their potential friendship.

Nice gesture, Kate thought, poised to reply with a polite no-thank you. Then she looked around the holiday let, which seemed boring and impersonal without Tony or any of her family there, and decided it was time to hold her feet to the fire. Venture into London alone for the first time since the rooftop incident? Look Emmeline in the eye and say sorry for shutting down during a tricky moment?

I'm game, Kate told herself, and hurried into the shower.

CHAPTER 33

The Happy Hen was one of those all-organic, locally-sourced restaurants that cost an arm and a leg, but always deliver on taste and quality. Kate's only quibble with the menu was, she couldn't get a fizzy diet drink in any brand she'd ever heard of. Emmeline, who'd been told to keep hydrated during her pregnancy, ordered water with lemon, so Kate did the same. As for the meal, they both chose brunch: Belgian waffles, warm blueberry compote, and an egg, sunny side up.

"I'm so glad you made it," Emmeline said. "I hate eating by myself."

"I had to come." Kate poured syrup over her waffle's golden-brown pockets. "I'm so sorry I—"

"Shut it," Emmeline cut across her, sounding more like her old self. She'd been a queen bee in school and at Uni, and it still showed. "I should've dashed for a guard. Let the professionals handle it. I didn't think, I just acted. Probably the sort of thing I'll be punishing my kid for in four or five years." She attacked her egg, closing her eyes as she chewed. "That's the ticket. I love this place. You never see yolks this yellow anywhere else."

"All-organic places are spreading," Kate said. "I was so hungry this morning, I snagged a banana on the way. At an organic kiosk by Baker Street Station."

Emmeline put down her fork. "Did you take the tube alone?"

"I did," Kate said proudly.

"How was it?"

She moved her hand back and forth to indicate, so-so. "I was nervous. Couldn't find my Oyster card and had to buy a new one from the machine. Felt like an alien on the platform. And of course there was a bloody weirdo in the carriage, looking at me. I pretended to read on my phone the whole time."

"I think that's grand," Emmeline said. "After what happened, Paul had trouble with crowds for a while. I think what helped him get over it is he's such an incorrigible daydreamer. He spends more time thinking about Marvel movies and streaming rubbish than anyone I've ever met. It's hard to maintain crippling vigilance when you can't stop fantasizing about lifting Thor's hammer."

"Now that sounds a bit naughty," a woman at the next table remarked.

Kate burst out laughing. So did Emmeline. From that point, they were off to the races, talking about everything and nothing. They'd moved on to plans for Christmas when Emmeline, who was facing the front window, said, "Don't turn around, but a homeless woman's been out there ever since we arrived. Dressed in nothing but crochet rags. Poor old sod. Most of the year, I only worry about myself. At Christmas time, I start thinking about other people a little more. It's probably the stupid carols," she added, gesturing to encompass the Happy Hen's sound system, which was currently blaring "Rudolph the Red-Nosed Reindeer."

"I know," Kate said. "Tony and I are blessed. We probably ought to do more. We met a nice family who could use a hand up. There's endless possibilities. But I suppose I'd have to pull my own head out of my arse first." Deliberately dropping an unneeded piece of cutlery, Kate turned in her chair to retrieve it so she could see the poor soul Emmeline had mentioned.

The woman, it seemed, was too cold or desperate to feign indifference to the scores of people eating inside. Like a child staring at toys behind a plate glass window, she peered directly into the Happy Hen. Her hands were covered in fingerless crochet gloves. Her crocheted tam sat crooked on her head. Beneath it sprouted masses of long, improbably thick white hair.

"Hang on." Kate pushed back her chair with a loud scrape.

"Are you going out there?" Emmeline, startled, reached for her bag. "If you're going to give her money, let me add some. I never carry cash, but I might have—"

"Hold that thought." Without even pausing to collect her handbag, Kate strode rapidly toward the front of the restaurant. The woman with long white hair spun away from the window. She was darting toward a clothing shop when Kate caught her arm in a steely grip. It was almost like old times.

"Nice wig," she said, staring down into a pair of dark, familiar eyes. "Come with me."

CHAPTER 34

"I don't like spying. I don't like tailing people, as they say on telly," Sharada Bhar said obstinately. Without the fake hair and charity shop togs, she looked considerably less ridiculous. She was still wearing the crocheted fingerless gloves, however, of which she'd apparently grown fond. Having procured an extra chair, the Happy Hen's wait staff had added her to Kate and Emmeline's small table. Now sitting with a cup of tea and a croissant before her, she addressed only Kate, as if her new daughter-in-law wasn't positioned directly in her line of sight.

"But what else could I do?" she wailed. "Deepal shut me out. If I hadn't followed him, I wouldn't have heard him talking on his mobile to you about returning to London. I wouldn't even know he lives in Denbigh Street. Although what he's doing there," she added coldly, turning her face away from Emmeline, "I have no idea."

"Sharada," Kate said reasonably. "You knew Paul was dating Em. You met her, for heaven's sake. And anyone with eyes can see how things have progressed."

"I'm sorry things went off the rails," Emmeline began, once

more abandoning her youthful queen bee manner for a gentler, olive branch approach. "I never meant for this to happen. On our anniversary, perhaps we can renew our vows so you can attend. And when your grandchild comes…."

Sharada silenced her with an imperiously raised hand. "How dare you speak to me? And why should I believe that's *my* grandchild? When you're the slut who's done half of London?"

"All right, that's it." Kate's bray was loud enough to temporarily silence the Happy Hen's dining room. For a moment, Sharada only gazed at her in shock. Then her large black eyes filled with tears.

"And none of that," Kate snapped. "Look, Sharada, I like you. I like Emmeline. I don't want to take sides. But Paul's my best mate, and if he won't put his foot down, I will. Stop this. All of it.

"Your son is not a child. He's a grown man, married, with a kid on the way. Emmeline is not a slut, she's your daughter-in-law. And your best friend in the world right now, if you weren't too much of a thickie to see it."

Sharada blinked away the tears as rapidly as she'd summoned them. She was listening. So were the tables in Kate's immediate vicinity, but that couldn't be helped.

"Sharada. You're fighting a battle you've already lost," Kate said, looking hard into the other woman's eyes. "You tried to keep Paul a little boy forever. You've insulted and blamed every woman he ever brought near you. Now he's broken away and he's practically in hiding because you've driven him to it. He doesn't want to disappoint you. Or make you unhappy. But he loves Em, and they're having a baby. If you can't support him and make friends with his wife, you leave him no choice but to cut you off."

For a long time, none of them spoke. Gradually, the clatter of plates and cutlery rose, and the chatter resumed, until the Happy Hen's dining room went back to normal. As she awaited Sharada's response, Kate had to clench her fists under the table to keep from launching into the same speech all over again. Sometimes, after you've made your case, you have to let it stand or fall in silence.

It was Emmeline who broke the impasse. "Kate's right about one thing. I could be your best friend. Paul's not happy about dodging you. I think the whole situation's ridiculous. And you know how he gets out of hand sometimes. Think of the fun we could have, teaming up against him."

Sharada took a deep breath. "I want to start over. If it's all right with you," she added, smiling weakly at Emmeline. "Let's begin again."

CHAPTER 35

"You're sure you won't have a glass?" Tony asked. The cabernet had breathed long enough and was ready to pour.

"It smells funny," Kate said. "Just like the Riesling. Whoever stocked this place did a good job on the food, but thumbs down on the wine."

"More for me."

Carrying the wine glass into the living room, he sat down with her on the white Chesterfield sofa. It was something of an after-dinner tradition with them, sitting in the dark by the fire. From the foyer, the Christmas tree twinkled. Over Cantonese takeaway—dim sum, spicy prawns, and rice—they'd gone over the Galen case to date, including the photo Gulls had discovered in Bernsley. It seemed possible that someone held Galen responsible for Seraphina Doughty's death, and had exacted a bizarre and terrifying revenge. Though why anyone would wait half a century to settle the score was yet another unanswered question.

"I'm proud of you for going it alone on the tube," he said.

Kate made a rude noise.

"Did that sound condescending?" He sipped the red wine, which tasted and smelled perfectly fine, no matter what his wife said. "I suppose you'll object if I compliment you for brokering peace between Paul and Sharada?"

"Nope. Pour it on," Kate said. "I really gave her a piece of my mind. If she hadn't been desperate to get him back, I doubt she would've stood for it."

"Think you and Emmeline might become friends?"

She shrugged. "She's fun to talk to. I never knew anyone in the estate game. It's a bit like police work, with access to hidden knowledge."

Tony chuckled. "That may be overstating it."

"You scoff," Kate said. "But when Paul told her about Strange Mews, she looked it up straightaway. Told him it wasn't a holiday let at all. It came on the market on 30 November and a man called Anthony Hetheridge bought it on the same day."

He had another sip of wine. There was no point fumbling for a quick response. Whenever Kate caught him dead to rights, she always gave him plenty of time to compose his rebuttal.

"The thing is," he said at last, "speed was of the essence. And when it came to security features, there was nothing that hadn't been booked ages ago. Except this place, which I had to purchase if I wanted us to spend the week here."

Removing the stem from his hand, Kate placed it on the coffee table and climbed into his lap. Arms encircling his neck, she gazed down at him. "She told me how much you paid. An awful waste of money."

"We'll unload the property later."

"Probably at a loss."

"I don't care. I had to get you here. And look. It's day five, and you rode the tube alone," Tony said. "Vindicated, if you ask me."

Kate, still in his lap, wiggled her bottom against him in what would have been a very unfair tactic, had they actually been quarreling. She kissed him, still moving until she produced from him the inevitable concession.

"Upstairs?" she asked.

"We own this sofa and the other furnishings, too."

"Well, in that case," Kate said, and carried on.

CHAPTER 36

"Stop singing," Kate said.

"I can't." Paul had been singing Christmas carols for almost twelve hours straight, apart from sleeping or feeding his face. Funny old life. One minute you were pondering the blurry image of a woman who'd been murdered long before you were a gleam in your old dad's eye. The next, your wife and mum had solved their animosities without any effort from you, and existence was pure joy.

"At least learn the lyrics," Kate continued. "I'm sure 'Good King Wenceslas' has more than just the one line."

She was right, of course, but he didn't know it. The same snippet of tune cycled through his head: "Good King Wenceslas looked out... on the Feast of Stephen...." Sometimes he sung it and sometimes he hummed it, undeterred by the demands of his extensive caseload, including the murder of Barnaby Galen. And why shouldn't he be happy, when Kate had administered yet another wonderful shock to his system by coming to work that morning? She'd even asked HR to update her security badge and warrant card. Her sabbatical was officially over.

Over breakfast, they'd put their heads together, preparing for the complex interview that they might have conducted at the crime scene, had the CSI caravan not chased them away. Cy Smythe, Selma Harwood, Adrian Poe, Leona Bell-Brown, and Jacinda Cox had each agreed to meet as a group to discuss the case. Only Leona had tried to decline, but when Paul told her that meant they'd turn up at Fantastic Flights, the SoHo special effects factory where she was an executive, she'd reluctantly agreed. Adrian Poe, the youngest member of the Holywell mafia, had offered to host the gathering. Jacinda Cox, somewhat bizarrely, had sounded pleased to be included, and said she'd bake a cake.

"I'm home alone at Christmas. Like that American kiddie." Greeting them at the front door, Adrian pretended to slap his cheeks like the film's Macaulay Culkin character. "No parents, no hassles, am I right?"

Paul forced himself to nod pleasantly, though he suspected Adrian still had the use of his parents' full staff, even if Mummy and Daddy had decided to winter someplace warmer. The Poe house was certainly decked out for the holidays, although Holywell Street's only eyesore, the Galen house, spoiled the effect somewhat. The other neighboring homes were carefully maintained, with tall iron gates, brick walls, and large front gardens. On the way to Poe's, Paul had spied many styles, including Neoclassical, New Build, and Victorian. Most displayed Christmas greenery and red velvet ribbons, but Galen's house was tied up in blue and white crime tape. It was the sort of present only a detective could love.

"Be honest," Adrian said, leading Paul and Kate through the foyer. He took them through the living room, veering toward the resplendent solarium just behind it. "Am I a suspect? I've been telling girls I'm under suspicion of murder by Scotland Yard."

"You're a material witness," Kate replied, saving Paul the bother of playing along with Adrian for the second time in two minutes. "If you answer our questions fully and truthfully, the MPS will be grateful."

That was a good answer. Paul couldn't speak for Kate, of course, but during the background gathering phase of the investigation, Paul had forgotten Adrian's existence. The only thing remotely interesting about him was his appearance: a nose ring, an eyebrow ring, several earrings, and bright blue hair. His birth date fixed his age at twenty-seven, but he looked seventeen.

"All right, ducks," he called to the people gathered in the solarium. "The rozzers have come at last. It's all a bit Agatha Christie, isn't it? Anyone need more coffee? Another helping of pudding?"

Jacinda Cox beamed from her place on the piano bench. Paul remembered her as the friendliest-looking of the kitchen lot. Heavyset and florid-faced; fifty-two according to her date of birth. Frizzy blonde hair floated around her head, thin at the scalp. Had she been entertaining the group with a song? Sheet music was out, and the keys' cover was up.

"I'm so pleased you enjoyed the torte."

"I didn't," the old woman in an armchair said. She had one of those low-pitched, gravelly voices that immediately reminded Paul of Agnes Brown, the drag persona of comedian Brendan O'Carroll, in the television program, *Mrs. Brown's Boys*. Dressed in what could only be called a muumuu, she wore a light, unobtrusive oxygen mask. Its generator was in a bag on her shoulder.

"You didn't?" Cy asked, looking around the room with a look that suggested everyone play along with the invalid. "We never would've guessed. You only said so twice before."

"I didn't." Selma Harwood sounded confused. A Zimmer frame was parked beside her. The carry-all suspended from it bulged with pill bottles, wet wipes, boxes of tissues, and infirmity's other essential items.

"Pain medicine makes you speak your mind," Cy told the room, still with that phony brightness. Paul knew it could be necessary, even unavoidable when dealing with certain sick people, but it was still distasteful. Especially since Cy delivered these reassurances, which weren't aimed at Selma, with his big, white, ersatz grin.

"If you're going to ask questions, ask them," said Leona Brown-Bell, looking very smart in tailored black trousers and a yellow silk blouse. Paul, who had an eye for ladies' fashion as well as men's, knew a couture ensemble when he saw it. Leona was fifty-one, but looked no more than thirty. Her makeup was expertly applied, and she'd probably had help from a surgeon.

"Some of us have work to do," Leona added.

Adrian reacted as if shot through the heart. "I'm an artist, darling. I work when the muse permits."

"I'm working right now," Cy said.

"Yes, we know, love," Leona said, thawing a bit. "I didn't mean you. You're lovely."

"Ought to give him the keys to the street," Selma muttered. She stared straight ahead at nothing, but her ears seemed to work quite well.

"She's cross with me," Cy told Paul and Kate. "I try to be Prince Charming, but sometimes reminding her about vitamins and protein shakes makes me come over like an ogre, I guess. And it's a bad day. Extra pain meds."

"Stole my money," Selma said, still looking at nothing. Her eyelids were heavy now.

"Spent your money," Cy agreed grandly. "Spent it on you, on all the things you need. If your son and daughter could be bothered to visit, perhaps they'd do things more to your liking. But I don't know. Seems like I'm your best bet, sweetheart."

"I know you're frustrated, Mrs. Harwood," Jacinda said, addressing the old lady in a very loud voice. "I advocate for the less fortunate. The homeless and food-insecure. It's a demanding job," she added, giving Leona a sidelong look, "every bit as important as the latest cinema fluff about superheroes and wars in space. If everyone were as selfless as Cy, instead of selfish, like Galen, I could retire in good conscience."

"You live in Knightsbridge just like the rest of us," Leona snapped.

"How do you know where I live?"

"The old bugger shouted it at you," Leona replied, casually self-assured. "He told you to go back to Cheval Place."

Jacinda sat up straighter on the polished black bench. "How do you know that?"

"I lived next door to the rotter for years," Leona said. "The older he got, the louder he talked. I thought I'd misheard him when he said Cheval Place. But there you are, in the directory. Maybe you ought to bring some of the homeless and food-insecure into your place. Charity begins at home."

Jacinda's red face turned redder. "It's none of your business where I live, or how."

Paul swapped glances with Kate. He couldn't remember the last time they'd had a group interrogate one another. And so far, he found the dynamics interesting.

"You know what else I heard him say?" Leona let that hang in the air for a beat as she examined her manicure. "He said he wasn't paying another penny, and you could take your story to *Bright Star* for all he cared."

Bright Star was a notorious print and online tabloid that few people praised and everyone, or so it seemed, religiously consulted. To Paul's left, Kate visibly perked up. Jacinda, on the other hand, set her jaw and looked angry enough to charge at Leona.

"He was a mad old bellend with delusions. He was cruel to his tenants and his P.A., Ollie. Half of what he said was nonsense. He verbally abused me so often, I had to take him to court. And I won," Jacinda added triumphantly.

"Yet you came back around his house last week," Leona said with false sweetness. "I wonder what you were holding over the old man's head."

"Yes," Adrian muttered softly. Paul, glancing at the young man whose existence he'd once again forgotten, realized he was filming the exchange with his mobile.

"Turn that off," he ordered.

Adrian looked hurt. "Somebody's going to confess to murder. Or murder for hire, more likely."

"Give me that phone," Kate said, holding out her hand until Adrian reluctantly passed it over. "You can have it back when this is sorted. Why did you say murder for hire is more likely?"

"Because that skeleton-thingy came up from under the bed," Adrian retorted, as if speaking to an idiot. "It was installed. A whole system. I can't even get an IKEA bookshelf assembled on a bet. Something with moving parts? Impossible.

"Besides," Adrian continued. "I hope nobody take offense, but look around. Old man Galen was a bitter pill. He dumped piss-pots in our garden once a week. He chased dog-walkers. He used to taunt Selma about her oxygen tank and say when you can't even breathe, take a hint and drop dead. He told one of Leona's man-friends that she had syphilis…."

"Ebola, actually, but the intent was the same," Leona broke in. "And that was my ex-husband, back for some of what he missed. Not a friend, but definitely a man."

"My mistake." Adrian grinned. "All I'm saying is, Leona, I adore you, but you'd never do anything that might break a nail. Jacinda over there is old, and Selma's even older. A basket case. Cy's kind of handy, true, but he's busy with Selma night and day."

"I'm fifty-two," Jacinda cried.

"And I'm sweet sixteen," Selma said. The pain meds must have been working their magic, because both eyes were closed now.

"I am handy," Cy agreed, flashing another smile at Paul and Kate. "But nothing compared to Nathan Vine-Jones. Don't misunderstand me. I wouldn't want anyone to even look his way. He's a good boy."

"True. I like him," Adrian said.

"Ollie and his entire family are above reproach," Jacinda said primly, looking as if the remark about her age still stung.

"A good boy," Selma muttered. Her chin was against her chest, and she was drooling slightly.

"The kid strikes me as above board," Leona agreed. "But why'd daddy happen to turn up around the time Galen was killed? And why'd he flee the scene with his boy's red toolkit in his hand?"

CHAPTER 37

*A*fter Leona's questions, everyone began talking at once. By the time Kate and Paul reasserted control, Selma was snoring gently and Adrian was picking at the remainder of the torte. Leaving Cy to turn his charm onto Jacinda, whom he assumed was a very youthful fifty-two, Kate insisted Leona recount her impression of Friday afternoon from the top.

"I came home a little early," Leona said. "Quarter after three, maybe. I had no idea anything was wrong at Galen's place. I hadn't seen Ollie let himself in, either. I only saw him go out because I was on the porch, sorting my post. Galen's front door banged open and there was Ollie, marching out fast like his hair was on fire, with Nathan's red toolkit in his hand. Next thing I knew, Cy was leading everyone inside the old dump like it was an open house. I went over to see what was happening, and I forgot about the toolkit. Until now."

"It's our understanding Nathan's toolkit had gone missing. That he'd searched the neighborhood a couple of times in person," Kate said. "This was the Saturday and Sunday right after Galen died. Why didn't you tell him his father had it?"

"Because he never asked. I was in the office all week. As I told you, I work," Leona replied. She wasn't a likeable witness, but her answers were clear and unstudied. If she was a liar, she was brilliant.

"You're the only person in Galen's life, at least that we know of, with a connection to show business," Paul said. "What's your impression of Granny? The skeleton contraption, I mean."

Leona laughed. "You poor dear thing. That's not show business. At most, it's an old school horror prop."

"Could you rig something like that up?" Kate asked.

Leona held up her hands and wiggled her fingers. "The boy was right. I'd never risk my manicure," Leona said. "I think anyone with modest mechanical aptitude and determination could've rigged that up. There are specs online and moving prop tutorials on YouTube. Someone with determination, patience, and reasonable skill could do it. If not the kid, maybe his dad."

"Are we finished?" Adrian asked. The torte had been reduced to chocolate streaks on a plate, and he sounded like a cranky teenager. "I have a date, you know."

"I'd like to get Selma to bed," Cy said. "Poor dear. She didn't mean to sleep through the interview. But when her pain is bad, she has to take the maximum dose. And it probably goes without saying, but she could never have killed Galen. Just wanted to state it for the record."

"Of course not," Jacinda said. "We're all just helping the police. I think the killer was probably a psychopath. One of those sick people who commits crimes for no reason."

"My thoughts exactly," Cy said, and made a sort of corny flourish, like a medieval knight saluting a lady.

Kate found the gesture borderline creepy, but Jacinda giggled. "As it happens, I do live in Cheval Place. You can walk there in five minutes," she told Cy. "If you'd like to stop by this evening, I'd love to continue our discussion about caregiving. I'll pop a roast in the oven and open a bottle of Merlot."

"It's been a long time since I've had what you might call a sensible conversation," Cy said, lowering his voice, although Selma was plainly asleep. "Will it be just the two of us? No boyfriend or roommate?"

"Just us. And my sweet Pooh. He's a Giant Schnauzer," Jacinda said. When Cy looked slightly alarmed, she added, "He's not vicious. He's a sweet heart. Anyone's for a strip of bacon, I promise."

"Not really a dog lover," Cy admitted.

"I'll keep him under wraps," Jacinda said. "Would you like some help getting your patient to bed?"

With Kate and Paul's permission, Cy and Jacinda left the Poe house together. Cy pushed the sleeping Selma in her wheelchair, and Jacinda carried the folded Zimmer frame. To Kate, it seemed that Jacinda was willfully pretending Cy was Selma's health care worker instead of her longtime, live-in boyfriend. If Selma wasn't long for this world, it was possible her replacement had already been found.

"I feel dirty having witnessed that," Paul muttered to her. "Before we continue, I think we should fact check a couple of things. Jacinda's financial profile, for one thing, and whether anyone's contacts at *Bright Star* know of a Galen story being shopped around the tabloids. Since Galen wasn't a public figure, it might be that what seemed like a story worthy of blackmailing him or his associates still wouldn't be juicy enough for the tabloids."

"What if it was murder?" Kate countered. "What if Jacinda knows something about Seraphina Doughty? Is Cox her married name, or her maiden name? She sounded Northern to me. Could she be from Bernsley?"

"Let's find out," Paul said. "But someone needs to confront Ollie. If Leona's telling the truth, he lied to us about why he fled the scene. And the toolkit."

Kate checked her phone. It was already past five o'clock, and dark. Most of Paul's team would be on the way home.

"Tony said he was going to spend today at Wellegrave House, trying to determine how much longer it's going to be," Kate said. "Let me give him a ring."

CHAPTER 38

"Oh. Lord Hetheridge. Good evening," Ollie said. The porchlight accentuated his pallor. He looked about as happy to see Tony on his doorstep as a politician would be to see reporters from CNN encamped on his front lawn.

"He's come to get you, Daddy," said Riteish, clinging to Ollie's waist and peeking around at Tony. "The bad man's come for you."

"I'm sorry to turn up unannounced," Tony said, "but it's a police matter. May I come in?"

"I think it would be better if I came out. Riteish, let go," Ollie said, prying the little boy's fingers off his trouser leg. "Stay inside."

"Can't expect privacy out on the street," Tony said mildly. He nodded toward a porch two doors down, where a couple were drinking bottled cider and watching with undisguised interest. Met ID in hand, he moved the card so Ollie could glimpse a flash of it, but Verbena Street's spectators could not. "I'm here as a Scotland Yard consultant."

Ollie folded his arms over his chest. "I understand. What do you want?"

"Today my colleagues interviewed one of Barnaby Galen's

neighbors. Leona Brown-Bell, who lives at 19 Holywell, just east of Galen's house. Have you met her?"

"Maybe in passing." If Ollie's clipped speech was meant to sound intimidating, it wasn't working. If anything, he sounded scared witless.

"She's a respectable person. Nothing in her public life or interview answers to give us any reason to disbelieve her. Did you realize she came home early from the office last Friday?"

"I said I don't really know her."

"She wasn't there when you arrived, but she must have driven up soon after. She was on the porch, sorting her post, when you exited Galen's house in a hurry. Mr. Smythe noticed you, too, as you'll remember. But Ms. Brown-Bell may have been nearer, because she mentioned you carrying something out of the house. A red toolkit."

Ollie said nothing. Despite the porchlight, his pupils were dilating.

"When you recounted the process of visiting 17 Holywell, knocking on the door, and ultimately using your key to enter the premises, you never mentioned the toolkit. After you discovered Mr. Galen dead, you told us you rang 999, tried in vain to call your wife, then called home and realized your youngest children were in danger of burning down the house. You *did* have the red toolkit in hand, didn't you?"

Ollie still didn't answer.

"My question is simple. Did you bring the kit with you, and take it away again? Or did you find the kit abandoned in the house and conceal the evidence? Because I couldn't help but notice," Tony continued, mercilessly turning the screw, "Mr. Smythe asked about the red toolkit when he dropped by on Monday. He said it belonged to Nathan, and Nathan was looking for it. If I were to enter your house and search for the toolkit, and I believe I have probable cause to do just that, would I discover the tools Nathan used to install Granny?"

"He didn't do it," Ollie burst out. "At worst, he helped, but even if he did, I'll bet Cy's pulling the strings. He must have manipulated Nathan. Tricked him into doing it!"

Tony rarely felt much pity for the suspects he grilled during an investigation's final stages, but he felt acutely sorry for Ollie, who looked on point of making a false confession to shield his son. If their places were reversed, would he be tempted to do the same for Henry?

"The truth is," Ollie said, taking a deep breath and visibly steeling himself like the terrible liar he was, "I used Nathan's tools. I put that skeleton under Galen's bed. He was an awful person and no one will miss him."

"Enough," Tony said sternly. "Stop talking before you force me to bang you up for obstructing an investigation. Is Nathan home?"

Ollie nodded. He seemed to be holding back tears by main force.

"Right. Let's go inside."

Once in the Vine-Jones home, Ollie regained a semblance of fatherly authority. Priya had taken the baby on a visit to her mother, leaving four children at home. Ordering the twins, Reena and Riteish, upstairs with Amara, who was apparently still poorly, Ollie called Nathan into the kitchen. Father and son sat down with Tony at the small kitchen table.

Nathan looked sullen. He did not, however, seem afraid. Rather than focus on Tony, the CID man who'd returned to make accusations, Nathan fixed on his dad.

"What is it? Why do you look like you're about to vomit?"

"Nathan. You know your mother and I don't care for Cy Smythe. His interest in you struck us as, er, unwholesome. If he's been at you, son, and pushed you into doing something you're ashamed of, now's the time to come clean. I won't judge, I swear it."

The boy frowned. He turned to Tony. "Is Cy a paedo or something?"

"You tell me," Tony replied.

Nathan shrugged. "I don't know. He never struck me as meaning any harm. Not like that. He did—well, he did start popping over to Mr. Galen's when the old man was away. Cy does power walks twice a day. For his gimpy leg. It's a kind of rehab to keep his joints from freezing up. Anyway, he lost the key to Selma's garden shed, so he asked me to help him break in. That's how it started. Mr. Galen didn't pay much for the work I did at his house, but Cy would always slip me a few pounds. I made loads more helping him out with odd jobs than I ever made with the old man."

Ollie seemed surprised. "You've been holding out on the family? I know Priya let you keep most of it for pocket money, but we expected you to show us everything you earned."

Nathan looked at the kitchen table top.

"So no funny stuff from Cy," Tony said. "You'd swear to that in court?"

"Yeah," Nathan said.

"Did he ask you to help him break into someplace besides Selma's garden shed? A locked classroom, perhaps, or a mausoleum?"

"You mean to get the bones to make the skeleton-thing that scared old man Galen to death? No," Nathan said. "That would probably be against the law."

"I never told any of you kids about the thing under the bed. How did you hear about it?" Ollie asked.

"Cy told me all about it. Just talking about it made him laugh until his chest hurt. Same with Selma. She got all choked up. Almost had to go back to the hospital for an emergency breathing treatment."

"When was this?"

Nathan looked stricken, as if realizing a mistake. "Um, Saturday. And Sunday."

"You weren't supposed to be over there. Your mum had forbidden it."

"I know. But I lost my toolkit, didn't I? I was sure I left it at Cy's, but he insisted it was never there. Sunday morning, I reckoned up how much money I'd need to buy replacement tools, and it was impossible. So I went back on Sunday and checked again. Either Cy nicked it from me, or someone else did."

"Cy likes to work with his hands?" Tony asked.

"Sure. Once he had a job assembling bicycles for a department store. Another time, he built sets for a cinema company called Hammer. He even hired himself out putting together furniture floor models before he met Se—"

"Hang on," Tony said. "Did you say, Hammer? As in Hammer horror movies, in the Sixties and Seventies?"

Nathan nodded. "I asked him if he met any stars. He told me they didn't even let blokes like him meet the writers."

Tony thought about that. Then he said, "You mentioned Cy has—what did you call it? A gimpy leg? Do you mean he has arthritis?"

Nathan gave him the blank, disinterested look of the young and healthy, who can't imagine a day when they might not be either. "He had cancer, years ago. The bad kind. The doctors cut out some tissue from his left thigh, or groin, or whatever. He survived the cancer, but his leg looks like he was sharkbit."

"When you say the bad kind, what do you mean?"

Nathan giggled uncomfortably. "In the goolies. Testicular. They cut one off."

Tony sat up straighter. "I see."

"How do you know all this?" Ollie sounded deeply alarmed. "Do you swear there was no funny stuff?"

"Cy never talked to me about his leg," Nathan said. "Selma did.

231

Cy says her meds make her gobby. Once the benzos start talking, she tells all."

Tony said, "Thank you for answering my questions. You've been very helpful. Now would you mind joining your brother and sisters upstairs? I'd like a word with Ollie."

When the boy could be heard ascending the stairs, Tony said, "That was reassuring. Tell me the truth now. You owe me that. I sent him away so he'll never know you misjudged him."

"I did misjudge him," Ollie said. Tears spilled from his eyes. He dashed them away with a trembling hand.

"Everything about my story is true, up to the point when I tried to ring Priya and couldn't get her. I didn't think I could leave the crime scene, and while I didn't want the kids home alone, I figured Priya would be back at any minute. I was downstairs, looking for a place that wasn't too filthy to sit and wait for the police, when I saw it tucked in a corner. Nathan's missing red toolkit. It was near the fireplace, not really obvious, but not hidden, either. As if he'd accidentally left it behind. I panicked. I rushed home and hid it in our community storage room. It's buried so deep, it might take days for me to dig it out. Then I made up a story about the twins trying to cook, and almost burning down our kitchen. Which actually happened over the summer."

"You really believed your son rigged up that contraption to murder Galen?"

Ollie sighed. "He's more like Priya than me. Spirited. A good boy, really, but when he's angry, he has to blow off steam. He heard me telling his mother about my latest firing. How Galen ordered me to live apart from my family for his convenience, and for no other reason than to prove who had the power. Nathan was furious. He was even angrier when I explained that we were losing the house. Moving might put us in a different catchment area, as far as the kids' schools. Nathan was already disappointed about not being able to attend a top-notch academy. He threw a full-blown tantrum."

"It happens," Tony said. "My son once threatened to run away and live with people who enjoy his company."

That earned a weak smile. "Fatherhood. Never a dull moment, eh? Anyway, when you live with someone like Nathan, who has the emotions of a child but a mechanical ability that far exceeds most adults, well… it's a bit intimidating. Maybe I was always a little worried that no good would come of his talent. It's not that I absolutely believed he created that skeleton device. But did I think it was possible? Yes."

"For what it's worth, so did I," Tony said. "Now. Chin up. I think I hear him coming downstairs again."

"Dad! Mr.—um, policeman," Nathan said lamely, shooting Tony an apologetic grin. A wrapped gift was in his hand. The paper was printed with Santas; the handtied ribbon was red. "Can I show you something?"

"It's not Christmas yet," Ollie said mildly.

"No. But this is your prezzie, Dad."

"I'll wait until Christmas like everyone else, thank you."

"No. Open it now. You'll see why."

Ollie caved in. Casting a quick glance at Tony, he untied the ribbon and tore the paper. This revealed a tissue box stuffed with shredded news print and wads of old plastic bags. Beneath all the padding was over a hundred pounds in coins and small bills.

"That's the extra money I pocketed from Cy," Nathan said. "All of it. For you, Dad. I mean, for the family."

Ollie, who'd held himself in check until then, burst into tears. Tony, satisfied by the interviews, decided the only decent response would be to show himself out, so that's what he did.

CHAPTER 39

"Good evening."

"Hallo, Trevor," Tony said. He was returning the M.E.'s call from the back of a cab bound for Strange Mews. "What's up?"

"It's ready." That chirpy excitement he'd displayed in the forensic pathology lab was back again; the boy magician was about to reveal a new trick. "A digital reconstruction of 976's face."

"Go on," Tony said, biting back excitement.

"The image quality generated by this software is incredible. Comparable to the work done in clay by artists," Trevor said. "There's still an extensive human component. My med students double checked the renderings and made small corrections whenever human judgment was necessary. The only true impediment was the missing mandible. Because we had to extrapolate in that area, I'd say the face is only about eighty percent likely to be accurate."

"I'll take those odds," Tony said. "Did you already transmit the file to me?"

Trevor chuckled gently. It was a sound Tony had heard before. Young professionals loved nothing so much as when an old dog made a technical gaffe.

"No. The file is huge and your computer wouldn't have the programs necessary to open it. But I can transmit a JPEG of the finished reconstruction product to your mobile right away."

"Then bloody well do it," Tony retorted with savage good humor.

"Done." Trevor rang off, still laughing.

BT's mobile network was having a good night. Within seconds, Tony's phone emitted the *swoosh* that meant an incoming image. He opened the file, looked at it for five seconds, then sent it to Kate and Paul. Next, he rang Kate.

"I just came from the Vine-Jones house," he said without preamble when she connected. "Nathan's in the clear. So is Ollie."

"We just finished with the Holywell Street mafia. Formerly known as the kitchen lot," Kate replied. "Adrian and Leona seem clean. Selma's probably in the clear, too, if only because she's in fragile health. Still looking into Jacinda, and Cy seems worse all the time. Like a career criminal who specializes in wooing sick old ladies. You know, bleeding them dry. Kicking them into the grave ahead of schedule, maybe, before moving on to the next one."

"That certainly fits," Tony said. "I have reason to believe Cy Smythe is actually Barnaby Galen's old partner, Monty Montgomery. Probably the poor sod in Manchester who was buried under Monty's name was the real Cy."

"What?" Kate's doubtful tone gave rise to a barrage of questions. "But how can Cy be Monty? Why would Galen tolerate Monty living under an assumed name, right there on his street? And what about access to 17 Holywell? How did Monty go in and out without being noticed?"

"Galen gave Nathan a key," Tony reminded her. "When Monty

saw the boy using it, he embarked on a special effort to befriend him. At some point, he must have lifted the key and made a copy. Once Monty realized Nathan had the mechanical aptitude to build almost anything, he must have decided he was the perfect fall guy. Before he killed Galen, he nicked the boy's red toolkit. He planted it in the Galen house for the police to find."

"Right. Except Ollie turned up and found it first," Kate said. "That's why he fled the scene, to get rid of the evidence. Well done you!" She stopped. "Hang on. I still don't understand—Monty went to prison and Galen got off a long time ago. Why did Monty wait so many years to get revenge? And it seems like Galen treated Monty exactly the way he treated the rest of his neighbors. Nothing personal, just general misanthropy."

Tony considered that. Then he said, "Do you suppose it was an accident that Monty chose Selma? That he came to Holywell Street for her, and just happened to find his ex-partner living there?"

"I guess it's possible," Kate said. "Talk about an uncomfortable reunion."

"Yes. Unless it wasn't uncomfortable at all. Because Galen was rich and powerful and forgot all about old Monty," Tony said. "Monty must've spent years imagining how it would kick off if he ever crossed paths with Galen. Yet when it happened, Galen didn't recognize his face or voice. Confidence men tend to have a high opinion of themselves. They consider themselves magnetic and unforgettable. I think Monty would have found being forgotten insupportable."

"You're raining on my parade," Kate said. "I was about to bet it all on Jacinda Cox. I thought maybe Galen had done her mum or grand-mum wrong. That she knew the story of a dead woman and a plastic rain bonnet, and was using it to blackmail Galen. She's like Priya Vine-Jones—spent her whole life working for non-profits and living modestly. Then, boom—three years ago she moved to Cheval Place in Knightsbridge and started living like a queen. Leona overheard Galen tell Jacinda he wouldn't give her another penny. I thought she decided to kill him when he wouldn't pay, and hired Cy—I mean, Monty—to rig up Granny."

"I think most of that's correct, actually," Tony said. "I'll fill you in on the rest in a moment. First, disconnect and have a look at the picture I sent you. Then call back in conference mode with Paul and I'll finish my theory. Blackmailers tend to become very attached to their nontaxable income. After Galen died, Jacinda might have decided to shift targets. And that could be the death of her yet."

"All right. Give me a sec to download the file and I'll ring you right back," Kate said.

Mind spinning from the possibilities, as well as a strong current of pride, Tony put the phone on his lap. Only then did he realize the cab was already parked in front of Strange Mews, and the cabbie was watching him from the rear-view mirror.

"You are the most interesting fare I've ever had in my life," the driver said, turning to look on Tony directly.

"Yes. Er. Well. Very urgent business sometimes must be conducted in the most unexpected of places," he murmured. "I'm afraid I must ask you to forget this conversation, and never repeat it to anyone."

The driver raised his eyebrows. "Is that right? Sure, guv. Done."

Tony suppressed a groan. At least Paul wasn't here to witness this cockup, or he knew it would be decades before he ever heard the end of it. "What's the fare?"

The driver punched a button on his digital meter. Suddenly it read triple zeros. "Nothing. Are you kidding? I should be paying you. What's, er, your name, guv?"

"Roderick Hetheridge," he replied, falling back on his loathsome nephew's name, the alias he always used when things went sideways. Without looking backward, he strode toward the mews house, eager for Kate and Paul to call back with their reaction to the skull's reconstructed face. It bore an astonishing resemblance to Jacinda Cox.

CHAPTER 40

$\mathcal{W}$hen Kate and Paul arrived at Jacinda's detached house on Cheval Place, it was dark and quiet. If Cy had made good on his promise to visit Jacinda, he must have walked there, as no car was parked by the curb. Jacinda was cooking a roast. Even on the front step, the smell was noticeable.

Kate knocked. No one answered, but lights were on, and the big bay window's curtains were pulled back, revealing a padded window seat.

Paul elbowed Kate. "Top right," he whispered.

She looked up. A CCTV camera was installed there, pointing at them. If Jacinda was playing possum, her home security system had tipped her off to the police presence.

"CID," Kate shouted. "Jacinda Cox. Open the door. We have questions about you and your great aunt, Seraphina Doughty."

No answer. Inside the living room, the lights switched off and the curtain swished closed.

"Do me a favor," Paul bawled, sounding very much like an unstable TV detective, the kind who often turns vigilante in the third act. "We have the authority to force entry if you won't open the door. Not sure your neighbors would care for that. You're

241

finally living on the sunny side, Jacinda. You want a knock-down, drag-out the way they used to do it in Bernsley?"

"Please," Jacinda cried with what sounded like genuine distress. "I can't open the door. Go away. Please, go away."

Kate looked at Paul. He, too, seemed to think there was real fear in Jacinda's voice, and not just fear of the police. After all, Jacinda had happily joined the group interview a few hours before; she'd even baked a cake.

"Cy's probably in there with her. Do you think he's holding her hostage?" Kate whispered to Paul.

"Why would he do that?"

"If she recognized him... if she shifted blackmail targets...." There was more, but this wasn't the time for explaining every nuance. Cy was no longer young, but he'd been killing and conning his entire life. He was certainly capable of opening Jacinda's throat with a kitchen knife and legging it out the back.

To Paul, Kate said, "Climb the fence and try the rear door. And summon backup!"

As Paul headed toward the back garden, which was guarded by a tall privacy fence, Kate looked up at the CCTV camera and addressed it as if looking into Jacinda's eyes. "Look, I know you think you're in trouble, but we can help. Is Cy Smythe in there with you? Is he holding you against your will? I think he must be. Smells like your roast is burning."

No answer. Blood whooshed in Kate's ears. She trembled all over. Shifting her weight, she relieved the pressure on her titanium right knee.

"I just spent the last hour learning about Bernsley and the Montgomery family," she said loudly, looking around the festively-decorated porch for something, anything, that might help her gain entrance. Inside her silver puffer coat, she had the tools of the trade—truncheon and handcuffs. She also had two pepper sprays, left pocket and right pocket, and a set of brass knuckle dusters that absolutely weren't legal.

"The Montgomery family was despised. All of Seraphina's relatives blamed Monty and Galen for her disappearance, didn't they? The police tried to build the case, but her body was never found. What made you accuse Galen? The fact he left Bernsley with twenty thousand pounds you knew he must have stolen from your rich great aunt?"

On either side of the welcome mat were two potted miniature cedar trees, each wrapped in silver tinsel for Christmas. Kate checked under the mat. No key. But under the winter-bare shrubs planted along the bay window, Kate spied a gray stone in the shape of a turtle. It looked like a hidden key-keeper.

"Monty, if you're listening, you did a bang-up job faking your death," Kate continued, seizing the turtle. She turned it over, revealing the compartment on its underside. "Did you top a man, trade IDs, and leave him to be cremated as a public health burial?"

The turtle's "hidden" compartment opened easily. There was nothing inside.

From the rear of the house, Paul screamed.

CHAPTER 41

ate froze. For one split-second, she didn't know what to do. During their partnership, she'd often heard Paul shout in frustration, pain, and outrage, but she'd never heard him issue a full-throated scream.

Suddenly it was all clear to her. Inside the house was a fifty-two-year-old woman and a seventy-two-year-old man. Jacinda seemed unlikely to carry a gun; Monty/Cy had never been cautioned for possessing one. Maybe they'd surprised Paul, but there was no way they could handle Paul *and* Kate.

"You're nicked!" Kate roared, picking up the potted mini cedar tree and smashing its pot against the bay window's double-glazed glass.

The first blow shattered the outer pane and cracked the inner. The second blow knocked out all the glass. Slipping free from her grip, the mini cedar broke open against the window seat in an explosion of dirt and tinsel. Somewhere a dog was barking, but Kate's attention was on something else. Next to the mat, in the damp round circle where the mini cedar planter had rested, was a spare house key.

Turning the key in the lock, she threw open the door with all her might. What she found didn't surprise her.

Monty stood in the living room with a long kitchen knife, probably plucked from Jacinda's own rack. It was held against Jacinda's throat. She was immobile with terror, motionless except for the tears rolling down her cheeks.

"Drop the knife," Kate ordered Monty. Pepper spray was in one hand, her truncheon was in the other.

He lunged. At the same time, the rear door burst open with a terrific crack. Jacinda's Giant Schnauzer, Pooh, galloped into the house like an avenging angel. Bearing down on Monty, the shaggy black dog leapt for his throat. When Monty lifted the knife to defend himself. Pooh's teeth sank into his wrist, sending the weapon flying.

"Bloody monster!"

Pooh yelped as Monty seized him one-handed by the throat. Squeezing hard, he yanked his wrist free of the dog's mouth and choked him with both hands.

"No!" Jacinda cried.

"Get off!" Kate roared, and squirted Monty in the eyes.

One stream of pepper spray should've been enough to put the old man down. Kate's cuffs were at the ready, but Monty still had Pooh by the throat. Kate squirted him again, this time in the mouth and nose.

That did it. Whining more from terror than hurt, Pooh bolted to his mistress. Monty was whining, too. Far too distressed to fight Kate, he went limp as she pulled his hands behind his back and snapped on the cuffs.

"I'm sorry. I'm so sorry. You were right," Jacinda told Kate. She wrapped Pooh in her arms; the dog licked away the tears as they rolled down her face. "I was blackmailing Galen over my great aunt's murder. At first, he paid up. It's like he'd lived most of his life waiting for the other shoe to drop. But after a few years, he decided I'd taken too much. He couldn't let go of any more."

"Then it's true what Leona said? He dared you to go public?" Kate asked.

Jacinda nodded, stroking Pooh, who had folded himself in her lap like a puppy. "But Leona didn't hear everything. The last time I talked to Galen, he said Monty Montgomery actually killed Seraphina. He told me to go find his grave and blackmail it."

Kate turned to Monty. His face was beet red; his eyes and nose were streaming. Still, his breathing was more even, and she thought he might be able to talk.

"Why did you come to Holywell Street? Did you know Galen created Ye Olde Money Man? That he was a multimillionaire?"

"No." Monty's voice was harsh with pain and rage. "I came for Selma. Finding Galen was a coincidence. Or fate. I knew I should have stayed home with her, instead of walking here to see this ugly fat cow. Who told me her flea bitten mutt was safely put away."

"If it's any consolation, he bit me, too," Paul said.

"Paul!" Kate would have run to him, but she was still catching her breath. Apparently when it came to smashing windows and subduing geriatric killers, she was out of practice. "That scream. I thought you'd been murdered."

"No. It was so dark in the garden, I never noticed the dog. I was trying to jimmy the back door when Fido woke up and sank his teeth in. Did I mention I was bending over? Guess it was too tempting a target."

"Are you sure you're okay?" Kate felt a bit lightheaded. Usually the sight of blood didn't bother her, but she suddenly feared that if Paul's wounds were bleeding, she'd faint.

"See for yourself." Paul showed her the seat of his trousers, which had a tear and some snags, but nothing worse. "Maybe it was a warning bite."

"Maybe you were too much of a mouthful," Kate retorted.

"Anyway, as I was breaking down the door," Paul continued, looking at Pooh, "he must've decided Jacinda needed him. He pulled his lead off the peg and dashed inside."

"Why did you kill Galen?" Kate demanded of Monty.

He didn't answer.

"I think it was because he didn't know you," Kate said, floating Tony's theory. "He'd put you completely out of his mind. And that was unbearable, wasn't it?"

"He owed everything to me," Monty said wrathfully. "He never would have those twenty thousand pounds, if not for me. When we were young, Galen was good-looking, but useless with women. I never got old Seraphina to look my way, so I taught Galen how to run the game. She spent a little money on him, but in the end, he couldn't close the deal."

"Why not?" Paul asked. He'd switched on his mobile's recording feature, but if Monty noticed, he was past caring.

"He was a cold fish," Monty said, tears slipping from the cracks of his swollen eyelids. "Never understood you have to make 'em want you. I don't care if they're two hundred years old and they have a crevasse full of moss where the honey ought to be. You *thrill* them. He didn't, and Seraphina began to lose interest. If Galen had done it right, we might have taken her for fifty thousand. Every cent she had. Instead, we had to settle for gifts, and loans, and what she had stashed around the house."

"Is it true you killed her?"

"Of course I did," Monty said. "He was meant to club her in the head with a hammer. But she was spry, and he missed. I took the hammer and walloped her in the jaw. Shattered it. A piece of bone must've lodged in her throat. In half an hour, she was dead."

Something about these details made Kate feel unbalanced, as if her head was too heavy for her shoulders. She concentrated on taking deep breaths as Monty continued.

"Know what Galen did when she died? He cried. The bloody wanker *cried*," Monty said, laughing as much as his pain permitted. "He didn't even have the courage to put a pillow over her face. He just hid in a corner and cried while she gasped and twitched on the floor."

"You could've smothered her," Kate said.

"Ah, but where's the fun in that?" Monty grunted. Pooh the Giant Schnauzer didn't seem to like the sound. He growled.

"Afterward, Galen had nightmares about Seraphina wearing her stupid rain bonnet with the duckies," Monty continued. "Nightmares of her rising up from the grave, a zombie in a bonnet, and killing him. Or kissing him. Maybe both. Any road, I buried her at least four feet under, in a quiet spot where no one would ever look.

"But after I got out of the joint, and made the switch from Monty to Cy Smythe, I found that spot and dug her up. It was a place my old dad had used before, and his dad before him, whenever the family ran into trouble. I took enough bones to make a complete set. Turns out I hadn't, but close enough. In the pit, most of the clothes were rotted, but that plastic bonnet survived. With any luck, Galen's in hell now, and still howling at the memory of seeing that bonnet again after all these years."

"Maybe he didn't remember it," Paul said, probably just to provoke the man.

"He dropped dead, didn't he? That's good enough for me."

"When did you recognize Monty?" Kate asked Jacinda.

"In the kitchen at Galen's house," she said. "After Ollie found the body, he called me, frantic. In the beginning, I only befriended him to get close to Galen, but before long we were true friends. When he told me how Galen died, and asked me to come to his house and sit with him...." Jacinda sighed, clearly ashamed of herself. "I had to see if Galen was really dead. So I pretended to misunderstand Ollie, and went to Galen's house instead."

"I thought I saw Bernsley in your stupid fat face," Monty said.

"The charm factor has gone out the window," Paul said.

"Better watch your mouth. If you talk to Selma this way, I doubt she'll pay your legal bills."

"I knew Monty was playing me," Jacinda continued. "But I was playing him, too. It seemed like he was getting rich off Selma, so I thought he could spread a little my way. But he didn't take it very well."

"I would've killed you," Monty said savagely. "When I heard the police at the door, I should have done it then. But I thought I could still get away."

His voice seemed to be growing softer. Kate felt as if she were losing the thread. Now her whole body was heavy; darkness flickered at the edge of her vision. Suddenly she had no idea how Paul had got inside Jacinda's house. "Did you say you broke down the back door?"

"Indeed I did," Paul said proudly. "Only took me four tries. I'm going to tell everybody I got it in one. Oi, Kate, you're turning white. Why don't you—"

But Kate never heard his suggestion, or felt herself hit the floor.

CHAPTER 42

"*I* confess, I don't feel much like a detective at the moment," Tony was saying.

Kate had come round less than a minute after fainting. But despite her objections, Paul had insisted she be taken to St Thomas' Hospital for evaluation.

Before the ambulance arrived, police backup came on the scene. The ranking officer formally arrested Philip "Monty" Montgomery, who'd lived under the name Cy Smythe for several decades. Perhaps ironically, for a murderer and lifelong confidence man who'd killed his ex-partner by frightening him to death, Monty had begun experiencing chest pains soon after he was loaded into the back of a patrol car. So he, too, had been transported to St. Thomas' Hospital, where he was being treated for acute angina, dog bite, and chemical burns from Kate's pepper spray.

Jacinda Cox had also been arrested. Although the man she'd blackmailed was dead, she'd confessed her crime to Kate and Paul. Moreover, such offenses rarely occurred in a vacuum. Jacinda had probably crossed other ethical lines, so her lifelong financial dealings would soon come under the microscope.

"You had what we called the zombie stomach bug," Tony continued. He sounded perfectly calm, but looked a bit dazed. "You were nauseous on and off for two months."

They were in a curtained-off alcove in the Emergency Department. Kate had been placed under observation because she'd bumped her head when she fainted; these days, urgent care doctors were careful about the possibility of a delayed concussion. On admission, her symptoms had sounded intriguing. A shock two nights ago, resulting in emotional collapse; a police confrontation involving smashed windows and broken-down doors; fainting; hitting her head. Tony, who'd apparently nurtured a secret fear that Kate had some undiagnosed issue left over from the rooftop incident, had told the admitting nurse everything else: Kate's weeks of nausea, suddenly renewed appetite, fluctuating emotions, and sensitivity to smells, like the Riesling she'd believed had somehow gone off. The medical staff had administered an EKG, drawn three vials of blood, and collected a urine sample. The urinalysis had given them the diagnosis. It was obvious yet completely unexpected, because Kate and Tony had been told it simply wasn't in the cards.

"Five months," Kate said. "Once you're past the first trimester, the risk of miscarriage is small. There's no reason we can't tell everyone. Even Henry and Ritchie."

"Mrs. Hetheridge?" A nurse, neatly attired in petal-pink scrubs, announced herself before pulling aside the curtain with a rattle of metal rings. "Doctor says you're fit for discharge. We're just finishing the paperwork. Do you already have an OB-GYN, or would you like a referral for examination and ultrasound?"

Kate looked at Tony.

"We'll take a list of physicians. Private as well as the National Health."

After the nurse departed, Kate couldn't help but shake her head at him. "I don't think you'll need to hire a team of specialists. The most dangerous phase is past. We can start thinking about names."

"Names? Good lord. I don't know." Tony squeezed her hand. "Monty?"

"Granny?"

"Seraphina is an obvious choice."

"What about Ollie? Or Priya." She sighed, suddenly picturing the cramped little house Ollie and Priya's family had shared for over ten years. Inadequate though it was in some ways, they'd made it into a home, and Ollie had endured plenty of abuse to keep it. Now it was lost, and while he might land a better job, the Vine-Jones family had a lot to overcome.

"There's really only one choice, if it's a boy," Tony said with a grave face.

Kate, reading her husband's mind, put on an equally serious expression. They said it in unison:

"Paul Bhar Hetheridge."

Laughing, Kate climbed out of bed, shucked off her hospital gown, and got back in her own clothes. Those largest-ever sizes on her knickers and jeans now struck her as an especially obvious clue. Tony wasn't the only one who didn't feel like much of a detective.

"I'll ring up Harvey first thing tomorrow," he said, that dazed look replaced by determination as he shifted into planning mode. "I'll tell him Wellegrave House must be finished inside a month. I don't care if we have to hire additional builders. I'll even break down and bribe an inspector if I must. I want us back there by the time the baby comes."

"I'm sure we will be. Besides, we have Strange Mews," Kate said. "We can move the family in until Wellegrave House is ready. Lucky there's five bedrooms. And lucky you bought the ruddy thing, you maniac."

"Indeed." Tony looked her straight in the eye. "So we're not going back to Devon? We're sending for them to join us here?"

"As soon as possible. Then we'll all be together for Christmas in London." Fitting herself into her husband's arms, Kate closed her eyes, allowing the moment to unfold. It felt like another miracle in two lives which had seen, perhaps, more than their fair share. In this case, the human miracle, as Tony had called it. Man, woman, and child; life continuing, in spite of everything.

EPILOGUE

$\mathcal{A}$t half-past eleven o'clock in the morning on 25 December, someone knocked on the door of the Vine-Jones residence at 9 Verbena Street.

"Door!" Reena called.

"Door, Mum," Amara announced from the sofa. Her younger siblings had torn apart the Christmas garland she'd made from loops of red and green art paper. She was laboriously rejoining them with Sellotape.

"The Christmas monsters are at the door," Riteish told Reena. "You're going to die."

"Shut it," said Nathan from the dining room table. Toolkit out, he was optimizing his little brother's new electronic racer.

"Shut it," Reena told Riteish in a perfect facsimile of Nathan's tone.

The person at the door knocked again. From inside the kitchen, Priya called, "I'm busy with the pie. Can one of you get it?"

Ollie, on his way downstairs with his youngest child asleep in his arms, said, "I'll do it."

Opening the door, he beheld a courier standing on his

doorstep. The woman wore a yellow company hat and a uniform jacket with the company's slogan, COUNT ON US, embroidered above the breast pocket. In her hands was an oversized envelope.

"Am I being served?" he blurted. They would have to vacate Verbena Street in about three months. He knew letters and warnings were part of the process, but he hadn't dreamed it would kick off on Christmas Day.

"No sir," the woman said. "It's a letter for Oliver Vine-Jones. Are you he?"

Ollie nodded, mystified.

"Sign here."

She passed him an electronic device and a stylus. Juggling the baby, he scrawled his signature and accepted the letter. It was oversized, like a wedding invitation, in a posh vellum envelope.

"Happy Christmas," the courier said, turning away.

"Yes, Happy—oh, wait," Ollie said. "Let me get you something. I don't have my wallet, and even so...." Over his shoulder, he asked, "Does anyone have any coins? Nathan? Amara?"

"Never mind that," the courier said. "Prepaid."

"Oh. Well. Happy Christmas!" Ollie called, making up in forceful sentiment what he lacked in cash at hand. Closing the door, he handed off the baby, who was making fussy noises, to Amara. Then he carried the envelope into the kitchen where Priya was finishing a mincemeat pie.

"There's nothing in here for you," she told him on sight. "Go away. Eat a candy cane until I tell you lunch is ready."

"I'm not looking for food. This came," he said, holding up the letter.

"Look at that stationary." She eyed the seal on the back. "Is it from your parents?"

"I doubt it. But maybe."

"One way to find out."

Feeling unaccountably nervous, Ollie broke the gold foil seal, which looked very festive indeed, and pulled out a thick piece of card stock bearing a hand written note. With the note came four printed photos of a mews house. There was an exterior shot, an upper terrace shot, a view of what looked like a master bedroom, and a view of the living room, which included a fireplace and a spiral staircase. Ollie read quickly. As he did, the photos slipped from his hand, scattering across the lino floor.

"What are they?" Priya gathered them up. "What's this all about?"

Ollie stared at his wife, more beautiful at that moment than on the day he married her. When he'd said "I do," he'd felt as if fate was smiling down upon them. Now he felt that way again. The sensation was humbling.

"It's our new home," he said.

"A house to let? Already?" She stared at the pictures of the mews house's exterior. "Good heavens, can we afford it?"

"Not to let. Our house. Our own," Ollie said, and handed her the note.

DEAR OLIVER AND PRIYA,

WE HOPE this Christmas finds you well. The Galen case was a sad one, of course, but meeting you and your lovely family was the silver lining. To come straight to the point, we made an impulsive real estate purchase this month: Strange Mews, in Marylebone. It's proven unsuitable for our family, long-term, and we have no wish to play landlord or hire a firm to manage the property. Nevertheless, the house is large, comfortable, and appropriate for a family like yours. Photos are enclosed. Our home phone number is written on the back of one.

As you may know, gifting a freehold house presents certain tax challenges. Selling a property for a nominal fee, however, such as £1, may be the better course. If you're willing, please consent to dine with us one day this week. We can discuss the particulars in greater detail and obtain the necessary legal advice. Our intention is to put the property irrevocably in your hands with minimal state fees. It would please us very much to see you and your children living in Strange Mews by February next, if not sooner.

MERRY CHRISTMAS and Happy New Year,

TONY AND KATE Hetheridge

THE END

FROM THE AUTHOR

Thank you for reading this book. If you enjoyed it, please consider returning to the vendor where you purchased it, or to Goodreads, and leaving a review. Honest reviews are priceless. They make the difference between a book that sinks like a stone, and a book that gets discovered for years to come.

I'm often asked if I'll write more Lord & Lady Hetheridge mysteries. The answer is yes! Please sign up for my newsletter* or follow my Facebook author page**to receive announcements. And thank you again for being a reader.

EMMA JAMESON

*http://eepurl.com/crIfYH
  **https://www.facebook.com/emmajamesonbooks

Made in the USA
Middletown, DE
19 June 2022